Small Town Haven

a novel by

Charlie Hudson

 American Quilter's Society

PO Box 3290
Paducah, KY 42002-3290
americanquilter.com

Located in Paducah, Kentucky, the American Quilter's Society (AQS) is dedicated to promoting the accomplishments of today's quilters. Through its publications and events, AQS strives to honor today's quiltmakers and their work and to inspire future creativity and innovation in quiltmaking.

EXECUTIVE BOOK EDITOR: ELAINE H. BRELSFORD
COPY EDITOR: CHRYSTAL ABHALTER
GRAPHIC DESIGN: LYNDA SMITH
COVER DESIGN: MICHAEL BUCKINGHAM

American Quilter's Society
P.O. Box 3290 • Paducah, KY 42002-3290
Fax 270-898-1173 • e-mail: orders@AQSquilt.com

Additional copies of this book may be ordered from the American Quilter's Society, PO Box 3290, Paducah, KY 42002-3290, or online at www.AmericanQuilter.com.

Text © 2013, Author, Charlie Hudson
Artwork © 2013, American Quilter's Society

Library of Congress Cataloging-in-Publication Data

Hudson, Charlie, 1953-
  Small Town Haven / Charlie Hudson.
    pages cm
  ISBN 978-1-60460-112-1 (alk. paper)
  1. Quilting--Fiction. 2. Murder--Investigation--Fiction. 3.
Georgia--Fiction. 4. Mystery fiction. I. Title.
  PS3558.U28945S57 2013
  813'.54--dc23
                                2013043006

*Cover photo used by permission
©2012 Kip McGinnis
Photography, Film, Video, Music & Advertising Production
VintageMoods.com / KentuckyHorseArt.com / KentuckyAVA.com*

Acknowledgements

I want to welcome the fans back for the second book with quilter Helen Crowder, her family, friends, and the town of Wallington. I am grateful to the American Quilter's Society for the series and the behind-the-scenes individuals who bring the production part of the book to life. I would also like to thank Brenda Grampsas with their wonderful Christian Outreach Center in Largo, Florida, and the terrific Quilter's Luncheon fundraiser they hold each February. As always, my wonderful husband, Hugh, provided me the support I needed whenever I was "stuck" on a plot point.

About the Author

Charlotte "Charlie" Hudson, born in Pine Bluff, Arkansas, and reared in Louisiana, is a 22-year career military veteran as well as a wife, author, and speaker.

After graduating from Northwestern State University in 1974, she entered the Army. During her extensive military career, Hudson was deployed to Saudi Arabia for Operation Desert Shield and Desert Storm as well as to Haiti in support of Operation Uphold Democracy. She retired from the Army in 1995 as a lieutenant colonel.

Hudson has a master's of science degree in organizational development from East Texas State University and is a graduate of the U.S. Army War College in Carlisle Barracks, Pennsylvania.

After retiring from active duty, she began to write and publish both fiction and non-fiction books. Small Town Lies is the first in a series of Hudson's novels to be published by the American Quilter's Society.

She and her husband reside in South Florida, where they enjoy their love of scuba diving.

CHAPTER ONE

Helen Crowder stood at one of the entryways into the conference center, taking in the sight of dozens of booths, the noise level moderate compared to what it would be later in the day. Becky Sullivan, Phyllis Latchley, and their newest quilting circle member, Alicia Johnson, were consulting their catalogs, trying to decide which direction to go. Helen and Phyllis hadn't been to a show for almost three years and this was the first time for Becky and Alicia.

"I know I've seen this on TV but, my gosh, there's so much," Becky said when they crossed into the main display area. "How are you supposed to know where to start?"

Alicia's head had moved from side to side, no doubt wondering the same thing.

"I have the class on Template-Free Quilting at eleven," Phyllis said, lifting her head. "Helen, you're going to the lecture on Amish quilts at the same time?"

"Yes, Bea Greer from Knoxville is giving it and I haven't seen

1

her since we went to the show in Lancaster." Helen looked at the two younger women. "Your class is later this afternoon, isn't it? You and Alicia are going to Three-Dimensional Appliqués?"

"At two o'clock," Becky said, Alicia still gazing at the crowded floor. "Do we want to split up and meet for a quick lunch?"

"Once you get among the booths, it's easy to lose track of time," Helen said with a soft smile. "And with all the food booths I'm seeing, grazing might be better. How about if we just plan on drinks at the hotel for happy hour before dinner? Tomorrow will be another full day."

"I like that," Alicia said, breaking out of her temporary trance. "I think I want to walk the entire floor, see how things are laid out, and then begin to poke around."

The women double-checked their watches, agreed that five thirty in the hotel lounge bar would give everyone enough time, and broke into different directions. There were twenty exhibitors this year, six special quilt exhibits, and twenty-three classes and seminars. Unlike some of the shows, they weren't running contests. Helen was excited about seeing Bea again, a woman who traveled to most of the major shows around the country and took in at least one international show each year. It was hard to believe this was the same girl she'd shared an English 101 class with in college before Bea dropped out to join VISTA, the domestic equivalent to the Peace Corps. Bea became entranced with quilting during her volunteer work in the Appalachians and set out to learn about the incredible diversity of quilting within all fifty states before turning her attention overseas.

After Bea's lecture and taking a few minutes to catch up on each other's lives, Helen couldn't resist a cone of warm cinnamon almonds followed by a refreshing peach sherbet, thinking she would have regular food at dinner. She strolled leisurely and spotted the

Click for Quilting booth, a major online company that was a leader in Internet sales. It had been started by a woman in North Carolina who just wanted her elderly mother to have better access to quilting supplies in the small town where she lived in West Virginia.

A quartet of white-haired women with bulging totes moved to the next booth, leaving alone a man who looked vaguely familiar. He was about her age, hair still full, although silver was liberally sprinkled among the brown. He wore his hair in a short style that came over his forehead. He was close to six feet and broad enough through the chest and shoulders to escape the term slender, no telling paunch beneath the royal blue polo shirt that topped his charcoal gray slacks. His gray eyes were fringed with thick lashes and his nose had a tiny bump in the center— not unattractive, but noticeable. The cleft in his chin was slight, as well, and a wide mouth stretched into a smile.

"Max Mayfield, Click for Quilting," he said in a voice that had to be bass if he sang. "How are you enjoying the show?"

"I'm having a great time," Helen said, looking at the two crib quilts affixed to the back screen of the booth. The table in front had brochures and a catalog and the narrow tables on either side were covered with a variety of quilting supplies. "I wasn't able to get away last year and it's been a while since we had a show in Atlanta. Some of the women in the circle didn't want to travel too far, so this is perfect."

He looked at her somewhat quizzically as if he, too, recognized her. "You're local then?"

Could they have perhaps briefly met at a show she attended? "Wallington," Helen said. "It's…."

He winked. "Two and a half hours unless there's not much traffic on I-20 and the state police aren't around. I've been known to make it in a tic under two hours."

Helen cocked her head.

"Edith and Burt Mayfield. Angela Hilliard is my sister."

"Oh my," Helen said, placing the face. "Helen Crowder. Well, Pierce then. How long has it been? High school graduation?"

He grinned. "I think so. I was a year ahead of you, if I remember correctly. I went straight to the University of North Carolina at Chapel Hill for the summer session instead of staying around town after I graduated."

She looked him over more closely, the younger face coming back in her mind. "You look terrific! Your mamma told me you had gotten into quilting, but I had no idea you were this big into it. Oh, I saw her maybe a couple of weeks ago when I was at The Arbors. She's such a sweetheart."

"She is that," he laughed and waved his hand around the booth. "I'm coming up on my tenth anniversary in quilting. You know that's something mother has always loved, and of course, back in those days, mothers taught daughters to quilt and dads taught sons to throw a baseball or a football." He motioned to the empty chair. "You certainly wear the years well, by the way. Come on inside and take the other chair while we're in this little bit of a lull. We can catch up, but the truth is, I'm headed your way as soon as the show is over."

"Coming for a visit?" Helen eased past the table and took the metal folding chair next to Max. The crowd had thinned and knots of women and those wandering singly stopped at other booths along the aisle.

"Sort of," he said. "Mamma is doing well considering her age and The Arbors is a wonderful place, but Angela goes to see her every day and that's something we think is important. I usually come in once or twice a year, and I took an early retirement from my company a few months ago, so I've cut back considerably from

4

the kind of travel I was doing." He adjusted the position of his chair and looked directly at her. "Angela teaches history at the middle school, but she's always had the desire to go on an archeology dig. A friend of hers was put in charge of a project somewhere in Belize and she's invited Angela to come down. The principal agreed and they have a substitute lined up. We don't want Mamma to be alone and even though Mamma thinks the world of my brother-in-law, Kevin, it wouldn't be fair to ask him to do the everyday bit."

"Well, that sounds like a lovely plan,' Helen said, briefly wondering how many men she knew who would be willing to do that. "Will you be staying with Kevin?"

Max laughed. "We're talking almost three months and that long isn't something either of us would care for. I've rented one of the apartments on the town square, the ones upstairs in that new building that has retail space on the bottom."

"Oh, those are nice as long as you don't need to be on the ground floor," Helen said. "A friend of mine has been there for about a year now and she loves it. They'd had one of the big old houses on Maple and after her husband passed away, she rattled around in it for years and decided to finally downsize. With all the restaurants on the square, she says she hardly ever bothers to cook and she can walk practically everywhere she likes to go."

Three women were approaching and Helen was beginning to feel the effect of having been on her feet most of the day. She wanted to go by the special exhibit area and see at least the Raining Cats and Dogs one. They both stood and she gave Max a quick hug. "It was great seeing you. Call when you get into town and we'll do this properly."

He handed her two business cards and a pen. "Keep one and jot your number on the back of the other," he said as he extended his hand to the women.

Helen thought about what a small world it is as she moved away from the booth. Max's father had died unexpectedly almost fifteen years ago of a massive heart attack. Helen had never been totally sure of what Max's job was that included traveling to remote parts of the world. Edith, stunned from Burt's death, hadn't wanted to delay the funeral and it had been a week later before Max was able to come home. His visits were usually no more than a few days and rarely followed a set pattern. Although Edith was excited and affectionate about his visits, neither she nor Angela seemed to mind his long absences. If Helen recalled correctly, he was divorced from a fairly short-lived marriage and there were no children. Angela and Kevin's oldest son and his wife had recently had a son, giving Edith that special pride that came with being a great-grandmother.

"Hey! There you are," Phyllis said brightly, her own tote brimming with items. "Have you been to see the *Raining Cats and Dogs* exhibit yet? I've been hearing good things about it."

"That's where I am headed," Helen said, "and you'll never believe who's at the Click for Quilting booth."

Helen filled Phyllis in and they spent the next hour taking in three of the six special exhibits and then caught the shuttle to the hotel. They had enough time to carry their totes up to their rooms and Helen stopped to do a quick refresh of her powder and to fluff her short, wispy bangs. She was due a trim to keep the layered cut at the right length, and she really liked this shade of chestnut. Edna, who had been doing her hair for years, changed it up slightly every few visits, but always within the same basic color. The little bit of eye shadow she'd applied that morning was fine. They had dined at the hotel last night and would probably go down the street to Cathy's Creole Café. Cathy was a chef as well as the owner, who relocated to Atlanta after her restaurant had been wiped out during Hurricane Katrina. Becky declared the cuisine to be authentic and Helen had fond memories of when she and Mitch had taken the children to New Orleans. Just now, she didn't need to change from her burgundy twill slacks with the pink-and-burgundy-striped knit top, although she did swap from her black walking shoes to a pair of leather burgundy flats decorated with black leather accents.

Phyllis was already at the elevator. She had changed into a new pewter-colored linen slack suit with a sleeveless turquoise silk shell. The jacket had no collar or lapels, but rather borders embroidered with a serpentine pattern in turquoise. The color set off her blue eyes and the white pageboy she refused to dye. When they made their way into the lounge, the spacious room was about two-thirds full, with most of the barstools occupied.

It was the usual sort of hotel lobby lounge with cherry-wood finishes and upholstered armless chairs at round tables for two and four. The color palette was browns and beiges and the carpet was a dappled type that hid stains well. The lighting was subdued, although not to the point that you couldn't see, and Alicia waved to them from a table near the bar. The hotel was one that offered discounted rooms as part of a package deal for the quilting show. Based on the number of women in groups who were not clad in business attire, Helen assumed many of the patrons were attending the show. It was an atmosphere of chatter with bubbles of laughter floating around the room.

"Draft and house wine are $3.00, bottled beer is $4.00, and mixed drinks are $5.00," Alicia reported, pointing to the waitress at the next table. There was a bowl of snack mix in the center, paper napkins strewn around, and a colorful menu card with specialty drinks. The waitress motioned she would be with them in a moment.

Phyllis picked up the card that featured martinis on the front. "Becky, does the Creole Café serve hurricanes? If I do one of those, I'll have a rum here instead of vodka."

"They do indeed and they pack a punch," Becky said and lifted a warning finger, "the kind that goes down smoothly and you don't feel it until later." Becky, never one to pay a lot of attention to clothes, had changed to blue jeans and a plain, dark red cotton sweater, opting for no jewelry as accessories.

"Oh, here comes the waitress," Helen said.

The pause in ordering allowed Helen to steer the conversation to the show and what each of them had seen.

"Here's to a wonderful day," Alicia said, lifting her beverage. "I had no idea it would be this much fun. Thank you ladies for including me."

"Of course," they said simultaneously, clinking glasses together.

Alicia, one of two new members of the circle that met every Tuesday evening at Helen's house, was only a year older than co-member Rita Raney, neither having celebrated their thirtieth birthday yet. Alicia, with a head of soft black curls and clover-green eyes, barely came to Helen's chin. Her short figure was curvaceous and she swore that avid cycling was the secret to keeping her weight under control. She was in stark physical contrast to Becky, a sturdy woman devoted to horses. The same contrast was obvious in their attire; Alicia was clad in a teal cowl-neck sweater and a fluid, black skirt that brushed the tops of her black leather boots. Her dangly earrings were gold teardrops with a teal enamel inset.

"We're still planning to try and be on the road around three o'clock tomorrow, aren't we?" Becky asked. "That should get us out of the way of rush hour traffic."

"I've signed up for two classes," Alicia said. "The one about fusible appliqué and one about designing a memory quilt that sounded interesting. Both are in the morning."

As they were settling the bill to leave for the restaurant, three men in suits sat at a nearby table, far enough out of hearing range for Phyllis's assessment not to be heard.

"It's too bad there are only three of them," she said, wiggling her eyebrows. "Their age range is perfect and none are toady."

Helen agreed with Phyllis's assessment if not her implied suggestion. The two men who were close to their age were attractive with a distinguished air, in suits that probably came from a men's store or at least an upper-tier department store. The third, who looked to be in his early thirties, was the tall, dark, and handsome sort that would have an Italian last name, if his ethnicity matched his face.

"Alicia and I are happily married women, so you and Helen can divide up the extra one," Becky said, double-checking the stack of bills they were leaving for the waitress.

Alicia glanced at the trio, and then seemed to stiffen and stare longer, distress flashing across her delicate face. Oh, dear, had Phyllis's remark disturbed her? It took a while to become used to the way Phyllis blurted things out.

"I can still appreciate an attractive package," Phyllis chuckled, as Alicia fumbled with picking up her purse from the floor.

"Better so on a full stomach," Helen said, standing. "I'm ready to try that crawfish étouffé Becky was telling us about."

"And the hurricanes," Phyllis added with a laugh. "Good food we can find anywhere. A properly mixed hurricane is another matter altogether."

CHAPTER TWO

I know, your back hurts and when you get into a comfortable position, the baby kicks." Helen set the mug of steaming cranberry and pomegranate tea in front of Tricia.

"Thank you," Tricia said with a smile. "If carrying high and having an active baby are signs of it being a boy, we might as well get everything in blue." Justin had agreed that they didn't want to know the sex of the baby beforehand.

"I was that way with Ethan," Helen said, noticing that despite the discomforts of the third trimester, Tricia's face had the glow of expectant mothers with that extra brightness in her brown eyes. "With the way he kicked during the last trimester, it didn't surprise me in the least that he loved football from the moment he could get his hands around one. Of course, that was before soccer was popular here. He might have been even better at that."

Tricia laughed and reached out her left hand to finger the small quilt folded across the back of the chair next to her. "I love this, Mamma," she said. "The design is so cute. Where did you get the idea?"

"I can't take credit," Helen said. "Deirdre Carter, the other new circle member, did one for her latest grandchild and I just made a few changes. Finding the striped fabric first is the key. Then you find the fabric to do the stars."

The quilt that could be used either in the crib or as a wallhanging was on a field of white with Six-Pointed Stars in three different sizes and in four colors of blue, pink, green, and yellow. The cutest part was the binding made from a striped fabric in the exact same colors as the stars.

Steam from Helen's mug of tea curled in a tendril as light from the late afternoon sun pulsed through the double window. "Do you want to call Justin and have dinner here? I have a whole pack of chicken breasts. I was going to freeze some of them, but we could go Italian, Asian, Southwestern, or comfort food depending on your mood."

Tricia took a sip of tea. "If I didn't have a stack of papers to grade and two more errands to take care of, I would love to."

Helen cocked her head. "I tell you what, then. I have a container of Brunswick stew in the freezer. Why don't you take that with you and by the time you get done running around, it will be partially thawed. You can either simmer it or microwave it the rest of the way."

"You are an angel," Tricia said, lifting her mug in a semitoast. "We have salad and some bread left from Always Fresh. Oh, have you been out there lately? They were able to open a pick-your-own pumpkin patch this year and they're doing hayrides on the weekend."

"I saw an article about it in the *Wallington Gazette*," Helen said, glad to see that Juanita and Kyle Lurley were apparently expanding their customer base. They had purchased the family farm when her widowed grandmother decided to sell and move into town with Helen's parents. The couple developed it into a combination of working farm, market, and petting zoo. Juanita had also created a line of herbal lotion and soaps that were gaining in popularity, too.

"Allegedly, the select-your-own Christmas tree section will be open next year, but they don't want to rush it," Tricia said and emptied her mug. "Oh, Justin will be painting the nursery Saturday. I thought I'd bring the curtains over and we can finish them here."

"Absolutely. We can stitch those up in no time." Helen stood and smothered a smile as Tricia rose awkwardly from the table, her rounded belly protruding under the long-sleeve front-pleated maternity top. The purple slacks set was a wonderful color for her and she noticed Tricia was wearing canvas walking shoes. That was a sensible choice at this advanced point in her pregnancy.

They originally thought the baby would be due at Christmas, but that was a miscalculation and there had been discussion about what to do for Thanksgiving if they were all gathered at the hospital instead of in Helen's dining room, as was the tradition. The first-baby-is-always-two-weeks-late anecdote might apply, but when Helen had Ethan, he had come within only one week of the anticipated delivery and Tricia's birth had actually been three days early.

Helen helped carry everything to the car and decided to go ahead and divide up the chicken breasts for tonight's dinner and freeze the rest. She would make one package of four for when she had company and the others in packages of two. She usually cooked two at a time to have leftovers and the idea of Thai was pushing out Italian. There was green curry paste in the refrigerator, a can of coconut milk, and a box of jasmine rice in the pullout pantry.

The pullout pantry next to the refrigerator had been part of Helen's dream kitchen when she and Mitch remodeled. There was a large set of floor-to-ceiling cabinets in the combination mudroom and laundry room that held bulky and extra items, but Helen had wanted the ones she used frequently in the kitchen while keeping most of the cabinet space for non-food storage. Even though they gained two extra lower cabinets when they installed the two-tiered island, most of that space was devoted to bakeware, odd-sized platters, and serving dishes. Not only did Helen love seasonal and special occasion tableware, she'd kept several of the old pieces from her grandparents' farm, like the blue-banded handcrafted pottery bread bowl she used when she made bread from scratch.

Helen moved around the kitchen comfortably in the expanded space that was created after they removed the original peninsula. Mitch had not been an avid cook, but he did have his specialties other than grilling, and he had never been the kind of husband to refuse to help with meal preparation. Even if all he did was make the salad and set the table, he'd spent a lot of time in the kitchen with her. She only wished there had been more time together before the cancer had taken him so unexpectedly. Helen never mentioned it to anyone, but there were moments when she reached for a pot from the rack over the island or took out the stool to get something from an upper shelf when she could sense Mitch's presence. She remembered how he often laughingly teased that if it weren't for opening jars and getting things from high places, she wouldn't need him. She felt a poignant pang that he couldn't be a part of this first grandchild on the way, then affectionately thought about how excited her dad was at being a great-grandfather. And there was no doubt that Justin's parents, Lloyd and Sue, would make the trip down from Baltimore. Even though Justin's brother and sister both had children, they weren't likely to want to wait long to see the newest addition to the Kendall line.

The telephone rang as Helen was wiping down the manufactured stone countertop in the milky color with blue-green flecks they'd chosen over granite. She'd decided that not having to seal it, combined with the ease of cleaning, were the main factors.

"Hello, Helen here," she said in her habitual greeting that was rather unnecessary now that she was alone in the house. Well, Tricia did sometimes answer the phone when she was there and they sounded a great deal alike.

"Hi, it's Wanda." There was a tiny pause with some sort of quick background exchange. "Sorry about that," she said. "Listen, I know you're planning to come by tomorrow, but Mamma called and needs me to drive one of her friends to the doctor in the morning and I have no idea how long it will take. Could you possibly scoot over now? I have something important to tell you."

"Sure," Helen said. "Want to give me a hint?"

"Only to say it's a good thing. See you shortly," Wanda hung up without saying good-bye. She'd never been one for long telephone conversations.

Helen was quickly on her way, with nothing in Wallington being a long distance. In fact, had she not been in a hurry, Helen could have made the twenty-minute walk to the beautiful antebellum house that had been in the Wallington family for five generations. The large, two-story home was graced with a deep porch and thick fluted Corinthian columns. Dark green shutters on the four sets of wide windows looked out onto the groomed lawn, punctuated with prizewinning azaleas and balanced with one large magnolia and one live oak. Both trees were older than either Helen or Wanda. The massive double front doors were striking with oval stained glass insets featuring honeysuckle blossoms and hummingbirds. The home had been routinely featured on regional magazine covers and there were two other similar ones in town that belonged to Wallington descendants. Wanda, originally being a Burton, came from an equally impressive lineage, for those impressed with such matters, and the marriage of two of the town's founding families had simply been the social event of the year. It had been as much pageant as wedding, despite the fact that neither Wanda nor Randy shared the pretentious nature of some of their family members. They had mostly acquiesced to their respective mothers' ideas of what the wedding should be like and escaped afterward for a honeymoon to Hawaii.

Helen, seven years younger than Wanda, had known of her, of course, but it wasn't until later that they became friends through a mutual love of quilting and Helen's work in Larry Shipley's insurance office. They were not in the same quilting circle, but there were overlapping activities, competitions at fairs and shows, and Helen could still remember the moment when their friendship solidified. It was the annual Fall Days Arts and Crafts Festival that was held on the town square the weekend after Labor Day when the weather was predictably beautiful. The streets were blocked off from traffic, businesses decorated, and booths were set up. Three of the local quilting circles had agreed to join together to display the members' quilts, demonstrate techniques, and run a raffle for a quilt from each circle with the proceeds going to the animal shelter. The planning committee had gathered suggestions for which cause to support and later drawn a slip from a bowl. Gertrude Jackson, the representative from her circle, had been in a huff because she had insisted they should all agree that the Women's Club should get the proceeds, no question about it.

Gertrude, with a perpetually pinched face and nasal voice that grated on most anyone's nerves, did not take kindly to being overruled. She had then constantly harped about where their booth was located, how were they going to make sure all the women who promised to show up to help run the booth would, and made other noises the rest of them ignored. As good committee members, Helen, Wanda, and Gertrude were there early the morning of the festival to finish setting up as women brought in their quilts. Gertrude managed not to be available the previous afternoon to help with the actual work of getting the tent, tables, and chairs assembled. Upon her arrival, she wanted to rearrange everything and was convinced the gray skies would not clear off as predicted. To top it all off, the youngest quilter in her circle, Annette, really more a girl at age nineteen, brought in a quilt that was quite nice, but admittedly plain and not the skilled design and stitching of someone more experienced. Gertrude started sharply criticizing the girl's quilt, questioning if something so amateurish was worthy of display. Wanda stepped over, gave the obviously distressed girl a quick pat on the back, and took the quilt from Gertrude's hands.

"Why, Annette, isn't this a wonderful example of starting with the basics? If you don't mind, we'll put that right here with our batch, and if you possibly could, I would love to have you come back for the two o'clock session we're going to have about generations passing on the love of quilting. You are the perfect role model for it."

Wanda had fixed Gertrude with an expression that said, *My words are coming out sweet as they can be, but it's time you be taken down a peg, and I'm just the one to do it.* Gertrude had thrown her shoulders back and made some nonsensical remark as she'd stomped off to harangue someone else. Annette had giggled, fully understanding what had transpired, and the next week joined Wanda's quilting circle. Wanda hadn't stopped there, though. As soon as she and Helen were alone, she'd held up her watch with mischief in her eyes. "I don't know about you, but I have no intention of putting up with her crap all day. I called Lucy Morgan last night and told her if Gertrude were here for more than one hour, I would probably strangle her. In approximately fifteen minutes, Lucy is going to desperately need help at the Women's Club booth and that should tie Gertrude up quite nicely."

"Bravo," Helen said before she burst out laughing, thoroughly enjoying the rest of the day that brought in more than a thousand dollars for the animal shelter.

16

She and Wanda had routinely lunched together after that, their friendship deepening. Like everyone else in town, Helen had been shocked when Randy died at only age sixty, collapsing after breakfast one morning, dead from a cerebral aneurism. Helen had been by Wanda's side to help as much as she could, never realizing their positions would one day be reversed when Helen, too, would be widowed at a relatively young age.

Although the Wallington children, Randolph III and Pamela, visited often, and Randy had provided well for Wanda, the huge house was a physical drain and required constant work of some kind or the other. Within a year of Randy's death, Wanda confided her desire to convert the house into a specialty store on the bottom floor and living quarters upstairs. A number of the large old houses had been completely transformed into commercial properties and Helen had been captivated as Wanda described her concept for Memories and Collectibles. The focus would be quilting in the magnificent ballroom. Of the other rooms downstairs, one would be devoted to dolls, another to candles, bath, and small gift items, one to scrapbooking, one set up for workshops for groups up to twelve, and the kitchen and final room as private staff space. The front foyer was large enough to accommodate a counter for the cash register and several customers without feeling cramped. There was really nothing like it in town and it was more than just the convenience of women no longer having to travel for supplies for their hobbies. It was the type of place where you could leisurely wander through and had the added benefit of being close to restaurants and the ice cream parlor on the town square less than two blocks away.

Jeff Lawson, the local architect who specialized in old homes and commercial buildings, was the obvious choice for the project, and Scott Nelson, Katie's husband, had a passion for old homes as a part of his construction business. Wanda's ideas were so well thought out that the two men offered few suggestions for changes, and within six months of opening, Memories and Collectibles was drawing customers from a three-county radius. Susanna Dickinson was the primary craft instructor, and Helen normally taught quilting every other Thursday: a class at three and one at six. She either drove the short distance home between sessions or more often pitched in with Wanda talking with customers and sorting through wonderful fabrics that came from a variety of sources. Helen hadn't wanted a weekly commitment in addition to the Tuesday quilting circle meetings, but twice a month was a nice fit for her. Susanna, a bubbly girl—well, woman, since she was Tricia's age—was a fabric artist and incredible seamstress. In addition to teaching, she did costuming and had a respectably profitable online business with a variety of products.

There were spaces enough for cars in the parking lot that had previously been a side lawn with a croquet court Wanda almost regretted losing. Practicality had won over sentimentality, though, and Wanda had the foresight to include a bicycle rack next to the handicap ramp. She'd also added eight rocking chairs to the porch. They were arranged four on each side in a slight semicircle with a round white wicker table in the center. These extras were as much for neighbors to drop by as for customers.

Helen stepped into the foyer and onto the parquet floors that had been updated with nothing more than refinishing and enough coats of polyurethane to hold up to constant foot traffic. As had been the custom when the house was originally built, the special flooring had been featured in the most public rooms and the rest of the house was done in hand-scraped hickory. The solution for the antique rugs downstairs had been to move them upstairs and replace them with stain-resistant replicas.

Lillian McWherter, Wanda's full-time assistant, was checking out two women Helen didn't recognize. Lillian, hovering somewhere around forty, had apparently never cut her auburn hair except for an occasional trim. Between her preference for wearing it up and a taste for high-collared blouses, mid-calf skirts, and low-heeled shoes, there was a turn-of-the-century look about her. In fact, as the resident doll expert, there were events when she dressed as a Gibson Girl, a Southern Belle, or a Suffragette, becoming literally a "living doll."

She glanced up and smiled. "Wanda's in back," she said, handing the first woman a medium-sized Memories and Collectibles bag.

"Thanks," Helen replied and went to the right through the bath, candle, and gift room, noticing that the smallest room that served as the office was empty. That meant Wanda was in the kitchen that doubled as the break room.

It was decidedly utilitarian for two reasons. The first being that Wanda had moved the period pieces and antiques upstairs and second was that she permitted catering for teas and luncheons and it had been more cost effective to go with the most basic equipment that met municipal code standards. The incongruence of stainless steel and linoleum floors was an acceptable trade-off when the health inspector popped in.

The rectangular table that sat eight was also significantly larger than the antique secretary desk in her office and a good place to spread out paperwork; an array she was peering at when she lifted her head.

"Hey, thanks for coming. You want a glass of tea or anything?" Wanda's round gold wire-rimmed glasses were partway down her nose as was often the case. She pushed them up into the proper position as she stood and set the papers aside.

"I'm good," Helen said, hanging her brown leather shoulder bag on the back of a chair opposite Wanda. "Is the mystery about to be cleared up?"

Wanda looked at her wristwatch, a silver bracelet decorated with amethyst stones. She accessorized with watches as she did with shoes, having only a slightly smaller collection of timepieces. Today's ensemble coordination included an eggplant-colored cowl-necked long-sleeve top that looked to be a silk blend, a pair of gray silk crepe slacks, and silver earrings with amethyst stones slightly larger than those in the watch. Wanda had adopted streaking her feathery short cut as soon as the first gray appeared, and she swore that a disciplined regimen of skin care was why most people didn't guess she was closer to seventy than sixty. The skin around her blue eyes crinkled and she motioned for Helen to sit.

"You, my dear friend, are one of the first to know that I am about to set off on an exciting adventure—or at least that's what I expect it to be."

Helen raised her eyebrows. "And that would be…?"

"Me teaching classes and giving lectures for quilting-themed cruises in the Caribbean for the winter," she said, her smile stretching wider.

Helen clapped her hands together. "Well, congratulations," she said. "Is Lillian going to run the shop while you're gone?"

Wanda laughed and shook her head. "No, but that's what I want to talk to you about, and no, I'm not trying to lure you into full-time work. It has to do with Max Mayfield, although I don't know if you remember him."

"Max! What a coincidence. I ran into him at the quilting show and he told me about coming to town for a few months. I didn't recognize him at first because it had been such a long time since I'd seen him."

Wanda nodded. "He isn't coming here only to help out Angela," she said. "Get comfortable and I'll tell you all about it."

CHAPTER THREE

Helen wasn't sure which part she wanted to hear first—about the cruise or Max.

"I'll start by explaining about the cruise," Wanda said, settling that. "You know we've been talking about taking one of those for ages." She didn't wait for Helen to reply. "Well, Nora Bledsoe, the new human resources manager at the factory, was in about a month ago with her cousin who was visiting from Fort Lauderdale. Nora was looking for a doll, but the cousin, Rachel, is a quilter and just the nicest person. It turns out, that of all things, she works for Sunstar Cruises. Of course, I wanted to know the inside scoop on them. We must have carried on for an hour."

Wanda gathered drinks for the two of them and Helen passed her a cracker with Brie. "Thank you," she said putting the cracker on a napkin. "Last week, Rachel called because one of the women who teaches and lectures has a family situation and wants to take the winter off, but, of course, that's one of their peak seasons and she thought of me as a substitute."

"Seriously? That's how it happened? I know you're going to have a wonderful time," Helen said, thinking how interesting it was that such a simple encounter led to this.

Wanda hadn't stopped smiling. "I think it's going to be loads of fun. There are two different itineraries, each one week—the Eastern and Western Caribbean. Even though it's not one of the mega ships, it has four restaurants on board and all sorts of lovely amenities. In fact, I think I prefer the idea of a slightly smaller ship instead of one that can hold half the town."

"What did your mamma have to say?" Helen was thrilled for her, but Miss Ruth was ninety and she and Wanda were quite close. How was she going to take to a three-month absence?

Wanda laughed and refilled Helen's glass before she could protest. "You know Mamma is all for adventure. She's fine at The Oaks and Kate and Randy Trey will visit more often, plus, after I learn the ropes, Kate is going to bring her to Fort Lauderdale for one of the cruises. It will be one of those three generations things. If Georgina was a little bit older, she'd bring her, too."

Helen took a chunk of Cheddar this time. "All right, it sounds like you have that part resolved. So what's the deal with the shop and Max?"

Lillian came in. "It's bridge night and I have to run by Forsythe's to pick up some of Lisa's carrot cake mini muffins," she said, placing the keys on the table. "The front is locked up." She winked at Helen. "I assume she's filling you in on the excitement? Isn't it just the most fun thing you can imagine?"

"It is," Helen said, not completely surprised Lillian would not be running the shop. She was an excellent assistant, but had commented more than once about not wanting the responsibility of owning a business.

"Got to run—see you in the morning," she said, waggling her

fingers.

"I did offer to let her be the boss," Wanda said when she'd left. "It seemed only fair and she turned that down almost before I'd finished asking the question."

"Okay, and how did that lead to Max, and are you saying he's going to take your place?"

Wanda ate the cracker before she replied. "Well, aren't you the clever one? The short answer is that yes, he is. It's another one of those fortuitous things that you have to wonder if it isn't fate intervening or something." She waved vaguely in the direction of the office. "I was reading Patchwork Penny's blog the day after Rachel called me, and she had Max as a guest blogger. At first I couldn't believe it, but, I mean, how many Max Mayfields originally from Georgia can there be?"

"You didn't know he'd gotten into quilting in a professional capacity, either?"

Wanda shook her head. "Not at all, but there are a lot of quilters that blog and write articles. Anyway, as you can imagine, I was intrigued and sent a comment for Max to e-mail me, which he did. When he talked about his semiretirement and mentioned he was looking to come back here for a while, it struck me as the perfect solution."

"You didn't ask him right away, did you?"

"Almost, but not quite. We talked about his involvement with Click for Quilting, and his business background is part of why he got started with them. It's strictly a freelancing sort of arrangement because he doesn't want to be tied down to any one thing. He said he was taking in the Atlanta show, would be over after that, and he'd come by. We chitchatted a bit more, I slept on it, and the next day I called him about running the shop while I'm gone. I explained my situation and he admitted that as much as he wanted to help Angela, he had been a little concerned about what he was going to do with himself that whole time. It's a perfect situation for both of us." She smiled again. "Lillie doesn't mind working extra hours for a short period if necessary, and Nelda always comes in to help for the holidays. In fact, she starts the weekend before Thanksgiving and goes through the first week of January."

Helen could see how it was a logical arrangement. "I have to say it does sound like a good fit. You're not going to be here for Christmas, though? When do you leave?"

"The first Tuesday of December. The cruises are the Saturday to Saturday kind, and I go through a few days of orientation. We'll have a huge Thanksgiving and Kate is already planning for Mamma to come to their place at Christmas. You're right in that it will seem a bit odd to be away, but everyone is thrilled for me."

Helen snapped her fingers. "Have you told the *Gazette* about what you're going to be doing? This is one of those stories you know they'll want to print."

"I hadn't actually thought about that," Wanda mused. "I'll give Denise a call tomorrow and see if they want to do an article." She plucked some almonds from the dish. "You said you and Max talked at the show. He didn't give a hint about this? It's not as if I'm trying to keep it a secret."

"Nope, but as it turned out, he was completely booked for the time we were there and he probably thought it wasn't his place to tell me. We agreed he would call me after he got to town."

A knowing look crossed Wanda's face. "See, that's another reason for me wanting Max. I would trust you or Lillie in a minute to run the shop and not carry on about every little thing that happens here. The truth is that Nelda doesn't have that good a head for business and I don't care for the idea of her—and I don't mean this unkindly—being privy to the intimate details of decisions I make about this place or why I run things the way that I do. As you well know from your insurance days, what a business looks like on the surface and what goes on behind the scenes can be very different matters."

"Oh yes," Helen laughed. "Customers who aren't always as nice as they seem, vendors who aren't as reliable as you might like, financial postures that may not be as solid as people think." She hoped that didn't sound cynical. "Sorry, I didn't mean you."

Wanda gave a half smile. "I know that, but it's true. Remember how shocked everyone was when Norbet Furniture went out of business overnight? Except, of course, it wasn't overnight because that worthless cousin of Don's had been skimming for months instead of paying the bills. What a juicy little scandal that was."

Helen easily recalled it since Shipleys had the insurance coverage for the store. That policy was one of the bills not paid, and when Helen had called at the store because she knew Glenda fairly well, the poor woman was on the verge of a breakdown. Jimmy, Don's cousin, was a likeable guy, and even though she knew he tended to live beyond his means, it never occurred to either of them that he would steal from his own family. Not that they could be convinced to press charges. It cost the Norbets practically everything they owned to settle the debt that had racked up and they didn't have the heart to try and start over. Fred Hillman, whom they had competed with for three decades, swooped in, offered them pennies on the dollar, and made certain to spread word around town about how clever he was. That was one of many reasons that Helen despised Fred. The Norbets moved to Valdosta to be near their oldest daughter and Jimmy had gone to Miami or Las Vegas, depending on which rumor you wanted to believe.

Wanda waved her hand around the kitchen. "Anyway, let's get back to how it's going to work with Max. He's taking care of his lease at the Uptown Apartments today and doing some other errands. The Uptown does month to month as well as longer, and is a great location. He can walk when the weather is nice if he wants. He'll be in tomorrow and we'll get started on everything he needs to know." Wanda paused. "Why don't you come up and we'll have an early dinner?"

Helen thought for a moment. The chicken would keep and Wanda was going to be gone for months. "Sure, or we can stroll to Amore or Copper Pot." The Calico Café and the Sandwich Stop weren't open for dinner.

"I have a flank steak, asparagus, and baking potatoes. We'll grill everything—well, microwave the potatoes—and I'll show you the brochures of the ship. Let's toss the trash and take the rest of the nibblies up."

"I'll get this, and you can lock up the back," Helen said, gathering the glasses. This would be fun. It wasn't as if she never had a spontaneous night out, but it didn't happen as often as it used to. She, as did her friends, had regular routines—although she hadn't yet reached the point in her life where the exact meal she ate was dictated by the day of the week or her desire to stay at home was because of what might be coming on television. Hmmm, now that she thought about it, with recording capabilities these days and whatever that thing was that let you watch television on a computer, did anyone refuse to leave the house because they might miss a specific show? Well, she guessed perhaps older people who weren't comfortable with technology, but then at that age, spontaneity tended not to be high on the priority list.

Ah, that led to the thought that while Wanda was gone, Helen would make certain to check on Wanda's mother, Miss

Ruth. Her deteriorating eyesight and a burst blood vessel in her left eye caused her to give up driving, which in turn had led to her decision to move into The Oaks as one of the oldest residents still able to live independently. With her wry humor, she had scoffed at the idea of moving in with Wanda, who offered to have an elevator retrofitted into the house. "I've been planning to go into The Oaks for years when the time came," Miss Ruth had announced. "I'm not near ready for The Arbors, but a one-bedroom apartment will suit me fine."

Although no one could consider Wallington a town on the leading edge of much of anything, the complex on the hospital grounds that had both independent and assisted living in addition to long-term care had been happily greeted.

Miss Ruth's inability to drive and read smaller print were really her only impairments and she was correct in that she could still live on her own. Even though Wanda was often available for chauffeuring, The Oaks had a shuttle service and they had set up the apartment so that anything that needed to be read was in very large print. Miss Ruth subscribed to an audio book service and she had one of the stand lamps with a large magnifying glass in her room to allow her to continue to quilt in at least small bursts. With the extensive menu of activities available to the residents, she was rarely in her room other than to sleep. There was no doubt she was living her golden years.

"That's all done," Wanda called from outside the kitchen. "You need me to carry anything?"

"No, I've got it," Helen said, the tray in both hands, purse slung over her shoulder. "Lead on, I'm right behind you."

Wanda's cooking and a good friend—it would be a nice way to spend the evening.

CHAPTER FOUR

"A male quilter? Well, it's not as if I don't think we should invite him, but I can't say I've ever met one," Sarah Guilford said, snipping a thread. "I know Edith and Angela, of course, but Max is not coming to mind at all."

"He had some sort of job that kept him traveling and his visits were no more than a few days whenever he had time," Helen explained. "I haven't spoken with him yet about the circle because I wanted to talk to y'all first like we always do."

It was their usual weekly quilting night, each member of the circle bringing whatever project they chose unless it happened to be a time when they were working on a quilt jointly as they did for several annual fundraisers. With the season having turned to fall, most of the women were working on presents or some type of holiday decoration. Sarah, her copper-toned wire- rimmed glasses creeping down her nose as they often did, was completing an adorable vest for her goddaughter's seventh birthday. She had cleverly found seven shades of pink to incorporate into the design that had been featured in a magazine.

"We popped by to see him at the show," Phyllis chimed in. She was sitting next to Helen tonight at the table, needing the space for the large medallion she was stitching. It was a beautiful one she was calling Butterflies and Blooms to connect quilting together with her second passion of gardening. "He's looking awfully good—has kept himself in shape for sure. I went back through the high school albums and he was a senior when I was a freshman, so it wasn't as if our paths crossed much. He was on the basketball team and then he did track in the spring—a hurdler."

"Angela is an absolute dear and she often mentions Max when she comes in. They're close even though he hasn't been around much at all since he graduated. I think it's wonderful he's willing to come here while she's gone," Carolyn Reynolds said and rethreaded her needle. She switched to a silver metallic thread she was using to outline stars bursting from a champagne bottle set against midnight blue fabric. It was a medallion for a set of holiday-themed placemats she was doing as a favor for one of her customers. She'd come directly from her shop, The Right Look, Ladies and Children's Apparel. As was her regular routine, she slipped off her two-inch green leather heels once she sat down on the sofa. Helen wasn't surprised that her shoes matched the color of her eyes and were the perfect touch for the navy-and-green print belted dress she was wearing.

"I can't believe the chance Wanda has gotten," Mary Lou Bell added, branching off-topic as she was prone to do. "Waylon and I did that Disney cruise last year with the kids and we went on a seven-day Western Caribbean one for our honeymoon. I think we definitely should schedule a quilting-themed one with the circle before too long. Wanda will be perfect for letting us know about what really goes on." She looked at Rita Raney and Alicia with a teasing smile. "I don't imagine y'all have been married long enough to want to take vacations without your husbands."

"Maybe not just yet," Rita laughed, fluffing her bangs of black hair. She was starting a new project she named PRETTY BASKETS. It was for her mother-in-law and it had taken her weeks to settle on a pattern.

Alicia had taken the chair next to her and Helen was suddenly struck by the resemblance of the two younger women, even with Rita's dark brown eyes and being a few inches taller. Alicia gave a half smile to Mary Lou's comment, concentrating on the square she was stitching. The quilt was a traditional Pyramids patchwork pattern and Alicia had said the fabrics she was using had come from when she'd bought a whole box of remnants at a garage sale.

"Max was a nice kid," Deirdre Carter said in her melodious contralto voice. "Angela was in the voice club and he would come early sometimes to pick her up. He would sit as quietly as you could ask, not making jokes like some of the jocks. I never knew if he might have some musical inclination and didn't want to admit it, or if he couldn't carry a tune in a bucket and just appreciated people who could sing."

Deirdre had joined the circle within a week of Alicia, an interesting bit of timing considering they were utterly different. Like several of the women, Deirdre was the fourth generation of her family in Wallington, and now the oldest in the group. You wouldn't know it by the few strands of silver hair and no more than faint wrinkles in her milk-chocolate colored skin. She'd retired at the end of the school year, agreeing to teach piano to a few select students and enjoying being the assistant choir director for her Baptist church. She came from a long line of quilters and ironically had been the youngest in the circle that had included her mother, one aunt, and friends of theirs. The truth was that as the members had passed on, they hadn't brought in new ones. Deirdre had been in the store not long after her mother's funeral and Helen extended the invitation to come for the weekly meeting. Deirdre's quilts routinely won prizes in the few competitions she entered and Helen hadn't mentioned that they had all speculated as to which circle Deirdre might join or if she would choose to start her own. The quilt she had with her was an example of her versatility. It was Homes Filled with Love and she'd taken photographs of her parents', grandparents', and grown children's houses; found cross-stitch templates to approximate those houses; and cross-stitched each one into a square. All the women in her family sewed, and she had used fabrics collected over the generations for the other squares, sashing, and binding. When Phyllis first saw the quilt, she asked how long Deirdre had been working on it, and Deirdre just smiled and said, "Oh, for a while now."

Katie Nelson, the only member missing, was coddling her husband through the painful aftereffects of having his wisdom teeth extracted the previous day.

Becky had brought the squares with red and blue stars she was incorporating into An Oath of Honor, a quilt she was planning to send to a cousin stationed in Afghanistan. "If you're asking for my vote about inviting Max, I say why not?"

Nods and murmurs of agreement made it unanimous and not entirely unexpectedly, Phyllis grinned with that expression that meant there was no telling as to what she might come out with. "What's his marital status, by the way? Divorced, I assume, if he can uproot for three months or so. We haven't had an eligible bachelor over the age of fifty and under eighty in town since Lorie Sanders got bored with Percy and dumped him to marry that mechanic over in Conyers."

"She married Lester Turnbull and he started out as a mechanic. He manages the Goodyear store now," Carolyn elaborated. "You are right about him being divorced—Max, I mean. Angela thought he made a mistake by marrying his wife to begin with—I don't recall her name—and when he finally admitted it wasn't working out, she was thrilled. That was four, could be five years ago."

Sarah chuckled. "Well, Phyllis, are you going to give the poor man a few days or pounce on him immediately?"

"He'll need someone to help show him around," she said archly. "There have been changes he might not be familiar with and it will only be neighborly to offer. Hey, is it break time yet? I'm hungry."

"You can wait another fifteen minutes," Becky said with raised eyebrows at the "only neighborly" remark.

"I guess all my appetites will have to wait for a bit," Phyllis predictably shot back to a collective groan. "Fine, I'll stitch and behave myself."

Helen smothered her laugh, seeing the same expression around the circle. The companionable quiet that descended was punctuated by the soft tick of the mantle clock, a piece she and Mitch had found in a secondhand store early in their marriage. The familiar scene was one Helen might not be able to articulate to anyone other than another quilter. The once traditional, oversized living room that had been used only a few times a year had been completely renovated and transformed into an ideal environment for quilting. There was a drop-leaf table; two hoop stands placed in an arc with a chair in front of each; then three more chairs curved around toward the sofa; an armoire filled with fabrics and quilting supplies; other custom-built cabinetry to include space for books and magazines; a sewing machine; and a concealed ironing board, all attractively and practically arranged.

She released an inaudible sigh of contentment and inserted her needle into the quilted pincushion on the right-hand corner of the table. "Okay, it's officially food time," she said and nudged Phyllis's arm.

They stood, a few stretching, and trailed into the dining room through the arched opening. The table her grandfather had made from a black hickory tree on their farm was covered as always with more food than they really needed. Helen had set out the slow cooker for the cocktail Swedish meatballs that Sarah brought and an electric warming tray for Phyllis's miniature shepherd's pies she said were one of the new frozen hors d'oeuvres the store was carrying. Helen had opted for two-bite pita pockets filled with chicken salad, Becky had sliced a quiche into slender servings, Deirdre's made-from-scratch cheese straws were becoming a staple, and Alicia had shyly offered a rustic onion and cheese tart. Carolyn, Mary Beth, and Rita had obviously been to Forsythe Bakery. Liz's signature double chocolate tartlets, butterscotch brownies, and caramel drizzled pecan cookies were recognizable without the box. They had all long ago agreed to never buy more than one dozen of each item for circle meetings. That kept the tempting leftovers at a manageable amount.

The flow of the evening progressed as it always did with an hour of quilting, the break for food that could be consumed while standing, a refill of beverages, and then reconvening to the projects for another half hour or so depending on how everyone was feeling. As the only business owner in the group, Carolyn usually left first with Rita, and Sarah not far behind. Becky and Mary Lou were toss-ups, Phyllis almost always lingered, and so far Deirdre and Alicia were among the early ones. As a young wife, Alicia might think a couple of hours out with the ladies was long enough to be away from her husband. Helen hoped everyone knew the invitation to stay and visit was genuine.

Tonight, it was only Phyllis who stayed and it was a sign of their decades-old friendship that they moved in an unspoken rhythm while cleaning up.

Phyllis brought the remaining dishes from the dining room. "Looks like we have a few munchies of shepherd's pie, chicken salad, and that minx Rita left four cookies. I'll zap the pies in the microwave when we're ready for them."

Helen put the electric warming tray in the wide cabinet of the kitchen island. One of the design elements had been to have space for awkward-shaped entertainment items that gobbled up space. She would leave the slow cooker out to dry and put it away in the morning.

Phyllis looked around the now-tidy kitchen, her hand resting on the island. "Sit here or at the table?"

Helen arranged the shepherd's pies on a plate and covered them with a paper towel. "I'm not sure I can hoist up on a stool."

Phyllis carried napkins and the tray with the chicken salad pitas and cookies to the table. "A full day does catch up with us, doesn't it?" She came back for the drinks as the microwave beeped completion of its short cycle and sat to the right of Helen's usual chair. "Speaking of a full day, how is Tricia holding up?"

"Really well, considering it's the last trimester. You remember what that was like for me delivering Ethan in late September."

"Lord, yes," Phyllis said, topping off their glasses. "Carrying through the summer heat made me wonder why you bothered to have a second one," she said, the affection warm in her voice.

Helen smiled. "I gave Mitch his son and thought a daughter would be a nice balance. I suppose if it hadn't worked out that way, I might have gone for a third."

Phyllis cocked her head. "Are you ready to be a grandmother?"

"I am so thrilled I can hardly stand it at times," Helen said with no hesitation. "I am so looking forward to rocking that tiny little baby and showing off the photos. I promise not to go overboard with it—no bumper sticker or tee shirt that says, Ask me about my grandchild."

Phyllis touched her glass to Helen's in a toast. "I'll remind you of that if I have to. Here's to an uncomplicated delivery and to what will, I'm sure, be the most beautiful grandbaby in the hospital."

"Of course, it will be," Helen said with a laugh. "There's no doubt about that."

CHAPTER FIVE

———⊰◆⊱———

Justin Kendall opened the door for Tricia and took her hand to steady her as she awkwardly climbed out of the car. He fought to keep a smile from his face at how it was the little things in a pregnancy no one told you about. How, when curled together at night, you could get a sharp kick from the baby, or how it became incredibly difficult to bend over and pick something up from the floor. The food cravings people joked about hadn't seemed to occur, although Tricia had developed a sensitivity to pizza, declaring it gave her heartburn after only one slice. Both of them hoped that would revert to normal after the baby was born. All the guys at the station assured him he was lucky not to have had a wife who was puking her guts out every morning and sending him to the store at midnight for strange snacks.

Fortunately, she hadn't suffered morning sickness or other ills, and each visit with the doctor brought a good report of progress. The first time they'd gone in for a sonogram, Justin watched in amazement as the technician explained what they were seeing.

There it was, their baby—no, no, they didn't want to know the sex—their baby, this human being developing and growing. It wasn't that he didn't understand the process of a child being born—it was that seeing the image and listening to the heartbeat gripped him with a sensation he hadn't felt since that night he'd met Tricia at a party. It was love at first sight—there was no question about it. He'd known it then and he knew it sitting by Tricia holding her hand as the technician's wand moved across her stomach.

"Ooof, let me stretch for a second," Tricia said, breaking into his thoughts.

"Take your time," he said. "I'll help you get inside."

She smiled, a look crossed between affection and exasperation. "I don't need your help with walking, sweetheart. Or, I suppose I should say I can waddle on my own. I'll lumber my way inside."

He laughed and retrieved her purse so she didn't have to reach in for it and let the passenger door swing closed. They were in Tricia's Ford Focus rather than his Mustang because the way those seats were designed did give her problems getting in and out. It was the same thing with parking behind Helen's Fusion instead of in the open spot in the carport. It was easier for Tricia not to have to maneuver in the narrow space between the car and the latticed wall of the carport.

As always, unless Helen was in the front quilting room, they entered through the combination mudroom and laundry room off the carport. And, as always, mouth-watering aromas preceded Helen's voice calling for them to come on in. He didn't know what Helen might be serving as sides, but, unless his nose wasn't working properly, the main dish was pork roast.

"Give me a hug," she said, opening her arms and lifting up her head to plant a kiss on his cheek. At five feet ten to her five feet six, he didn't mind bending over, even though she most often came up on her toes instead. "Let's get Tricia off her feet and I'll see if the potatoes are ready," she said.

Tricia laughed, her eyes sparkling with humor. "Mamma, I'm not that worn out from working all day."

Helen made a shooing motion with her hand. "Don't try and fool me, young lady. Being on your feet at this point is more tiring than you realize. Sit and relax. Speaking of work, what's Dr. Fraiser saying about when you should quit? Didn't you have an appointment this morning?"

He waited for Tricia's answer about how much longer she might be working. Police Chief McFarlane had already assured Justin that he doubted a major crime wave would interfere and they would schedule his shifts however they needed. That was before they'd received notice from the next county over that there were odd rumors about potential drug dealings they didn't normally encounter. He shook his head from that conversation, preferring to hear what Tricia had to say.

Tricia patted her belly. "Baby Kendall is as healthy as can be and so is mamma. I will admit I've been routinely going to bed around nine o'clock these days. But honestly, other than feeling like a beach ball and needing a bathroom break practically every time I turn around, I'm fine. We aren't setting a date yet because it's a little muddled with the due date being close to Thanksgiving. If the baby is late, I won't need the substitute until after the holiday, and right now, we're still looking at this little bundle being born two days after."

Helen punched a button to turn the oven off and slipped mitts onto her hands. "Did I hear that Melissa Lawson is going to be subbing for you? What a great recovery she seems to have made."

Tricia tucked a strand of hair behind her ear. "Yes, and we're both glad about that. She finished the really intense physical therapy about a month ago and is doing the rest at home. She said she doesn't need the cane for getting around too much and is hoping she'll be past that within another six weeks."

Justin tried not to flash back to the scene of the accident where he and Dave Mabry had managed to pull Melissa from the crushed car that had mangled her right foot and ankle. It had been one of those situations Justin had never encountered on the police force in Baltimore when, as dusk had closed in on Newling Road, a huge buck had bolted from the wood line, slamming into the front left corner instead of clearing the car. In struggling to regain control, Melissa hit a streak of packed mud that spun the car into a sizeable tree that had also been weakened by two days of torrential rain. Had the tree fallen slightly differently, it would have been the roof of the car that caved in rather than the front. Despite the unfortunate series of events, Justin and Dave were practically on-site when they received the call. Melissa had been coming back from dropping off her eight-year-old daughter at a sleepover, and there was an exceptional orthopedic surgeon at the hospital. As they were writing up the report, Dave explained that deer-related wrecks were as common for them as were drive-by shootings in the city.

"I've got the glasses out if you'll take the tea over," Helen said, bringing him back from that overcast evening.

He poured the tea. Justin felt extremely comfortable around Helen. Her cooking was definitely a benefit, not that his mother and wife weren't good cooks. He honestly didn't know what it was she did, but tonight was typical of enjoying dinner at her house. The roast pork would be so tender you wouldn't need a knife, the scalloped potatoes would be perfectly browned on top, the glazed carrots (that he had never particularly cared for before having hers) would have a great blend of honey and mustard, and she said it was her grandmother who taught her to make rolls and biscuits. He didn't see a dessert on the counter, which meant she'd probably made one of her meringue pies or it could be banana pudding.

Tricia put salad on her plate and pointedly looked at the mounded serving dishes. "Did someone else forget to come to dinner tonight?"

Helen laughed. "I want you to take leftovers with you. That will mean one less meal you have to deal with."

Justin wanted to accept quickly to keep Tricia from saying no, but he sensed that would not be a good idea. While Tricia hadn't been overly emotional during the pregnancy, there had been a few notably uncharacteristic outbursts he didn't want repeated.

"Thank you, we will," she said, to his relief.

The small talk that followed led them through dinner and clearing the table with insistence that Tricia relax and let them take care of it. Justin switched the coffee on while Helen removed the lemon meringue pie from the refrigerator. His mother could bake brownies, cookies, and cakes with the best of them, but she avoided pastries that included crusts. He vaguely remembered her saying it had something to do with not being able to manage the dough correctly, and as long as there were good frozen pies, she wasn't going to worry about it. He assumed Helen's pies were homemade since he watched Tricia occasionally make one. The truth he would never say out loud was that his mother-in-law's pies were some of the best he had ever eaten, and as a police officer, he'd been in a lot of diners with good pies.

"A small slice for me," Tricia said and grinned. "We'll be happy to take some of that with us, too."

When they returned to the table, Helen snapped her fingers and looked at him. "Dessert and Tuesday—that reminds me. We were at the end of our break and Becky asked me if you had mentioned anything about rumors of some sort of drug situation around here. She hadn't heard much except someone had said something to Bob about there being signs of problems, maybe. I told her you hadn't said anything, but that I would ask."

Justin swallowed the last bite and hesitated. Helen had the respect of everyone on the force, especially Chief McFarlane. "We don't have anything definite and we're hoping it's just talk," he said carefully. "There have been a couple of cases of uncovering signs of meth—methamphetamine—labs in rural areas in abandoned houses, or rather barns at houses. Not here, but not too far away, either."

Helen's face registered concern. "That's a terrible drug, isn't it? Very addictive?"

"Yes," Tricia said and gave a little sigh. "You remember what it was like in Baltimore, sweetheart. None of the neighborhoods were really immune from it and schools were constantly on the lookout. I mean pot was more common, and a lot of adults don't realize how often kids swipe prescription drugs from their parents." She moved the coffee cup to her lips. "Not having to cope with serious drug problems is one of the great things about living here. It's so sad to see in the cities."

Helen set her cup on the saucer. "That is correct, isn't it? What we have here mostly is marijuana? Well, I suppose if we're being honest, there are probably a few folks around who are heavy handed with their tranquilizers and sleeping pills, too."

There was no reason to alarm the women. He'd read the reports and checked some on-line sites. The problem is that meth is dangerous, yet not difficult to produce; and if someone is cautious, a lab can be set up and functioning without drawing too much attention. Houses with outbuildings like barns and sheds are ideal spots and all of the counties have hundreds of homes that fit the description. With Wallington being close to I-20, distribution east to Atlanta or west to Augusta made the area a target if someone was looking for a spot. Chief McFarlane had contacted his friend in the Georgia Wildlife Resources Division since their people knew the wooded areas well. He'd also had a chat with the fire marshal, and talked to everyone about responding quickly to any complaints that came from out-of-the-way houses. A sudden increase in traffic on normally quiet roads and suspicious fires at vacant houses could be indicators of drug activity. Wallington wasn't so heavily populated that seeking a market there was viable. It was production for transport to the east and west they needed to be concerned about.

He tried to keep those thoughts from showing in his expression. There was nothing concrete that pointed at Wallington. "Pot is one of the simplest things to grow," he said instead, "and from what I've seen and been told, running across a still is more likely than anything else."

"We do have a family or two that could possibly be engaged in that," Helen said with a smile. "Sort of a long-standing family tradition, you might say."

Tricia bounced her fingertips off her forehead. "Oh my Lord, do you remember when Mike Gable got caught with that trunk full of moonshine—or sort of got caught?"

Helen made a surprising snorting sound and turned her head to Justin. "Goodness, yes. You should get Cyrus to tell you all the details sometime. It was, I don't know, probably six years ago. They were getting ready for the annual Fourth of July barbecue and the men from the Lions Club gather at Wallington Park where they bring in the big smoking rigs and build fires to cook up huge kettles of Brunswick stew. They cook all night between how long it takes to barbecue the whole hogs and the quantities of stew they make up. I mean, at least half the town goes out there on the Fourth to either eat or get to-go meals."

This was evidently another of the involved stories that people enjoyed retelling.

"Well, some of the men are there all night, and of course, there's a cooler or two around. Wayne Turner, God rest his soul, had apparently made arrangements with Mike Gabler to come out with a rather stronger delivery, if you know what I mean."

Tricia wiped her mouth with a napkin. "Chief McFarlane never mentioned this to you?"

Justin shook his head as Helen continued. "It was maybe mid-afternoon and for some reason, Cyrus stopped by, and I guess Wayne and Mike were in the middle of their transaction when someone saw his patrol car coming. There's only one way in and out and Cyrus wasn't a big fan of Mike, so he figured Cyrus would hassle him just for general purpose, although if you think about it, this was exactly why Cyrus should check to see what he was up to."

"Get to the good part, Mamma," Tricia grinned.

"Okay, Mike jumped into his car, put it into reverse, and backed it right into Wallington Pond—I mean up to the front seat with him scrambling out the window and over the hood. From what I was told, everyone was about falling over laughing and Cyrus was cussing up a storm. By the time they got Mike's car pulled out, there was nothing in the trunk, of course, since all the glass jars had smashed and the liquid was mixed with the pond water that had poured into the trunk. Wayne had hidden his jar in the carcass of one of the hogs they were going to barbecue and no one would tell Cyrus that. Cyrus was mad about it for a while and then figured losing a whole trunk full of moonshine was punishment enough for Mike." Her eyes filled with laughter. "It's my understanding that the family for whom Mike might or might not have been making deliveries determined he was not really cut out for the business. Allegedly, that was the end of him dabbling in moonshine."

Having had one conversation with Mike Gabler during an investigation, Justin had no problem believing the story.

"There have certainly been some interesting happenings in preparation for the Fourth of July barbecue over the years." Tricia folded her napkin and couldn't stop the yawn that escaped.

"Okay, you two, time to get you home and in bed," Helen said affectionately. "I'll package up those leftovers and we can talk tomorrow."

Justin carried the bag and Tricia's purse to the car while the women took their accustomed fifteen minutes to say good-bye. He would have plenty of time to go back in and give Helen a hug. After the farewells, as they drove the few miles to their house and Tricia chattered about something that he wasn't paying attention to, he thought of her comments about drug problems in the city. That was definitely not one of the things he missed about Baltimore and he hoped it was going to stay that way.

CHAPTER SIX

⟿⟡⟾

T he telephone rang as Helen stepped across the threshold, purse across her shoulder and a quilted shopping bag over each wrist. Her voice mail was set to answer after four rings, so she set the heaviest bag onto the counter and grabbed the receiver.

"Hi, it's Rita. I hope I'm not catching you at a bad time."

"No, I'm good," Helen said, slipping the other bag off her wrist and letting her purse slide off.

"I need a favor, but seriously, it's fine if you can't do it," she said without the distress that accompanied some requests.

"I'll be glad to if I can," Helen assured her. She had a special affection for Rita who had gone through a bit of a rough patch with her husband, Steve, traveling a great deal for work and the sort of misunderstandings that can occur early in a marriage. Rita gave Helen far too much credit for having helped her out with that, although the shoulder to cry on that teary night she'd spent with the young woman in her kitchen had seemed to work.

"We close at three and I was wondering if I could come by

with my quilt. I'm following the pattern, but I'm thinking about making some slight changes about how I place the squares and now I can't decide about the alternating fabrics. I really want this quilt to be perfect."

"Oh sure, I'm planning to be here the rest of the afternoon, so come over when you can and we'll take care of it." Helen didn't think it would do much good to explain that few quilts were perfect. Part of being experienced was learning that lesson.

"Thanks ever so much and I'll bring cookies," Rita said. "It will be about three thirty, if that's not too soon."

"Cookies aren't necessary, I have some left from the church bake sale, and the time is fine," Helen said. She had plenty of tea on hand. Rita was a light drinker rather than a teetotaler and she appreciated the assortment of teas Helen usually kept in the handcrafted tea box that had been one of her last gifts from Mitch. It was an antique he'd found at Yesterday's Treasures while they were remodeling their kitchen. He'd gone to the hardware store next door for something and had seen it in the window. He'd asked the owner, Betty Johnson, to keep it at the store until their kitchen was complete, and he had brought it home as a finishing touch.

Helen put the groceries away, taking the empty bags to the laundry room and also depositing her purse on top of the washing machine by the door. She hung the bags on a hook on the section of wall between the dryer and white chest freezer she hardly used any longer. The quilted shopping bags had been Katie Nelson's idea when she'd bought an almost full bolt of fabric at a closeout sale. It had been one of those impulse buys quilters were familiar with— don't pass up a great price on a cute fabric even if you don't know exactly what you're going to do with it. The colorful pattern of fruits and vegetables had been what caught her eye. With reinforced stitching of the seams and using tubing and heavy interfacing to create handles, it was a practical, completely machine-washable shopping bag. The creativity was in the part that was quilted and the addition of a monogram. Everyone in the circle thought it was clever and other fabrics were used after the original bolt was depleted. Most of the circle members had made them as little presents for friends—the sort of casual thing women exchanged among each other. They were sturdy and definitely not mass produced, unlike the ninety-nine cent type at the grocery store.

Helen arranged cups, saucers, small plates, spoons, and the sugar bowl on a tray. Neither she nor Rita used cream in tea. She went into the quilting room to check that she'd left the table leaf up as she thought she had. The outside temperature had fallen a bit and she decided to turn on the fireplace. It ignited with the press of a button and even though it didn't truly match the authenticity of a crackling wood fire, there was also no hauling of split logs, bits of bark and wood scattered on the floor, no coaxing kindling to light, messy ashes, or too much smoke if the damper was in the wrong position. There was merely the friendly glow and leap of flames, providing comfort and ambience, courtesy of modern technology. Her grandfather, who grew up on their farm, would no doubt have laughed derisively that anyone would have invented such nonsense. Perhaps not, though, since cutting and hauling firewood was a time-consuming chore.

Rita arrived through the front entrance a few minutes before three thirty. She'd removed her veterinarian's assistant lab coat and was wearing taupe thin-wale corduroy slacks and a deep orange, round neck cotton sweater that was an excellent color for her complexion, which had olive undertones. They chatted amiably while managing the logistics of getting settled in the quilting room. Rita spread out her project. She glanced at the fireplace. "I really love those gas inserts. They make so much more sense than bothering with the real thing, don't you think?"

"It was Phyllis's idea and Katie's Nelson's husband, Scott, is the one who put it in," Helen said.

Rita looked around the room. "I think what you've done here is great. With just Steve and me in the house, we have a guest room and we use the third bedroom as a combination office and craft room." She smiled shyly. "We're starting to try for a family, though, and will have to decide what to do about that when we need a nursery."

Helen smiled, hearing the softness in Rita's voice. "There are a lot of options—finding those hidden spaces that don't get used well or moving to a bigger place," she said. "If you like your neighborhood and need to remodel, I can certainly recommend Scott."

"We've been talking about different ideas because we're thinking two and maybe three children. It is a nice neighborhood and there are some larger houses, so we're keeping our ears open in case we hear one of them comes onto the market," Rita said and took the chair next to Helen. "My mother-in-law has this incredible collection of baskets in all sizes, types, and from I don't know how many places. I've been collecting fabrics with baskets on them for a while until I had enough for seventeen squares. I have plenty of different floral fabrics to make the other squares, but maybe I don't want to do that and some solid fabric squares mixed in would be better." Rita pointed to the stack of squares she had already completed. "I like the larger basket in the center, but I can't decide if I should replicate that in the corners or have only the one large one and all the others as small. Or, should I include a third size? I have some on another fabric."

The pattern was straightforward with the basket in the center a half size larger than all the others, but Helen could see Rita's point about using that same size in the corners as well. The pattern showed floral fabric for the other squares with solid-color sashing and binding.

Helen knew that for someone who was still somewhat a novice, simplification was the key. "This is a good pattern," she said. "The idea of different size baskets is nice if you have enough to give that symmetry it sounds like you want. Since you have solid colors for the sashing and binding, I think you'll be better staying with that. Let's see what all you have." She suspected that Rita had not spread the quilt out before she started on it and laid out the intended squares to see the full view. That really was an important step.

It didn't take long for Rita to see that making the single change of having different size baskets was really all she needed to do to achieve the right look. The floral fabric was a nice balance to the baskets and the moss green fabric she had for the sashing and deep rose for the binding worked well.

Rita looked at their work with satisfaction. "Oh my, that was a lot easier than I thought it would be and you're correct. I looked at the picture and started right in on it instead of taking the time to really lay it out properly. This is part of why I joined the circle. Aside from the fact that I enjoy everyone, I've learned so much from all of you. I was talking to my mom the other day and she thinks it's great. She loved the quilt I sent for their anniversary."

Helen turned her head to look at Rita. "We're happy to have you. If we don't bring in new members like you and Alicia, we wind up in the same situation as Deirdre. Her mother and aunt were sweet ladies, but the whole group was so set in their ways they couldn't deal with the idea of letting younger women—oops, I guess since we're planning to invite Max to visit, I ought to say younger *people*—in."

A giggle escaped Rita. "I'm sorry. I know it's stereotyping to be surprised that a man would want to be part of a circle. Have you talked with him yet?"

Helen shook her head. "He's been very busy with Wanda and I thought I would give him a day or two before I go by."

Rita stood, folded the quilt, returned it to her tote, and hesitated slightly. "Uh, if you don't mind, there is something else I'd like to talk to you about." She smiled quickly. "Nothing bad— not at all. Oh, and I need to pop into the bathroom."

"Certainly," Helen said, pointing to the door into the hallway. "It's through there and to the right, in case you don't remember. I'll put the kettle on for a fresh cup of tea if you'd like."

"That would be nice," Rita said. "Be with you in a few minutes."

Since they were both drinking the same orange-rosehip blend, Helen used the porcelain teapot Tricia bought for her when they visited a lovely teashop in Baltimore. Every foot of Totally Tea was decorated in lace, frills, crystal, china, and silver, an absolute monument to the pleasure of tea. Helen first noticed the teapot, a classically rounded shape with indigenous flowers of Maryland painted on a pale blue background, as they were waiting for their table to be cleared. Tricia insisted on buying it as a souvenir of their afternoon.

Rita's return put a stop to her musing and Helen waited for what she assumed would be a favor. Rita's eyes, the color of heavily steeped tea now that she thought of it, had a hint of mischief. "You know I am still incredibly grateful for what you did the night you were at my place. Under the circumstances, I feel like I can be very candid with you."

"I didn't do as much as you think," Helen said with a smile, "and, yes, despite our ages, one of the best things about having girlfriends is that we can have frank discussions—the kind that make men blush when they overhear us."

"Not this time," Rita laughed. "Actually, I guess I need to start with a question. The night you rescued me, you seemed really good with Toffee. I mean, you petted him and didn't mind that he was all over you and on the furniture. I've never heard you talk about having pets, though."

Helen was sure she knew where this conversation was heading. To be honest, it was something she'd considered. "Why don't I have a cat, dog, or both? I suppose it's rooted in the fact that both sets of grandparents, mine and Mitch's, were originally farmers. There were animals everywhere, of course: hunting dogs, cats, chickens, pigs, cows, a horse for plowing, rabbits for my grandparents, and a couple of goats for Mitch's. I think when you grow up with animals like that, you aren't as prone to the idea of having them in the house. Mitch's father left the farm when he shipped out for World War II and took a job in town after that. My mother had no brothers and neither she nor her sister was interested in the farm, but it stayed in the family until I was in my early twenties. The kids spent a lot of time out there so they had plenty of animals to play with even when my grandfather stopped keeping the livestock. Once he passed away and my grandmother sold the farm, the kids were sort of beyond wanting a puppy or kitten."

"Is it something you might like to do?"

Helen silently tapped her forefinger against the cup. "I know people are always asking you if you can find homes for animals. Is there something special about one or are you looking for homes in general?"

Rita moved the cup around on the saucer before she answered and lowered her eyes momentarily. "I try not to get emotionally involved when people drop strays off in the middle of the night. We usually patch them up as best we can and shuffle them off to the shelter." She raised her eyes to meet Helen's questioning gaze. "This one, we've started calling her Tawny because of the color of her coat, was heartbreaking. One rear leg had been broken in the past and healed badly so she has a bit of a limp. She was terribly thin and had awful ear mites."

Helen could hear the catch in Rita's voice.

"With animals that have been abused, they tend to be either difficult to deal with or so grateful for kindness that they just droop into your arms."

"I gather that Tawny is the second type?"

Rita let a sigh escape her curved mouth. "I was first to the office and it had been raining during the night. I'd come in the back like I always do and when I went to unlock the front, there she was, wet and shivering and with eyes just begging not to be hurt. We have that recessed entryway and she'd tucked into it as far as she could."

"It must have been a sight," Helen said quietly.

"We've had worse," Rita said. "I got some towels, and the moment I wrapped her up, she gave my hand a little lick as if she understood I was going to help her."

"Then she's a small dog?"

Rita's head bobbed. "She's a chug, if you can believe it."

Helen wasn't sure she'd heard correctly. "A chug?"

"A cross between a Chihuahua and a pug. Despite how it sounds, she's cute as she can be. The Chihuahua features soften the pug's face so you don't get the usual snuffling from a pug and the sturdier pug body offsets the more delicate Chihuahua one. What you have is a small, short-haired dog with really the best features of both."

"You haven't taken her to the shelter yet?"

Rita turned her cup again, the tea probably tepid. "Dr.

Dickinson wanted to make certain the ear mites were cleaned up. They don't need that problem at the shelter and Tawny is so sweet she doesn't get in the way or anything. He thought Mrs. Murdock might be willing to take her and that didn't work out. We've been checking with everyone who comes in and so far, no luck. I called the shelter yesterday and they're almost at capacity, so I'm afraid that if I take her...."

Helen understood now. "If they have too large a population, they have to euthanize some of them."

"Yes, and I'm sure it wouldn't be Tawny as a new arrival, but I'd hate it to be one of the others on account of her." Rita finished the tea and rested her hands on the placemat. "I would take her except we do have Toffee and the cat and we are trying to start a family. Adding another dog into the mix right now is asking a bit much of Steve." There was no question that Rita was sincerely concerned about the dog.

"I have occasionally thought about a pet although more about a cat simply because that's what single women tend to do." Helen cocked her head. "She's at the office with you?"

Rita nodded enthusiastically. "Does that mean you'll come take a look?"

"No promises. It will be a day or two before I can come."

Rita's smile stretched wide and she raised both hands in either a prelude to a clap or silent supplication. "I understand, I do. I'll keep looking around too, and someone could come in tomorrow, see her, and whisk her home." She dropped her hands and pushed her chair from the table. "And speaking of home, I've taken plenty of your time and need to get myself moving. Thank you for everything, Helen. You do know you're a wonderful person, don't you?"

Helen laughed at the exaggeration. "It was my pleasure, and

while I am flattered, that doesn't mean I'm taking your little Tawny."

"You'll still be wonderful." Rita said as she gathered her belongings and left after a prolonged hug.

Helen stood at the door for a moment and Rita tossed a wave as she drove away. The temperature had dropped another few degrees, and when the wind blew chill across her, Helen closed the door, glad she'd turned on the fireplace. A dog? A chug, of all things! She was still having difficulty envisioning Tawny, but it sort of made sense. Lord knows, the strays that used to show up at her grandparents' farm were some odd mixtures.

She wandered into the kitchen, reflecting on the idea. Despite the size of the living room and kitchen, the house was not the huge size of some of the newer ones. Three bedrooms and two baths had once been considered large. Their master bedroom was not a big suite, being only slightly more spacious than the two others, and no one could mistake the master bath as spa like. It was comfortable, though, a lived-in house, the remodeling giving her the kitchen she'd always wanted, the quilting room that she knew was the envy of many a quilter that saw it, and the coziness of the den where she could feel cocooned in books, quilts, and music or television. All of that was supposed to have been with Mitch, the two of them sharing the life they'd built.

Helen cleared away the tea items, not ready to contemplate dinner, and she listened to the quiet of the house. A dog would be a definite change for her. And, she was about to become a grandmother. On the other hand, it wasn't as if she would be going to Baltimore to be with the baby. Thank goodness for that. A small dog? Well, she would give it serious thought, but it wasn't a decision she needed to make at the moment.

CHAPTER SEVEN

⬥

Helen waited to laugh until after she replaced the receiver. Today, it was Alicia asking if she could come by. Heavens, hopefully Alicia wouldn't have a cat she wanted adopted. Her timing was good, though. Helen hadn't been home long, having been at Collectibles to teach a class and see how Max was fitting in. Everyone seemed to be having a good time and she had issued the invitation for him to come to Tuesday's quilting circle meeting. He'd accepted with a smile, asking about all the women he remembered from high school. And yes, he was planning to have dinner with Phyllis on Saturday. She certainly hadn't let many days pass. Well, they would no doubt have fun, and who knew, Phyllis might be exactly what Max needed.

Helen checked the refrigerator for the pitcher of tea and she still had a half-dozen Cokes™ and diet Coke if Alicia wanted something cold to drink. Was Alicia coming with a quilting project? Helen realized she hadn't said that specifically, and now that she thought about it, her voice had sounded a bit strained. Twenty minutes later when she opened the front door to Alicia,

Helen knew this couldn't possibly be about how to lay out squares for a quilt or adopting a cat. Her tentative smile did not reach to her green eyes and Helen knew too well the signs of leftover tears.

"I'm sorry to just call out of the blue like that…"

Helen automatically pitched her tone to one that Carolyn once told her conveyed sympathy, concern, and the assurance that confidences would be held. "It's no problem at all," she said. "And unless I miss my guess, maybe we should have a seat at the kitchen table. I gather you don't have a quilting question."

"I guess the happy face I'm trying isn't working all that well," she said, tilting her head up a little. "I just didn't know who else to talk to."

Helen motioned to the kitchen. "Hot beverage or cold?"

"Coffee would be good if you have some." Alicia let her burgundy leather shoulder bag slip to the crook of her arm. Helen recognized the burgundy slacks and coordinated burgundy, lightweight merino wool square-neck sweater with flecks of navy from Carolyn's shop. Navy ball earrings and a double strand of navy and gold beads completed the look.

"It won't take more than a few minutes to make," Helen said. "Why don't you sit here at the island while I put it on?" She angled sideways to keep an eye on Alicia as she moved around with the quick preparations. "Shall I ask how you are?"

Alicia draped her purse over the back of the stool, a sigh mixed with her words. "I honestly don't know how to answer that, and I wish I did. I think that I have a problem, and then again, maybe I'm letting my imagination run away with me. I've spent the last few days trying to convince myself there's nothing wrong, but I can't shake the feeling. That's why I thought getting someone else's perspective might help."

"I take it to mean you haven't talked to Hiram?" Helen had only met Hiram one time, and while that had been pleasant, it had been no more than brief social chatter.

"No, no, I… it has to do with my ex-husband."

Helen saw Alicia's face tighten and she leaned onto the island so she could look into Alicia's eyes and spoke gently. "Ah, that can be a difficult subject."

Her mouth trembled, but her voice was steady. "Helen, I don't mean to impose and what I need to talk about is pretty personal. I just…"

Helen felt the familiar surge of concern when someone turned to her with an apparent dilemma they were struggling to articulate. She honestly couldn't say when it had been a conscious choice with her to genuinely listen to people, to provide the proverbial shoulder to cry on. Even when Mitch had teased her about "Helen's Kitchen and Counseling Service," he'd done so with the understanding that her sympathetic nature did not extend to handholding of drama queens. She had no patience for those who created their own problems while simultaneously seeking to blame others. For most, though, tangled emotions were like balls of yarn. Put two or three into a bag and inevitably strands worked loose, becoming ensnared together until you had a knotted mess that could only be unraveled with patient attention. Well, at least it was that way for women. Men often seemed to find other solutions that had nothing to do with patience.

She fleetingly wondered if she had moved the box of tissues away from the telephone. There was a good chance they might be needed. "It's okay, Alicia, really. You haven't been in the circle for long and some of us have been friends for more years than you've been alive. You don't develop that kind of closeness overnight, but I think you've seen that we all have a special friendship. At least I hope you've seen that."

Her mouth relaxed. "Yes, and that's part of what gave me the idea that you would be the right person to call." The coffeemaker beeped and Alicia cocked her head at the sound. A flash of chagrin crossed her pretty face. "If I'm going to pour my soul out to you, it will be better to start from the beginning, if you honestly don't mind."

"I don't," Helen said with a soft smile. "These walls have absorbed a lot of confidences over the years. Let's get coffee ready and move to the table. I have some cookies if you'd like."

"I haven't had much in the way of appetite lately," she said, sliding off the stool and taking a filled mug. "What else can I carry?"

"Sugar and sweetener are on the table. Do you need cream?"

"No, I usually drink mine black unless I'm having one of those frothy jobs," Alicia said, following Helen and sitting to her left. "Where did I say I was going to start?"

"The beginning," Helen prompted. "Although I'm not sure which beginning that would be."

"Not me as a child," Alicia said. "Well, a thumbnail sketch, I suppose. You know I was born and raised in Vicksburg. No big traumas there. My mother is still a schoolteacher, my father is a contracts administrator for the city, and I'm an only child—good grades in school, never in trouble, dated appropriately, and went to my parents' alma mater, the University of Mississippi." She paused for a sip of coffee, her eyes not leaving Helen's face. "All very normal and predictable."

Ah, the emphasis on the word predictable.

"I joined a few clubs, didn't set any academic records, majored in English because I didn't know what I honestly wanted to do, and that seemed to be something useful if you're not very good at math. My dating life was active, but not anyone who gave me the feeling that here was the great romance I was expecting."

"I graduated, and thanks to one of my English professors who noticed that I do have an eye for detail, I was steered into copy editing, and hooray—a job in Jackson, which makes sense as to where such jobs would be available." She ventured a smile. "I'm rambling, aren't I?"

"Laying the foundation," Helen said.

"Yes, so here I am, independent, a good job, all of twenty-three years old, and off I go for a weekend with a girlfriend to Biloxi. We did what girls do and that first night, we're in the lounge of the hotel where we're staying. It was one of the big ones that gave us a great weekend rate. And there he was, already at the bar with a friend." Her voice dropped.

"If I said tall, dark, and handsome, would I be far off?"

"If you added impeccably dressed in an Armani suit with a gold Rolex, you'd be exactly right." She gave a tiny shake of her head. "If you used the word electric or the phrase instant chemistry, you would have the whole picture. Even now, I can't deny that when he looked at us, nudged his friend with his elbow and said, 'Please tell me you're both single, because if I don't have the chance to at least buy you a drink, I will consider the night a complete waste,' I practically melted into the stool next to him."

"That's not a bad line," Helen murmured.

"Leo had more than good lines," Alicia said, probably not aware of the frown tugging at her mouth. "After things fell apart, my girlfriend who was with me said she had wanted to warn me that everything moved much too fast, but she simply didn't think I would listen." Alicia ran her forefinger around the rim of the mug. "She was right. I wouldn't have listened because I couldn't hear, think straight, and could barely breathe. I had walked into an incredible romance and I was showered with attention, fine dining, champagne, dancing, and a promise of more to come. Do you know what he did instead of just saying good-bye?"

Helen raised her eyebrows. "Not proposed that weekend?"

"Not quite," Alicia said. "He paid the bill for our room without telling us. He said he would be in Jackson the next weekend, and sent me home with a dozen long-stemmed roses in one of those boxes where each stem is in a tiny vial with water so they would be fresh when we arrived. Oh, and he included a case of champagne so there would be some left when he came for his visit."

"That would have been impressive," Helen agreed.

Alicia sighed. "Oh yes, and it was a beautiful, different type of bouquet delivered to my office every day and a telephone call every night about how I'd stolen his heart and he couldn't wait to see me." She shrugged. "He was living in New Orleans and his plan for the weekend after Jackson was for me to come there. I was so overwhelmed I couldn't see straight and the girls in the office were just as impressed." She momentarily dropped her eyes, then raised them again. "I called home and told my mother I'd met this great guy, and if I had been able to understand what she was telling me at the time, she was trying to convince me to slow down."

The memory of a similar call from Tricia when she'd met Justin pinged across Helen's mind and it was obvious that the outcome of Alicia's love-at-first-sight hadn't turned out as theirs had.

"So, after this extravagant weekend in Jackson, well, as extravagant as Jackson was, I naturally agreed to go to New Orleans." She lifted the coffee mug partway to her mouth. "Except when Leo greeted me at the airport, he said he had a better idea." She made a quick swallow despite the fact that the coffee was now lukewarm. "He had tickets for Las Vegas. Less than twenty-four hours later, I was Mrs. Leonardo Luigi Rosso. We flew back by way of Vicksburg where we breezed by my parents' home. He apologized for the impetuousness and laid the charm on, but as you can imagine, they were stunned. Ten days later I had quit my job. What little furniture I had was given to the Salvation Army and even most of my clothes, Helen."

"What?"

"Uh-huh," Alicia said, a faint blush to her cheeks that instantly faded. "It was like I was this pretty doll. We get to New Orleans to this fabulous apartment on Poydras and then it's the chauffeur taking me to this exclusive shop where the manager is waiting to create my new wardrobe."

"Goodness," was all Helen could think to say.

"It was literally like being under a spell and it was sheer perfection for the first month."

"I'm listening," Helen said, taking both mugs for a refill. Alicia turned sideways in the chair. "Then it was like, *Okay, I have this taken care of—a pretty little Southern wife.* Had I known about his family in New York at the time, I would have realized I was not what they were expecting any more than my parents expected Leo. Not that I ever actually met his family," she added.

"Things changed for you?"

Alicia took the fresh coffee. "He started staying out all night, coming home still drunk. Again, if I hadn't been so naïve, I would have recognized it was more than booze. He told me he was in the import/export business with a little real estate development on the side. He had lots of international clients that required dinners and late nights. What was I complaining about? Didn't I have everything I needed?" She blew a stream of air across the mug. "I don't want to get into all the details, and Lord knows, I've analyzed it a million ways since then. I was as much a toy to him as was his powerboat and his Ferrari."

"What happened?"

"He never hit me, if that's what you mean," Alicia said with a bleak smile. "But, it was as if I was supposed to simply stay on the shelf until he was ready for me to go with him somewhere to show me off and that got very old, very quickly. We'd had a couple of fights about it, and one night before he went out, I accidentally overheard him on the telephone with someone." Her hand trembled slightly as she lifted the mug and then put it down without taking a drink. "I don't know who he was talking to, but there was no question as to what he was saying—cursing and using terms like *bury the bum, no one treats us like that and gets away with it,* that sort of thing. He saw me, and I'm sure I had this shocked expression on my face because he laughed and said it was nothing, that everyone in business talked like that."

"You didn't believe him?"

Alicia lifted the mug again. "It was the look on his face when he turned, before it registered with him that I had heard. Helen, it was more than anger. There was this wildness in his eyes that genuinely frightened me."

"What did you do?"

"I pretended to laugh it off and asked him to stay home instead. I suspected that in his frame of mind, that was the last thing he wanted to do, and sure enough, he was gone within minutes." Alicia held up one finger as she took a drink. "I was truly struck with the sensation that if I didn't get out of there right away, I might never leave. I'm still not sure I can accurately describe the feeling that overcame me. I packed one bag of the least expensive clothes, left the jewelry because I took part of the stack of cash that he kept in his dresser, and wrote him a note. I told him I was gone and I didn't want to hear from him until I sent the divorce papers."

"He accepted that?"

Alicia drew in a deep breath and exhaled it. "I went directly to my parents' house because I couldn't think of where else to go. He called me the next afternoon, and I swear, Helen, it was as if he was no longer interested. He said if I had no better sense than to leave him, he could replace me with the snap of a finger and not to bother with a divorce. He would arrange for an annulment."

"Did he?"

"I had the paperwork within four months. I couldn't face

going back to Jackson, and a friend of my mother had a cousin in Augusta who said she would help me find a job. It seemed like a good place to start over."

"It is a nice city." Helen said.

"I found an apartment within bicycling distance of my job, took on as much work as I could, and began recreational cycling as a way to release my energy. I began quilting, thanks to one of the women in the office, and I stayed out of bars and away from men for almost a year."

"You were still very young," Helen pointed out softly.

Alicia bobbed her head. "I know, but more than anything, I needed to regain my balance and figure out how I let myself get into a situation like that."

Helen was only partially surprised with Alicia's revelations. If it was one thing she'd learned in listening to people's problems, it was that what you saw on the surface, what you thought you knew about anyone was often not true. The town of Wallington might be small and many of the residents were familiar with each other over multiple generations, yet a façade versus the reality of people was common. "You apparently did so."

"Yes, and it was the simplest answer of all. I fell for Leo's looks, money, charm, and the notion of love at first sight. Small-town girl meets handsome stranger so very different from anyone she'd ever encountered." Her smile was crooked this time. "I'm not knocking love at first sight, but it's not usually actual love, is it?"

Once again, Helen set aside her own initial misgivings when Tricia had claimed that same "he's the one" about Justin. The difference, well, one of many differences, was that she and Justin had waited several months before getting married. "Instant attraction can be deceiving," was what Helen settled for.

"Yes, and if you stood Hiram and Leo side by side, there isn't much doubt as to which man women would flock to," she said, the corners of her mouth curving upward. "I met Hiram by accident in a way, or maybe it wasn't if you believe in fate. The company where I worked had multiple periodicals we published. Not all of our clients were local and a gentleman who was the editor for one of the smaller magazines was also in Kiwanis and he was in town for a conference. He knew Hiram from other Kiwanis events, and when my boss asked me to go to dinner with her to make it a foursome, I thought, hey, why not? I mean two guys in Kiwanis—that should be a safe enough evening."

She placed her hands loosely around the mug. "It was, in a way. Hiram, as you know, and I say this in a loving way, does not fall into the eye-candy category."

Helen couldn't argue that, thinking of his average height, a slim build almost to the point of being skinny, prematurely receding hairline, and almost lashless brown eyes behind less than fashionable glasses—a nice smile, though.

"He was interesting and could carry on a decent conversation and we'd exchanged business cards, of course. It turned out he worked less than a block from where I did and lived close by, too. There was a special exhibit at the Morris Museum I had mentioned during dinner and he called to see if I wanted to go with him. It was all very low-key and the more time I spent with him, the more I came to see what a good man he was—sweet in little ways, nothing at all flashy."

Helen didn't want to ask if perhaps Alicia had deliberately selected a man who sounded like the complete opposite of Leo. That wasn't really important.

"All I told him about my marriage was that it had been a mistake I regretted, and he said he hoped it hadn't completely set me off of the idea." She blinked rapidly to hold back tears. "We dated for not quite five months when he proposed. It was a small wedding but a lovely one, and we did it the right way."

"At home or in Augusta?"

"Oh, the church I grew up in," she said quickly. "It was the kind of wedding my mother had always envisioned. We hadn't been married for long, though, when the accounting office that Hiram worked for was bought out by a large corporation, and it wasn't something he really wanted. He preferred the small firm."

"That's why y'all moved here?"

Alicia nodded. "Yes, Mr. Longley is also in Kiwanis, and they've known each other for a while. He was looking to bring on someone younger and it was a good fit. Mr. Longley has been able to cut back and the plan is for Hiram to buy him out at a mutually agreed upon time." Her blinking didn't stop the welling in her eyes and Helen pushed a napkin toward her.

"Thanks," Alicia sniffed and dabbed her eyes. "So, here we are, in a wonderful little town. Hiram has what is basically the perfect job for him, I've been successful in switching to freelance, I love being in the quilting circle, and then…"

Helen waited.

"It was the trip to Atlanta," Alicia said, her voice low. "Leo was there, Helen. He came into the bar that night before we went to dinner. He was with some other men and I tried not to react. I was hoping he wouldn't see me."

"Ah, you're certain it was him?"

"Yes," Alicia said. "There was no mistaking who he was and I couldn't wait to get out of there." She took a shuddering breath. "I didn't think he saw me, and I went straight to my room when we returned from the restaurant. Now, though, now I'm wondering if he's in Wallington. There are some things I can't explain, but maybe it's only my imagination."

"Oh, dear," Helen said. "Okay, why don't you tell me what's been happening?"

CHAPTER EIGHT

Helen touched a finger against her forehead before Alicia said anything else. "You know, perhaps I should call Justin and ask him to come over if he can."

Alicia took her hands from around the mug. "I wouldn't want to bother him if this is all my imagination."

"Unless he's in the middle of something unexpected, he isn't going to mind and what I'm thinking is that he probably has more experience with this type of thing than you or I. He doesn't need to know the details of how you were married, and quite frankly, he won't ask."

Alicia nodded thoughtfully. "Uh, that does make sense. Why don't I run to the bathroom while you're calling?"

Considering how quickly he agreed to come over, Helen assumed Justin was stuck behind the desk doing paperwork. In the short span before he arrived, she made another pot of coffee and tempted Alicia with the white chocolate macadamia nut cookies she knew Justin would want at that point in the afternoon.

Alicia stepped close to Helen, the sound of a car door slamming. "Helen, I can't thank you enough for this."

"I haven't done much yet," Helen said gently.

"Just being able to talk about it has helped," the younger woman said. "I know I may need to tell Hiram, but I wasn't sure how to even start."

Justin came into the kitchen looking official in his uniform, and as he often did, unbuckled his belt that held his pistol and other equipment and draped it over the back of a chair within easy reach. Helen made introductions, and his smile to Alicia seemed to put her at ease.

"I was explaining to Helen that this could be nothing. I might be imagining things just because I was so startled at seeing my ex-husband."

Justin, two cookies on a napkin in front of him, didn't have his notebook out. "Our instincts are frequently correct," he said, breaking off a chunk of cookie. "Can you give me a little background before you tell me about what has your senses on alert?"

Helen appreciated his manner, not that she had doubted he would handle it correctly, and Alicia repeated much of what she'd told Helen without the emphasis on why she'd rushed into the marriage.

"You never knew for certain what sort of activities he was involved with?"

Alicia shook her head. "Only that it, or something, paid for a high-living lifestyle and that a number of his business acquaintances had foreign names." She dropped her eyes briefly as she had done before; then she looked directly at Justin, her face still. "Once I was out of there and beginning to think straight again, it was pretty obvious he was no stranger to recreational drugs. Cocaine, I suppose, but I don't know the real signs."

"It sounds like you're probably right on that," he said. "Was he ever violent toward you?"

Alicia hesitated. "Not actually. When we started fighting about—well, when I started objecting to—how I was being treated, it was more placating than anger; how I should relax and enjoy being taken care of, and let myself be pampered. The next stage was impatience. He couldn't understand what I was upset about."

Justin nodded, silently chewing a cookie.

"I still don't know exactly how to describe the panic I felt that night I left. There was something about the expression on his face that I…"

"Did the smart thing," Justin said quickly. "Domestic violence cases are much more common than people realize and the first explosion can come in the blink of an eye. Your description sounds like a classic control situation and you were wise to run."

Alicia gave him a grateful look, and if it had been appropriate, Helen would have given him a hug. What a supportive thing for him to say.

"Now, if you don't mind, can you tell me the sorts of things that have been happening?"

"Yes," Alicia said immediately. "Really, it started two days after we returned—a telephone call I thought was a wrong number because as soon as I answered, it was disconnected. I didn't recognize the caller ID number. Then it happened three more days in a row, but at different times."

"You work from home?"

"Mostly. I'm a copy editor and proofreader and I do that remotely. I've been taking training for my real estate license, too, so I'm out of the house for that."

Helen remembered Alicia had mentioned she was going to

start the class that Clarissa Grigsby ran three times a year. As far as Helen was concerned, she was the best agent in town and the right one from which to learn.

"I'm not sure when this part started, but I guess it was the third day of these phone calls that I went to the grocery store. For some reason, I noticed a black Cadillac parked two rows behind me. Well, I say for some reason. It was because Leo had a black Cadillac with a driver that he—we—used. The car reminded me of him."

"And then you started seeing it more often?"

Alicia nodded once. "Yes. It was never very close and I mean, really, it is a small town, so there aren't that many different grocery stores and banks to go to. Anyone could be driving it."

Helen fleetingly wondered what kind of car Max drove. He had arrived in town right after the Atlanta show. Wouldn't that be a coincidence?

Justin finished the second cookie and his first mug of coffee. "There's something else though, isn't there?"

Alicia cast a quick look at Helen, then drew a deep breath. She held it and exhaled slowly. "I think someone was in the house yesterday while I was gone to class."

Oh my, that would explain the telephone call.

Justin leaned forward slightly. "Not a real break-in, you mean? Not a robbery?"

"I, no, I mean, no, not the door damaged or a window broken." She twisted the mug around on the saucer, her eyes not leaving Justin's face. "We don't keep a key under the doormat or anything, but it's not like we have an alarm system, either. I came into the house and I'm always good about turning out the light when I'm not in a room. My daddy was big on that. I went into my office and the light by the desk was on. Then I noticed the stack of files

I'd been working on that morning didn't seem to be in exactly the place I'd left them." She half smiled. "Our cat, Blaze, sometimes jumps on the desk, though, so she could have done that and moved them."

Justin smiled encouragingly. "What did you do next?"

"I had this creepy feeling and I walked around to look, I guess, is what I was doing."

Helen noticed how Alicia's jaw was tightening. "I went into our bedroom and it was the same thing. The closet light was on and my jewelry box was a couple of inches over from where I usually keep it. Nothing was missing, though, nothing in the house, and there were no muddy footprints or anything like that—not one single thing I could have called and put into a complaint without sounding like a paranoid person."

"Did you ask to see if your husband had perhaps come home unexpectedly?" Justin's voice was neutral.

Alicia shook her head rapidly. "He was out of town all day yesterday on business. He left half an hour earlier than usual and didn't get home until almost six o'clock." She relaxed her jaw and glanced at Helen. "I've been stressed, though, and leaving a light or two on or bumping a jewelry box without realizing it isn't beyond something that I could have done."

Justin took a pen and a notebook from his front pocket, a small black spiral one. "I don't know either, Alicia, but I'm glad Helen called."

"You are? Then you don't think I'm jumping to conclusions?"

Helen heard the thinly veiled relief.

"What you're describing is not unusual," Justin said. "It might not be anything, and maybe you have been distracted and left lights on and so forth. I'd like to get your ex-husband's name, though, his address, and any friends or business contacts you might know.

And I'm going to give you a card with my cell phone number. If you see the black Cadillac again, try to get at least a partial license plate, or just call right away with the location."

"Thank you," Alicia said, her face genuinely relaxing for the first time that afternoon. "I really appreciate this, both of you, I mean."

"No problem," Justin said, shook Alicia's hand, and gave Helen a good-bye kiss after he copied down the information.

"Oh, Helen, I honestly hope you don't mind me coming to you, because this takes such a load off of me," Alicia said as they stood at the table.

Helen wanted to reassure her. "This has not been the least bit of a problem for me. Are you going to tell Hiram?"

Alicia sighed, grasping the back of the chair she'd been sitting in. "I really should, shouldn't I? He's asked me a couple of times if I'm feeling okay, and I've made some silly excuse. Hiram is such a sweetheart that I haven't wanted to worry him."

"I understand that," Helen said. "You know how we women are, though. He might be wondering if he's done something to upset you that he isn't aware of. And, if your ex-husband is here lurking about, having two sets of eyes on the lookout for him would be better than one, don't you think?"

"Yes, of course," Alicia said, slipping her purse over her shoulder. "You've been such a dear. Thank you again."

Helen walked her to the door, their good-bye hug prolonged as she planted a kiss on top of Alicia's head. That brought another smile, a recognition of the maternal warmth of the gesture. Well, Alicia was practically the same age as Tricia.

Helen paused in the quilting room, seeing the group as they had been on Tuesday. It was funny how she could see it differently now, Alicia being more quiet than normal. They always chattered among themselves and especially so if Phyllis was wound up. The topic of inviting Max to the circle had certainly gotten everyone's attention and that had dominated the conversation for most of the evening. She wandered to the table with the quilt she was working on waiting for her. She stood, thinking she might finish a couple of squares before she bothered with the few dishes in the kitchen.

While she sympathized with Alicia, the story was a bit disturbing. She was no expert, but Justin had taken the possibility of her ex-husband stalking her seriously. Was stalking the right term? She couldn't recall having ever had a situation quite like this in town. It wasn't out of the ordinary for estranged or ex-husbands and boyfriends to not want to let go of a relationship, but it was overt, not slipping around. Lord, she remembered when Edna kicked Wally out of the house. It had been a long time coming between his drinking and his unwillingness to find steady work he would stick with. She'd finally had enough and he would come around the beauty parlor at all hours of the day begging her to give him another chance, show up at the house after the bars closed, and made a total nuisance out of himself. Edna put up with it for a while until one day when she had every chair booked and had brought Rosa in to give her a hand. Wally had stumbled through the front, waving around a batch of wildflowers, swearing he was a changed man and would do right by her. She'd stopped in the middle of cutting Helen's hair and walked to the counter where she kept the .38 underneath the register. She'd yanked it out and told Wally he could leave of his own accord and quit bothering her or she'd call the chief, or put a round right through his lying heart, depending on how the spirit moved her, and he had exactly three seconds to decide. That had been the end of Wally's attempts at reconciliation.

Based on the way Alicia described her ex-husband, she didn't think he was as harmless as Wally. The idea he might have been in

Alicia and Hiram's house was definitely upsetting, and yes, now that she thought of it, a little quilting and some music was what she needed. She turned the television to one of her favorite music channels, and as the sound of Celtic Women floated through the room, she sat at the table.

Helen was two-thirds of the way through the quilt she was intending to send to Justin's mother, Sue, for Christmas. It was a ribbon quilt with three vertical panels of a lovely fabric with seventeenth- and eighteenth-century sailing ships with two panels of solid medium-blue fabric separating them. The five panels were bordered with a thin navy-blue cord and the binding was reminiscent of a ship's sail, although in a lighter weight fabric than real canvas. It was a simple design with limited colors because they had only visited the Kendall's Baltimore house once and they had stayed in the front rooms. She didn't think she could go wrong with a nautical theme.

Her mind flowed between the stitches and the music, thinking of Alicia's comment about taking up quilting as a hobby. Most young women who became quilters did so because they were from generations of quilters, or they were skilled in any of several fabric arts such as sewing, embroidering, crocheting, and knitting, and quilting was an aspect they admired. It was a hobby that could indeed occupy your mind as well as your hands. For most of them, it easily became a passion even if someone didn't identify it that way. There was such a richness in quilting with an endless variety of designs and projects. It had such a practicality to it. Someone could never move beyond the basics, creating quilt after quilt to contribute to good causes, or use it as a source for clever gifts. Quilted objects were popular even if they'd done something as simple as a shopping bag or the stacks of placemats and napkins that Tricia had produced in her early quilting years.

The artistry of quilting edged her thoughts to Max. As far as she knew, there were no male quilters in Wallington, or at least none that belonged to a circle or attended events. Edith, Max's mother, had bemoaned the fact that Angela had shown no interest in the craft, and she had probably discussed that with him during a visit. It didn't seem likely that Max simply woke up one day and decided he wanted to try his hand at quilting. Now that she was focusing on it, Helen did remember being at The Arbors with a group of the women in the main activities room off the dining room. There were five or six of them and everyone was actually working on different squares or panels and not whole quilts that day. Edith had made the comment about Max, and of course, the idea of a son who quilted sparked lively discussion. How funny she had completely forgotten about that day.

Click for Quilting, the company Max was representing at the show in Atlanta, was well known among quilters and they had branched out from mostly patterns and supplies into having a newsletter, a blog, hard-to-find and antique quilting tools, and memorabilia.

Ah, the Atlanta show. She had never been to a show she didn't enjoy and there was something special about introducing quilters to their first show. What a shame it was marred for Alicia and none of them realized what a fright she'd experienced. She was so glad Justin was involved now. He was an excellent police officer and she didn't think that only because he was her son-in-law. She felt confident he would get to the bottom of it quickly.

CHAPTER NINE

Everyone on the force was still trying to become accustomed to referring to Chief of Police McFarlane as Chief McFarlane. The county had issued a memorandum that municipalities should immediately use the term sheriff only as it applied to the county sheriff, and all respective towns would use the term chief of police. It wasn't that anyone really minded the change, however, it was always a little awkward to reverse years of habit.

It was easier for Justin since he was still the newest member of the small force and chief was the title of his former boss in Baltimore. This was one of those stray thoughts that passed across Justin's mind as they sat in familiar spots. Just now, Justin was in the wooden chair in front of the uncluttered desk with the chief propped on the corner. He had listened to Justin's explanation of the discussion at Helen's, his brown eyes attentive. His short brown hair salted with white and skin leathered by outdoor hobbies of canoeing and fishing made him appear older than Justin knew him to be. Even in this casual posture, he sat erect, without being stiff. He barely missed being six feet tall and he either deliberately kept his muscled weight a little under two hundred pounds or his physique was a natural product of his physical activities.

The rectangular fluorescent light fixture glowed white light in the utilitarian office, the afternoon sun obscured by clouds that may or may not bring rain depending on variables that the weatherman had explained on the noon news. The heavy dark blue curtains that could be drawn across the two street-side windows for privacy were open, and there was little traffic at this time of day.

"You do a search on the ex-husband? What did you say his name was?"

"Leonardo Luigi Rosso," Justin said, not bothering to emphasize the pure Italian sound of it.

Chief McFarlane raised his eyebrows. "I suppose it would be politically incorrect to make assumptions based on his name, a wealthy lifestyle, and having foreign business associates."

"His current address is New Orleans with most of his life spent in his native New York."

"Isn't that interesting? What else do we know about Mr. Rosso?"

Justin had spent half an hour on the telephone with a contact in New York whom he'd met when he was on the force in Baltimore, during several days of a joint investigation that involved a murder suspect fleeing New York. "Mr. Rosso is the youngest of four sons and one daughter in the family of David Enrico and Catherine Isabella Rosso. The family has a number of business interests that include New Jersey, Miami, and New Orleans."

"One son in each and the oldest stays in New York?"

Justin had quickly learned the chief's easy-going style was more style than reality. Little happened in town or the county that he was unaware of, he kept up to date on state and regional crime news, and he subscribed to professional periodicals that were delivered to his home where he could read them at leisure. "Yes, according to my contact. This is one of those families that mostly keeps a low profile, or at least not many arrests, and definitely no convictions."

"Your contact does know of them, though?"

Justin nodded. "They are indeed known within the organizations that keep an eye on these things. Leo Rosso has been arrested on minor charges that disappeared before prosecution could proceed, except for one assault and that also disappeared when the individual refused to press charges."

Chief McFarlane squinted his eyes briefly, a sign that Justin learned meant he was calculating. He gave a little grunt. "Don't think I have any contacts in New Orleans. Your guy have any speculation about the youngest Mr. Rosso?"

"His reputation is as the least discreet of the sons, and that could well be why he is in New Orleans rather than closer to home." He shifted in the chair that was worn smooth by many years of use. "Do we want to put in an official request for information?"

Chief McFarlane rubbed a palm across the top of his hair. "Sure, can't hurt. What are your thoughts about the Johnsons?"

Despite Justin's position as the junior officer on the police force, his experience in Baltimore and his performance had been recognized by the chief and amicably accepted by the others. He was the first to admit he was still puzzled by what he viewed as peculiarities of life in Wallington, but when it came to the potential that big city crime might be touching them, he was the right person to offer some perspective.

"I could see this either way. Mrs. Johnson was obviously rattled by seeing her ex-husband, and that could have upset her to the point that she's having ordinary mental lapses such as leaving lights on without realizing it and is reading too much into all of this. On the other hand, I've worked a few stalking cases, and while this one is pretty mild compared to those, the pattern would be correct."

"Yeah," the chief drawled, "around here, guys don't want to let go. They're more open about it, likely to make fools of themselves, get in a fight and what have you, not sneak around. Did Mrs. Johnson tell her husband about this?"

"My impression is that she was going to," Justin said. "I thought I would call her, see if I could meet with them, and talk through a couple of precautions to take."

"That sounds like a plan," the chief said, rising from the desk. "I don't think we have more than a dozen black Caddies in town. Fred Hillman won't own anything but a red one. Folks that buy those kinds of cars are a mix between Caddies and Lincolns and Walt Wallington bought his wife a Mercedes last year. We'll keep an eye out for one that doesn't fit in." The chief grinned. "We don't need to tell Sheila yet. I would hate to think we've got some legitimate businessman in town looking to bring us jobs, and he gets labeled as a nefarious out-of-towner."

Justin couldn't suppress a laugh at the accurate assessment. Sheila Tipton, who in many ways was the real linchpin to the department, had a formidable network that extended throughout the town. She had come to work at the station right out of high school as a clerk, and within a year, she was the dispatcher and on her way to being an astute administrator. Her lack of formal education was no impediment to her stature among people who came to the station for help or in running afoul of the law. In their open environment, and with more than forty years at her job, she was privy to a lot of information about the citizens of Wallington. She might not have the computer skills of their part-time employee, Kelly Gleason, but they hardly operated with cutting-edge technology. Sheila's memory, ability to connect with people, and sternness when called for, were characteristics that were as respected as they were well known. She was not a woman you wanted to cross. Her wiry five-foot-five frame was capable of exuding a don't even think of messing with me attitude that could be flipped on like a light switch.

Justin stood, the conversation at a close. "I've got it," he said, leaving the chief to whatever tasks he intended to complete before he greeted the night patrol. The other four desks in the open bay were unoccupied and Sheila was at the reception counter, the frosted glass double doors behind her propped open as usual. She was on the telephone, though, with her back to him, and he made the call to Alicia Johnson to see if he could stop by on his way home. She thanked him again and asked if he could give her an hour to break the news to her husband. With that set up, Justin called Tricia to see how she was feeling and let her know he would be a little late getting home.

Despite what Tricia said, she sounded tired to him, a condition that made sense at this point in her pregnancy. "I have to go right by Bess's Place on the way back, so why don't I pick up that salmon you like? That way, you can just relax and not worry about dinner."

He imagined her smiling into the phone. "What a sweetheart you are. I think I want the chicken, though—that new recipe with a mushroom sauce."

"I'll get the salmon for me, and if you change your mind, you can have some or all of it," he said, making a note of her preference. He would get a slice of their triple chocolate cake, too. Although her craving for sweets had been intermittent, it was a strong urge when it struck. He sneaked a look around, relieved he was alone and knowing that, in all likelihood, he had a silly grin on his face. There were these moments when he was struck with the thought of what it was going to be like to be a father—not a father, a dad.

He hadn't had the opportunity to know Tricia's dad for long before cancer took him, but he'd liked him and had heard a lot of stories since they moved to Wallington. His own dad and his two uncles were all great role models. In his dad's case, he had made his way from apprentice electrician to owning his own family-run store with two vans to handle their workload. He was a man who lived the ideals of his word as his bond, working hard and taking Sunday as a family day. Sure, he had guys to handle emergencies, but not to have the store open on Sunday. He'd carved out time for Little League, too, stepping up to be a coach and not cutting his sons any slack if they got sloppy. He hadn't missed many ball games, either. He was in the stands middle through high school as much as he could. He appreciated the value of education and made sure there was money for college for all of them. These were quiet sacrifices Justin hadn't understood until later. Not that his mother wasn't a part of that, of course she was. She and his sister had that same mother-daughter bond he saw between Helen and Tricia. With fathers and sons it was less open, yet he didn't think that made it less strong. There were those games of catch in the backyard, drinking a cold beer watching Sunday football on TV, having the occasional outing to the stadium, or fishing in the Chesapeake—they didn't need verbal exchanges of affection for that. Discipline had been swiftly applied when it was required. Groundings or extra work in the dirtiest part of the shop were a reminder when boyhood pranks got out of control. Justin mostly felt confident he could pass that along to his son or daughter if that were to be. He would be less than honest if he didn't acknowledge there were flashes of worry about becoming a new dad, and he was just as certain he was not alone with that, not that he would ever bring the subject up to anyone.

A ping on his computer alerting him to an incoming e-mail broke into his thoughts, and he read the message from his contact in New York asking if he needed any more information about Leo Rosso. He replied with a request asking if he knew anyone in the New Orleans Police Department, not expecting that he would. When he confirmed that as a "no," Justin pulled up the directory for New Orleans and looked through to see if any names might be familiar. No luck. He selected a name that sounded like the correct person in their hierarchy to call as a matter of routine inquiry. The individual with a noticeable "Who dat?" accent passed him to another office, linking him to a Sergeant Robbichaut who was only marginally easier to understand. In what he thought was a longer conversation than necessary because they shifted to the topic of why the New Orleans Saints would be Super Bowl contenders again, the man assured Justin that his request would be processed. The time frame was difficult to say unless it was urgent and Justin couldn't make that claim. Probably no longer than a few days? Yes, that would be fine. Saints going to the Super Bowl again? Sure, they were playing well, but the Falcons were on a roll, and his Ravens had recovered from a stumble early in the season.

He logged off the computer and waved good-bye to Sheila who waggled her fingers, the receiver still pressed to her ear. Bess's Place's parking lot was almost full as he drove past. Happy hour prices offered ten-cent wings and $3.00 nachos in effect until 7:00 p.m. He planned to call his order in as he left the Johnson's. A blue Toyota Camry and a silver Highlander sat side by side in the carport of the older split-level home that either the Johnsons were remodeling or updates had been completed before they purchased the house. The dark gray paint of the brick below the windows was fresh, the lighter gray shingle siding above new, and the white trim had no telltale stains of age. They had the closed gutter system that he was thinking about having installed and two small satellite dishes instead of one, which probably meant they had a very high-speed Internet connection. That was a reasonable assumption with Mrs. Johnson working remotely and passing large files.

The front door was recessed rather than having a porch. A circular pewter doorknocker was mounted on the six-panel white steel door with a pewter cover for the bell that chimed pleasantly when pressed. He took note that the lock was the type that could be easily jimmied with no sign of forced entry.

The man that greeted him with, "Please, come on in, I'm Hiram Johnson," was so ordinary that if Justin asked a witness to describe him there would be a pause as the individual tried to summon a memorable feature.

"You already know my wife, Alicia," he said, motioning to the two steps that led up from the foyer. Justin noticed a longer set leading downstairs. "We'll be in the living room."

Justin imagined the hardwood floors had replaced shag carpeting and an oval mirror with a frame made from overlapping pewter discs broke up the expanse of the off-white wall.

"Would you care for tea, a Coke, or something else?" Alicia called over her shoulder.

"No, thank you, I'm fine," he said, hoping his stomach wouldn't rumble in response to the delicious smell wafting from the unseen kitchen. He envisioned perhaps a pot of simmering beef stew.

One of the reasons he didn't care for split levels was the tendency for rooms to be separated instead of having a more open plan and this was a typical layout. It was an airy room, however, with a set of three windows across the front, the dark red Roman fabric shades topped with a padded printed valance. Cushions on the deep red and gold striped sofa were of the same fabric as the valance with the two upholstered easy chairs in a cream color. The coordinating cream, red, gold, and green colors of the area rug that protected the floor were muted to where it might be an antique.

The coffee table in front of the sofa and matching occasional table between the chairs were mission style with a shelf below where magazines were displayed. The top of the smaller table was bare. A shallow, dark-green ceramic bowl in the center of the coffee table held an arrangement of dried flowers. The paintings on the white walls were still life all being framed oils of different sizes featuring fruits and flowers.

Justin took the chair to the left of the sofa where the Johnsons sat. Justin noted Alicia's hand tucked loosely into her husband's. She hadn't completely erased the tension from her eyes, although the tightness had disappeared from her face.

"Alicia explained the situation to me," Hiram said, his voice calm. "She isn't given to fantasy and I was not home yesterday. We'll have one of the combination security, fire, and carbon monoxide alert systems installed this week. It's something we had previously discussed. What are your other suggestions?"

Direct and to the point, that was a change from the usual rambling approach that most people in town took, and Justin returned the courtesy. "I think that's a good idea. We've requested a police report on Mr. Rosso in case there is something of interest. We will quietly keep an eye out for the car you described, and I would ask if either of you see it, to call me immediately with as much of a license plate number as you can get." He handed his card to Hiram. "I'd be glad to ask the patrol to increase their presence in the neighborhood if you'd like."

A trace of a frown creased Hiram's high forehead and Alicia sucked in her lower lip. "I don't think we need to do that yet, Officer Kendall, although we will yield to your advice."

Justin wasn't surprised. "I agree with you, although I did want to make the offer. I'm sure your neighbors will notice the security system sign the technicians usually put in the yard and that will probably cause them to be extra observant for the first few days. It's a natural reaction."

"I have no doubt that the telephone will be ringing the second the installers leave," Alicia said with what was almost a smile. "The ones who've been urging us to get with the modern age will want to know what we went with and the others will want to make sure that we're okay."

Justin stood, his stomach threatening to let loose with a loud growl. "Don't hesitate to contact me if you think of another question and do call the station directly if anything else happens," he said.

"I'll walk you out," Hiram said, giving Alicia's hand a squeeze. He stepped outside with Justin, the temperature having dropped as the sun arced downward.

"Thank you for coming by and for taking Alicia seriously," he said, holding out his hand. "I wished she'd told me when things first started and I don't want to press her about her ex-husband. What happened then hasn't ever mattered to me, but if you find anything disturbing, you'll let me know right away?"

Justin heard the note of urgency beneath the calm and there was a firmness in Hiram's eyes that Justin recognized. This was the kind of man who, as a boy, would have been ignored, if not subjected to bullying, with the mistaken notion that he was a weakling. Perhaps he'd even been the turn-the-cheek type— once. Then he would have landed a punch with enough force to get his point across and offered to tutor the jocks to keep them academically eligible to play.

"I'll do that," he said, the promise sealed with a handshake. He sat in the car for a minute before cranking it, not wanting the squawk of the radio to interfere with the call to Bess's Place. His stomach gurgled in either approval or impatience, he wasn't sure which.

CHAPTER TEN

Helen didn't expect to see many cars in the parking lot at ten o'clock in the morning with no class scheduled. She promised Rita she would come see the small dog, Tawny, and she wanted to complete her other errands first. She'd mentioned the idea of adopting Tawny to Tricia last night.

"Of course, you should if you want to," she said without the slightest hesitation. "She sounds like the perfect size and if she's housebroken and old enough to be out of the chewing phase. I don't think it would be a bad transition for you."

Helen put those comments in the mental pros column she had to admit was longer than the cons, that consisted of only two entries: never had an indoor pet and would have to clean up dog poop.

She had spoken with Tricia right after Alicia called to thank her again for her help. She'd been particularly relieved to hear how Hiram had taken the news and that they were both impressed with Justin.

Helen entered the Memories and Collectibles foyer, breathing in a delicious scent from a lovely arrangement that sat on the marble topped table to the left of the door. She paused to look at the woven-twig harvest basket filled with dried moss. Three ceramic pumpkin-shaped candleholders were nestled in the moss: one candle in cinnamon, one pumpkin spice, and one nutmeg, according to the peel-off labels. Dried brown-toned protea, creamy-colored plumosum, and yellow-tipped echinacea were arranged around the candleholders for a low enough profile that it could serve as a centerpiece.

Lillian was on the telephone and smiled a greeting. Helen could see the backs of two women in the main quilting room. They were looking at one of the quilts hung on a floor-mounted wooden frame. Wanda had three of them set out from the far wall with a quilt mounted on each side of the frame to simultaneously display six quilts. She also took quilts on consignment and would usually feature them on the frames. She preferred to have different styles whenever possible, and at the moment, there were patchwork quilts, hand-tied quilts, and two with autumn-themed appliqués.

"Helen, it's good to see you, but you just missed Wanda. She'll be gone for an hour or so," Max said, coming from the doll room, or more likely the office. He held up a mug, one with a quilt motif. "I have a fresh pot of Guatemalan brewed."

"One of my favorites," she said, suddenly realizing she hadn't seen Max since he arrived in town. "I know you and Wanda have a lot to do in a short time and I didn't want to be in the way."

He laughed, his wide smile welcoming. "I can't imagine you ever being in the way. Come on back for a cup of coffee and we'll talk. Lucy Morgan and Sherry Gleason are looking for inspiration and they don't need any help with that."

No, they not only didn't need help, they preferred to be alone. Helen knew from experience that the cousins could spend at least an hour wandering among the quilts absorbing ideas. Lucy had won more than one ribbon in competitions based on her intricate designs.

She followed Max to the kitchen, settling at the table where she'd sat so many times with Wanda. It was going to feel odd with her being away. "How are you and how is your mamma?"

"She's great. She's absolutely thrilled with this whole business, although she's half convinced that Angela will be eaten by a crocodile or python while she's in Belize." He raised his eyebrows. "Angela swears they all carry around pistols expressly for that purpose and so far, they haven't lost a single person at the site."

"I'm sure it will be a wonderful experience for her," Helen said, thinking that visiting Belize would be nice, but spending two or three months under what she assumed were fairly austere conditions was entirely too much work. Wanda's time spent on a cruise ship sounded like more fun.

"And I'm getting to know the town again," Max was saying. "Not too many changes and most of them seem for the better. Although I noticed Fred Hillman appears to be prospering. Guess that can't be helped." His gray eyes sparked humor. "Hope he's not a friend of yours."

Helen was startled to hear herself give a little snort. "Not hardly, for a list much too long to get into."

"He's been a piece of work as far back as I can remember, always throwing his family name around and dividing people into the *right* and *wrong* kind. One of those guys that if you could buy him for what he was really worth and sell him for what he thought he was, you'd make a hefty profit." He dismissed the thought with a wave. "Oh, I had dinner with Phyllis the other night over at the Copper Pot. That's definitely on my list as a favorite place. I went for comfort food with the chicken pot pie. I meant to take some as leftovers and ate it all instead. I compromised and only ate two bites of the peach cobbler and took that with me."

"They get most of their ingredients locally," Helen said. "That's a goal they set and so far, it works well for them. They keep their regular menu fairly limited and their specials are based on what they can get. As a matter of fact, they grow their own herbs."

"I'm not surprised," Max said and patted his stomach. "I like having choices, although I don't mind cooking for myself."

Helen peered over her mug. Phyllis's account of their dinner together had been that of simply two people sharing a meal and it didn't sound as if Max had viewed it as anything more. "Did Phyllis remind you about the circle for Tuesday? We'd love to have you come." She hesitated. "Of course, you may already have invitations to other circles. It doesn't take long for the news to get around."

The cornflower-blue cotton sweater Max was wearing brought out a hint of blue in his gray eyes and the creases around them deepened as his smile stretched wider. "I have indeed received one or two other invitations and I would love to make your Tuesday my first, but I promised Mamma I would be her substitute bridge partner that night. The following Tuesday will be okay?"

"Certainly, everyone is looking forward to it."

Max winked at her. "It's okay to ask, Helen, really it is."

Helen didn't feel a blush to her cheeks and wondered if they had pinked beneath the light make-up she wore. "Well, it's just that…"

"I couldn't resist a little bit of tease," he said, laughter lacing his words. "I never intended, much less expected, to get into quilting. It's sort of like when football stars are interviewed and it turns out they knit or read romance novels. Sure, men are all over the place with fashion design, but most people do view quilting as exclusive to women. You want a refill?"

"I'm good," Helen said, wanting to hear more about how he came to the hobby.

He scooted his chair back a bit. "I bet you guessed that the starting point was Mamma with her carrying on about Angela never being interested in it."

Helen nodded, having remembered.

"Like I said, it's been almost ten years now. I was in this high stress job. I loved it, mind you, but there was a lot of traveling, and I mean traveling to places where you weren't always sure what time zone you were in. One of my worst trips was a meeting in Paris that I dashed out of to catch a plane for Tokyo where I finished up and headed to Bangkok."

"Goodness gracious," Helen said instinctively. "That must have been exhausting."

"You get used to it," he said with a shrug. "Then you make an exit plan for yourself and let the younger, hungrier guys take over. Where was I?"

"Visiting your mamma, I think."

"Yes, this was when I was sort of at the height of my career and that kind of travel and the focus on my job hadn't helped my marriage much either. Not that there weren't other issues," he said, flicking his hand. "I was in town for only two days, which was about what I normally did. I would schedule to fly through Atlanta when I could and tack the time for here on either end of that trip. So, I'm at The Arbors with Mamma and we're in the activities room with her and two other ladies who are working on some squares. I was sitting there, watching them, answering questions about whatever and I don't know, it…"

Helen could have supplied the words and waited to hear if she had guessed correctly.

His smile flashed from humorous to poignant. "There was this incredibly deep bond with the women that you could practically feel as they stitched and smoothed out the squares. They were talking about where the fabric had come from and then Mamma needed her ruler. She'd left it in her room and I told her I would get it. I went in and I suppose I had never paid much attention to how the place was decorated. There was the quilt on her bed and another one folded across the end. There was a small quilt across the back of the rocking chair and two on the walls instead of paintings. Her tissue box holder was even quilted. I found the ruler, took it to Mamma, and started asking questions about the different quilts they'd made over the years."

"That's like asking someone about their children and grandchildren," Helen said with a laugh.

"So I discovered," he said. "It was fascinating and we sat there until dinnertime, me listening to their stories." He set his mug aside and a hint of sheepishness entered his voice. "I went a little earlier to see Mamma the next day and we were alone in her room. I asked her to show me how she was doing the squares. I could sew on a button and stitch up a short rip, so it wasn't like I didn't know how to thread a needle. We spent most of the morning on a crash tutorial and I discovered one of the secretaries in the home office was a quilter. She was glad to give me a few lessons." He glanced at the clock on the wall. "If you think about it, quilting makes for a great road-trip activity. Squares don't take much room and don't require any equipment to speak of if that's all you're working on. I would take a stack with me, bring them back completed, and put them together when I was home."

He grinned again. "I mostly do carry-on luggage when I fly and after I had one pair of small scissors confiscated, I started using a nail clipper, and that works fine. Renata, the lady I was telling you about, was a big help, even though I never joined her circle."

Helen cocked her head. "And how was it that you got from basic quilting to working for Click for Quilting?"

"Fairly easy, as it turned out. Internet is a way of life for me, so I found several bloggers I liked, read no telling how many articles, and found a number of books to order. As you know, there are a lot of quilters in North Carolina. Once I decided to cut back on the travel I was doing in my job, I had more time to spend quilting, and I started playing with designs."

Helen snapped her fingers. "You designed and did a lap quilt for your mamma, didn't you? It was a lovely piece with all of her favorite flowers in bud and full bloom. Oh, and you added in heart shapes in the corners."

"Mamma's Hobbies was the name of it," he said with a nod. "She did love her gardening. The bay window in her room is filled with African violets." He reached for Helen's mug. "Anyway, I met Lorie, who founded Click for Quilting, at a quilting show. We got together for dinner, and by dessert she offered me a job I could do with telecommuting. It was the perfect setup for me. The company I was working for was looking to move out some of the senior people. I received an attractive severance package and struck a deal with Lorie."

"That's certainly an interesting journey," Helen said. She could imagine what a surprise it must have been to Renata when he initially approached her.

"Enough of that, though," Max said, rising with both mugs in hand. "Sure you don't want a refill?"

"No, I started early at the house. I'm usually up around 6:00 a.m. or so."

Max poured the coffee, turning sideways where he could see her. "Me too. If I sleep in past 7:00 I feel like half the day is gone. Now, it's your turn. I know you come from a long line of quilters. How was it that you started teaching classes for Wanda?"

Helen checked her watch. "It's a bit involved. Do you need to check on Lucy and Sherry?"

"Are you kidding? They know their way around the place better than I," he said and took his seat again. His eyes softened. "I'm sorry about Mitch. That must have been very difficult for you and the kids."

"Thank you, it was," Helen said quietly, the response she'd learned to give without the prick of tears that had been with her during those first months of loss. "But as for my career, I actually helped Larry Shipley get his business started. It was the two of us and a tiny office on Third Street when he decided to leave the national office and go out on his own. He'd always been popular with people and it wasn't much longer than a year before we moved into a bigger place. He managed the growth well, and before we knew it, he had the biggest independent insurance agency in town." She allowed a small sigh to escape. "I kept working after Mitch died, as much because I wasn't sure what I wanted to do as anything. Then one day, Larry and Alicia decide they want to travel the country in an RV while they were still young enough to enjoy it."

Max raised his eyebrows. "Really?"

"Oh yes," Helen said. "They picked up a nice one and downsized their car to a little sub-compact that was easy to tow, and bought a couple of bicycles. You should have seen them. They had the entire country mapped out by region and season." She felt the affection in her voice remembering the expression on their faces as they described their plan, map posted up on the wall in Larry's office. "The catch for me, though, was him selling the business."

She lifted her hands in a what-can-you-do gesture. "Larry offered it to me at a great price, bless his heart. Aside from the fact that it was really more generous than he should have been, I simply couldn't see running my own business. It wasn't that I didn't understand everything there was to do and the four women that worked there were like my second family. I just didn't want that for me. I never had." She felt the tug of a frown and consciously gave a half smile instead. "Unfortunately, Tommy Hillman made the best offer by far."

Max grunted. "I assume the apple didn't fall far from that tree and he's like his mamma and daddy?"

"Worse, in my opinion," Helen said. "The man's a bully even though he puts on a good act for customers. That's the same sort of thing his daddy does. Larry was well aware of how I felt and he broke the news to me as soon as the deal was made so I wouldn't find out about it from someone else. It took me about ten seconds to decide I was retiring."

"I can understand that," Max said sympathetically.

"It turned out quite well in spite of my initial disappointment," Helen said, waving her hand toward the doll room. "Larry and Alicia insisted I take part of the proceeds, and combining that with my other resources meant I didn't have to work if I chose not to. Wanda called me practically on my first day as a lady of leisure and suggested I take on some classes here. I love the shop and I have a wonderful time with the classes."

"I bet you're the perfect instructor," Max said with such assurance that she almost blushed. "Loving quilting is one thing. Being able to teach it requires a special kind of personality, though. Wanda said you are one of the best she's ever seen."

"That's sweet of her, but a slight exaggeration," Helen said with a laugh. "We do have fun together and Susanna is the true artist. Have you met her?"

"I have and you're right about her talent," he said, scooting his chair back toward the table. "In fact, if you have a few minutes, can we go into the classroom and go over the schedule? I think I've got it, but I don't want to accidentally let anything drop off if there's more to it than Wanda and I discussed."

"Oh, sure," Helen said. "We have the regular classes set up and there are one or two that some women had inquired about that I don't think have been firmed up yet."

They moved into the spacious room that had been created from two small parlors or whatever the original term for them had been. The only drawback of no windows had been overcome with an excellent design that combined recessed lights and twin chandeliers.

The advantage to a lack of windows was that the walls were devoted to quilts of all types that were both decorative and teaching tools. Even the whiteboard in front had a sliding quilt-covered panel that could be closed over it when the room was used for events. Teaching supplies and two sewing machines were tucked away in custom built cabinetry that had been expertly antiqued. The four folding tables set in two rows of two were long enough to accommodate three people side by side. There were smaller tables available if a new configuration was required and it took surprisingly little time to transform from classroom to luncheon or tea setting.

Lillian was an artist in her own right when it came to tablescapes and Wanda had one of the storerooms filled with tablecloths, napkins, candleholders, and items collected from thrift shops and yard sales. Helen had seen the room decorated in classic Victorian, whimsical fairyland, and all the traditional seasonal variations.

Max walked Helen to the door when they finished with the schedule. Three more women were in the quilting room and Lillian was showing something in a magazine to another woman at the counter.

"It looks like I'd better start circulating," Max said and opened the door for her. "Thanks for coming by and I'm really looking forward to working with you."

"Me too," Helen said with a wave that Lillian didn't see. The sun had broken through the morning grayness to provide swaths of blue, although it wasn't supposed to completely clear until the next day. She was warm enough in the lavender long-sleeve brushed cotton sweater she put on and she'd left the quilted jacket in the car, confident that the temperature was going into the high sixties as the weather lady had promised. One more errand to take care of and then it was on to Dr. Dickinson's to see this little Tawny. What was she going to do about that?

CHAPTER ELEVEN

—⟫◈⟪—

As a non-pet owner and not being a customer of Oak Tree Bank, Helen knew Wilfred—Will Dickinson and Maureen only on the social side. It was Will's grandfather that she thought was originally from Philadelphia or perhaps it was New York, who'd been in France during World War I with Wesley Turner and heard stories about Wallington as they survived the deadly trench warfare. Ralph, his grandfather, had come to visit, bought a small farm, and never left. His two sons, Will's father and uncle, had not been enamored with that life and both moved when they married—Will's father to Atlanta and his uncle to Charleston. Will, however, if not given to the smell of freshly plowed earth, had always enjoyed animals and spent most of his summers with his grandparents. Maureen was originally from Brunswick and they'd met when Will was in veterinarian school. In one of those fortunes of timing, Doctor Roberts, one of only two vets in town, was looking to cut back on his hours as Will was looking to become established. His grandfather put the two together and then sadly died of a stroke before the year was out. Well, maybe it had been a heart attack. At any rate, his grandmother couldn't possibly manage the farm on her own and Will and Maureen moved in with her after building a large master suite onto the main house. He slowly converted fields into meadow that they subsequently leased, then sold most of the property after his grandmother passed. He maintained five acres around the house and barn where he kept two horses of his own, and allowed boarding for up to another five. Helen knew the family history from Will and Maureen's niece, Susanna, when they chatted about things at Collectibles. The Dickinsons were Methodists and Maureen was not a quilter, so Helen's personal interaction with them was limited to the usual pleasantries exchanged in the course of town events, or saying hello at the grocery store.

Will started out in Doctor Roberts' office, but needed more room as his practice expanded and he'd moved into a building that had been an electrical supply store. The warehouse section was easy to convert into kennels for the animals he had to keep overnight. It was also less than two miles from the animal shelter, which made it convenient for his volunteer work. His office was the standard red brick set with a recessed entry. Wide double glass doors showed *Dickinson Veterinarian Services* in black block letters and a sign with their hours posted below. Open Monday-Friday, eight to five and nine to twelve on Saturdays, closed Sundays and holidays. There was a big window to the left and Helen could see the young lady and the back of a man's head at the reception counter.

The lobby was larger than she expected. There was a beige laminate front counter that was not quite chest high, a computer workstation with an extended surface perpendicular to it, and a five drawer black metal filing cabinet fit next to that. The telephone was to the right of the thin profile computer and a short stack of file folders was in a black box to the left.

There were two molded dark-green chairs against the wall with the windows and four more against the adjacent wall, all of them placed far enough apart to allow animals to sit between them. The floor was green-flecked gray linoleum and the white walls were covered with posters showing different breeds of cats and dogs. There was a large bulletin board crammed with fliers, notices, and business cards mounted by the door of the back wall. Only two chairs were occupied. A heavyset woman that she thought looked familiar was holding a red miniature dachshund in her lap and an older black gentleman with his eyes closed had a beagle resting at his feet. The beagle looked old as well and briefly raised his soulful eyes to Helen. Norm Greenfield, the retired choir director for the Methodist church, was the man at the counter, a black plastic pet carrier on the floor with the yellow fur of a cat pressed to the side of the carrier.

"Thank you, Terri," he said, scribbling on a charge slip. "That should do it for this year." He picked up the carrier and turned. "Why hello, Helen. How are you?"

The old man in the chair didn't open his eyes, but the woman with the dachshund gave a smile and the dog pricked his ears forward, although he didn't bark, whine, or growl.

"I'm fine, thanks," she said. "Is everything good with you and Sylvia?"

Norm, who was always in popular demand as Santa Claus, chuckled. "Oh yes, can't complain. Sylvia's sister is in for a few days, so I told them to go off and do girl things and I'd bring Tiger here in for his shots." He tilted his head. "You have a pet in with Doc?"

"Uh, no, I dropped by to see Rita for a minute," Helen said, not wanting to explain. "Be sure and give Sylvia my best."

"I'll do that and you have a good one," he said.

Rita appeared in the doorway before the young lady, Terri Gabler, according to the name tag, said anything.

"Mrs. Bryant, we're ready for Rex." She noticed Helen and gave her a thumbs-up. "Be right with you," she mouthed and stepped aside to let the woman pass her, cradling the dog in her arms like a baby.

Terri barely looked old enough for a work permit. She had a round face, deep dimples, big brown eyes, and faint eyebrows. She smiled to reveal a mouth full of braces. She had the bubbly sort of voice that probably erupted periodically into giggles. "Hi, Helen, can I help you or is it just Rita that you need?"

"Uh, Rita, and…."

"Tawny," Terri semisqueaked, snapped her fingers, then pointed. "You're the lady that might take our little girl."

Helen hadn't seen the cushioned dog bed underneath the desk, but at the sound of her name, a small dog stepped out where she could be seen, shaking her body as if flinging off water. She sat and cocked her head to Terri. The girl swiveled her chair, rose, scooped the dog up, and supported her hind legs on her arm so Tawny's paws were on top of the counter. Tawny gave the girl's hand a single lap and looked at Helen. What an utterly adorable face. Her fur was light caramel, her eyes like shiny lumps of coal, and her muzzle was black. Rita was correct. Her nose protruded more than a pug, but not with the sharpness of some Chihuahuas. She gingerly licked Terri's hand again as if questioning Helen's intentions.

Helen extended her hand, palm up, and felt the wet nose touch it delicately. Then the tongue followed with two laps.

Terri's face was mischievous. "Would you like to hold her?"

Helen hesitated as Terri effortlessly lifted the dog onto the counter. Helen took her, feeling momentarily awkward as Tawny snuggled into her stomach, tongue lapping at one hand.

"Should I take a photo?" Rita had come through the door while Tawny was burrowing into Helen's heart.

"She is easy to handle," Helen said, attempting to focus on the practical instead of the sensation of affection washing over her.

"Not to mention free of ear mites, shots up to date, and spayed," Rita said, ruffling Tawny's ears.

"You got a dog, and treat it right, you got a friend your whole life," the man sitting in the chair said in a gravelly voice. "Had Basie here since he was a pup and his mamma before that."

"Is he all right?" Helen asked, hoping the man wasn't there to be given bad news about his companion.

"Basie's been with us for years," Rita said before the old man answered. "He got into a bit of a tangle with a porcupine a couple of weeks ago and Doctor Dickinson wanted to check to make sure the punctures in his mouth are healing properly."

"Dog shoulda' had more sense, but he does forget sometimes," the man said with a pat to Basie's head.

Helen thought of what a mess that would have been as Tawny gave a contented sigh.

"We'll be with you in about ten minutes, Mr. Tipton," Rita said to the man and motioned to the door. "Helen, would you like to bring Tawny back and we can talk for a minute?"

"Take your time," Mr. Tipton intoned. "Basie and me are relaxing."

Helen carried Tawny, trying to pretend she hadn't made her decision. After all, she wasn't the first person in the world to get a pet at her age.

Rita's office was just large enough for a black metal desk with a chair, one matching three-shelf bookshelf and a single chair like the ones in the waiting room that had been placed to the side of the desk.

Helen sat, Tawny on her lap. "How do we do this?"

Rita pulled out a form. "We haven't entered her into the animal shelter system, so it's pretty simple. I assume you'll want to use Doctor Dickinson as your vet and I thought we would go ahead and do that paperwork so we have it on file. I imagine you'll have some questions." She grinned. "I ran off some information about chugs for you."

Helen didn't think she was that predictable, but perhaps she'd given more signs of acquiescing when they first discussed it than she realized. "Why am I not terribly surprised? Would it be okay to leave her for one more night? I'd like to pick some things up and get the house ready."

"Oh, sure," Rita said. "I wasn't kidding when I said she's no trouble. It's just a relief that she'll be going to a good home."

The paperwork was quick and Helen insisted on paying for the treatment Will had provided. He did enough discounted and free work for the animal shelter. She was adopting Tawny and she might as well become accustomed to the costs that came along with owning a dog. When she re-entered the waiting room, Mr. Tipton and Basie were apparently in with Doctor Dickinson. A woman who couldn't possibly weigh more than a hundred pounds had taken a seat, a huge dog that looked to be a mix of German shepherd and something perhaps equally large was sitting next to her. Helen hoped she had a yard for him to run in—walking an animal that size would have to be difficult if he decided to take off after a squirrel or something. The woman gave a nod, and like the dachshund before, the dog pricked his ears forward, but made no move toward them.

Terri stood and took the paper that Helen had filled out. All set?"

"Yes, thank you, and I'll be picking her up tomorrow. Probably early afternoon."

"We'll be here, won't we girl?" Terri said, and as Helen surrendered her, the pink tongue lapped her hand again. Terri gave Tawny a squeeze before setting her on the floor. She smiled at Helen. "I'm really happy to see her go to someone like you. She's a sweetheart and I think you'll be perfect together."

"Me too," Helen said, mildly surprised at the confidence in her voice. It did feel right.

Her next stop was at Wallington Feed 'N More. It had originally been established as a standard feed store but had grown into much more. Wallington did not yet have the mega home improvement stores and certainly not anything like a dedicated large pet store. According to Rita, Feed 'N More had significantly increased their line of pet supplies and Helen imagined it was no doubt the second generation of owners who determined there was a market gap they could fill. The store she thought had been built in the 1960s had the look of an oversized farmhouse with a rough-hewn weathered wood exterior. A porch stretched the width of the building, less the short loading dock to the far left of the main entrance. Two pickup trucks—one black, one brown, both mud-splattered and neither new—were parked alongside the dock. Helen watched men carrying large bags slung over their shoulders move in and out of the store, transferring the bags into the trucks.

Helen stepped inside, memories coming back to her of trips to the feed store that her grandparents used. It had closed long ago and just like that one, the grooves of this wooden floor had been filled over the years with bits of debris that resettled after being swept, tiny particles packed tightly by feet that trod the boards. Bins of dried corn and different types of other feed gave off their own slightly musty odor. The interior of the building was dim with an old-fashioned light fixture hanging from the ceiling throughout the store rather than rectangles of florescent lights. She stood to let her eyes adjust and a skinny kid wearing a red Feed 'N More apron stopped next to her, a plastic pet carrier in each hand.

"Can I help you with something?" His voice was deeper than she expected, and on closer look, his build wasn't exactly skinny. The muscles in his forearms where the sleeves of his chambray shirt were rolled to his elbows were clearly defined. His narrow freckled face was topped with brown hair that he probably kept as short as he did because it would otherwise be a tangled mop of curls.

Helen extracted the list of recommended supplies she'd printed out before leaving the house that morning. "I'm getting a dog tomorrow," she said. "A small one that will be inside," she added, looking closely at the list for the first time. Collar, leash or harness, food and water bowls, food, some sort of chew thing to control tartar, shampoo, chew toys, dog bed optional. Did they have everything?

"I'm Tim," the boy said with a tilt of his head. "Our pet section is pretty big and we add to it depending on what customers ask for," he continued, leading her two aisles over. "Products for dogs and cats, this aisle, hamsters and gerbils next one over, birds, reptiles, and others after that, and aquariums and fish are on the back wall. Want me to get you a cart?"

Helen looked at the full shelves, amazed at the different items to select from and glad she had a list. "It looks like I'll need one," she said. The item that was not included was a doggie door she thought would make life easier.

She'd called Scott, Katie's husband, before she left Doctor Dickinson's office and he told her he would drop by right after lunch to take measurements and discuss options. He said he would pick up whatever they decided on and add that in for a total package cost. Helen didn't mind letting Tawny in and out of the backyard for a few days, but her having the ability to come and go as she pleased seemed to make the most sense. She'd briefly considered an electronic fence for the front yard when she saw an advertisement on television and thought that might be more complicated than she wanted.

In fact, thinking of the fence brought to mind that the front yard was lovely, as it had always been, and it wouldn't take a great deal of effort to bring new life to the back. Landscaping in the late fall wasn't her usual approach and she wanted to stay with low maintenance plants anyway. The yard was actually balanced with a large oak in one corner and a big pine in the other. She could put in beds around the trunks to mimic the front and only put mulch in until it was time to plant marigolds, daffodils, and petunias. She would bring in clematis to climb the sections of fence that were bare and those simple additions would add the bursts of color she wanted. Phyllis, who loved gardening as much as she did quilting, would be glad to help her and they could make it a weekend project. Phyllis, who had three cats and two dogs, had repeatedly suggested that Helen take in a pet and she would be pleased to hear the news. She would give Phyllis a call when she got home to see when she was available.

After Helen unloaded her purchases from the car and Phyllis had enthusiastically said she'd come over bright and early Saturday morning, Helen slipped out to the backyard. The lots in the neighborhood were all close to an acre each, and the Sherwoods to the right had a double lot. The parcel adjacent to hers was where Rick had a shed with his riding lawnmower and a workshop. The Murphys to the left were like she and Mitch had been. The backyard was a playground for children rather than an entertainment area for adults. The clothesline Cathy rarely used now was within a few feet of the hurricane fencing that was meant to last for a lifetime. Goodness, how many balls had flown into adjoining yards—football, catch, soccer—whichever sport it was at the moment? It had, of course, been bicycles and skateboards out front, a neighborhood where everyone admonished their children as to proper safety, and all the adults kept a watch when backing up or turning down the street.

Helen's gaze drifted to where the swing set had been, a gleaming structure Mitch had put into place as Ethan and Tricia eagerly awaited the signal that it was ready—the source of one of many trips to the emergency room when Ethan hadn't been content to merely swing in a normal manner. No, not when he could shimmy up the side pole, grasp the top pole, and perform acrobatics until he lost his grip. Fortunately, the simple fracture had been to his left arm. How many injuries had they coped with during his adolescence? The broken arm, stitches to his forehead, oh, that nasty cut on his foot, and the concussion that had frightened her most of all. Thank goodness he later channeled his energy into baseball.

Tricia's habit of digging around in the dirt for worms and such had been messier, but she'd managed not to get bitten by anything dangerous. And now, there was to be a grandchild. Well, it would be a few years before a new swing set was needed, and Rita had assured her Tawny would be wonderful with children. A grandchild and a dog! Yes indeed, interesting changes were on the way.

CHAPTER TWELVE

⟞⟞◆⟝⟝

Justin watched the ambulance crew slam the door shut, lights rotating. The boy, whom Dave Mabry identified as Johnny Jenkins, was unconscious, face a mess, degree of head trauma unknown, and no way to guess if there were internal injuries. The damage to the 2001 green Chevy Blazer was easier to determine, considering the boy hit a tree that was at least eight feet in diameter. What made him lose control was the question because it didn't look as if there had been any attempt to swerve. Getting the blood alcohol test would have to wait until they made the initial determination at the emergency room about whether they could treat him. Despite being a small town, Wallington's hospital was well equipped and staffed for standard traumas and Justin didn't think they would have to transport the boy to another hospital.

Dave, his hat pushed to the back of his head, stood next to Justin, thumbs hooked into his belt. He nodded to the tree, where the truck had torn a short path from the poorly maintained road, small seedling trees ripped away, weeds and grass yanked loose.

"This how you found it?"

"Yeah," Justin said. "If he hadn't had his seat belt on, probably would have thrown him out. Don't know if that would be better or worse."

Dave scratched the belly that hadn't yet begun to overlap his belt. At six foot two, the solid bulk that made him a high school football star was something he struggled to keep under control as an adult. College had never been an interest and he made the Army recruiter's day when he strolled in to see him a few months before graduation. For Dave, it had been the single four-year tour he signed up for, serving in the infantry with no desire to tack on specialties such as airborne. He hadn't minded the assignment to Fort Polk, Louisiana, ready to return to Wallington after his initial obligation ended. Justin wondered if his worldview would have been expanded if he'd been stationed somewhere like Hawaii or Germany instead.

"Johnny's not the worst kid around, but he ain't in the running to be an angel either," Dave said, turning his head to spit. "He for darn sure shouldn't have been out here at this hour on a school day. Roger got a snootful in him; he'll be hard to handle, too. You okay with it, I'll go on to the hospital, see what I can find out, and be there in case there's problems with Roger."

Justin never minded passing on interacting with parents in situations like this. "Sounds like a plan. Chief McFarlane knows about it?"

"Sheila knows, he knows," Dave said, taking a cigarette from his front shirt pocket. He lifted his hand as the ambulance driver signaled they were ready to move.

"I got this. You go on," Justin said. The crash occurred less than two miles from the county line, but like most officers, handling an accident that had the potential to be ruled a fatality was not something you argued to be a part of. The county officer who'd joined him briefly stayed only long enough to determine that Justin did not require assistance.

Louis Walker, a gnarled black man driving a truck that looked as if he'd owned it for many years, had come upon the wreck soon after it happened. In fact, the engine was still warm when Justin arrived within ten minutes of dispatch issuing the call. Mr. Walker explained that Jenkins was bleeding and unconscious, but with an unquestionable pulse. There had been no evidence of gas leaking or threat of fire and Mr. Walker folded a handkerchief and held it to the boy's forehead, assuming he shouldn't move him unless it became necessary. Justin assured him it was better to allow the paramedics to do so whenever possible and they were only a few minutes behind.

Mr. Walker had been on his way into town for a doctor's appointment and Justin agreed he could go ahead in exchange for his contact information and a promise to go to the station to make a statement after his appointment. Mr. Walker confirmed that Dealy Road was not well traveled and the boy was mighty lucky he'd come along when he did.

The silence that descended after Dave left was not in fact actual silence. Once the sound of vehicles and sirens faded, the natural forest noises resumed their interrupted rhythm. A squirrel scampered up a nearby pine tree, a mockingbird shrieking at its presence. Other faint snaps could be heard, whether from birds he couldn't see moving about, chipmunks rustling through the underbrush, or any of several small animals. Insect buzzes carried from deeper in the woods. This particular stretch of road had no shoulder and little clearance on the side that Jenkins plowed into. A thicker stand of trees abutted a weed-filled shallow ditch on the opposite side. Had the truck swerved in that direction, his momentum might have slowed before he impacted a tree.

Justin slipped on a pair of the translucent surgical gloves he always carried. It was a habit from his Baltimore days that he saw no reason to change. He wanted to examine the truck carefully, looking for any obvious sign of beer cans or liquor bottles, or perhaps the scent of marijuana soaked into the interior. Both doors had popped open in the crash; the front end was smashed with the engine block shoved back. The windshield was shattered and the front tires were flattened.

There was around two hours of good sun left before it angled too low to pierce well through the trees. Most of the leaves had been stripped from the hardwoods, but pine was almost as prevalent. Justin leaned into the truck, the smell of tobacco present without being overwhelming. The ashtray was empty. If anyone had been smoking something stronger, it wasn't immediately noticeable. A jumble of crumpled papers, wadded up cash register receipts, gum wrappers, a stained rag, straws, and fast food wrappers were scattered on the floorboards that hadn't seen a vacuum cleaner any time lately.

There was a gun rack—an option around Wallington he'd come to accept was as common as a radio. The Winchester lever-action .30-30 rifle was secure in the rack and Justin assumed he would find a box of ammunition in the glove compartment. He moved from the driver's side and peered into the bed of the truck. There was black bedliner with an accumulation of dead leaves, chunks of bark, mud, and a locked stainless steel toolbox fastened to an eyebolt by a short link of heavy chain. A stained brown tarp partially covered an axe, tire iron, lug nut wrench, and a jack. The bundle was obviously thrown loose during the collision. A red plastic gas can was on its side several feet from the truck with a bottle of drain cleaner close to it. Justin walked over and toed both objects to see that they were empty and not likely to be leaking into the soil. He picked them up and placed them into the bed, wondering vaguely why Jenkins had drain cleaner with him. As Justin was preparing to lean in on the passenger's side to check the glove compartment, he saw a raw streak on the tire rim. He braced one hand against the truck and leaned in for a better look, then dropped to one knee to run his hands across the freshly scraped metal.

This was a bullet strike. There was no doubt in his mind. It was probably a .30-06 or something similar. That changed things. He rose to his feet, his mind shifting with the revelation. He slowly turned a circle, his eyes scanning the quiet woods, listening intently for sounds of humans or distant shots. Hunting season was underway, and while mid-afternoon was hardly a prime hunting time, it wasn't unheard of. He didn't know the exact statistics, but there were incidents every year. A .22 short bullet could travel over a mile and a high velocity cartridge, such as a .30-06, could send its bullet triple that distance. He'd never gone after deer or other game. He'd done a little duck hunting with his dad and brother until they all decided that getting up predawn in the cold wasn't really all that much fun. A common problem with hunters was firing without a clear target and sending at least one and maybe more bullets carelessly zinging into the woods, oblivious to the fact that the final resting place for it might not be a nearby tree. The round hadn't lodged in the tire and Justin made an immediate search to see if he might luck out and see it embedded in the tree Jenkins had plowed into. He wasn't the least surprised not to find it and even if he had, it probably wouldn't be of any forensics value. Well, he'd better call the chief and see if he wanted to send for a team or have Justin snap the photographs. He had a digital camera in the patrol car and had worked enough accidents over his career to know what kind of photos they needed.

It was nearing the end of the day shift when Justin entered the station. Sheila was in Chief McFarlane's office with a small stack of papers he was signing. Justin noticed the coffeepot was barely a third full which meant it was probably left over from the mid-afternoon brewing and would have been sitting for at least an hour. He grabbed a bottle of water from the refrigerator in the break room instead.

Sheila came out of the chief's office and gave him an update. "The Jenkins boy is stabilized, but still unconscious. No internal injuries, for which they can thank the good Lord. Dave talked to his mamma and daddy and there was early dismissal from school today, so he wasn't playing hooky—not that he hasn't on other days, mind you. That boy's been skirting around trouble since the time he could walk. Both him and his big brother take too much after his daddy. Got little respect for authority, less for women, and too much liking for the bottle. It's no wonder Isabelle left Roger last year. That's what comes from marrying beneath you in the first place, and it took her longer than it should have to figure that one out."

"Thanks, Sheila," he said, taking note of her commentary. He wondered if she would be disappointed to learn the wreck hadn't been caused by underage drinking. Well, he wouldn't know for sure until they had the toxicology report.

Sheila was already past him and turned. "Oh, and Dave said to tell you he had a lead on that stolen riding lawn mower he was going to check out. The hospital knew to call one of you if the Jenkins boy came to."

Justin lifted his hand in acknowledgement and waited to see if there was anything else before he went in with the chief.

Chief McFarlane swiveled his chair and motioned Justin into his usual spot. The leathery skin around his eyes crinkled. "Guess Sheila filled you in?"

"Complete with her opinion of the family," Justin said, taking a swig of water and the setting the camera on the edge of the desk.

The chief didn't reach for it. "Yeah, well, both boys have always been a handful. Jared's the oldest and he managed to scrape by and graduate from high school last year, then took off for somewhere. Never officially arrested him, but he's been in for questioning a few times. Suspected vandalism, petty theft, but nothing major. Roger's had his share of warnings. He likes to pick fights when he's had one too many and he has that pretty often. I would have guessed booze in Johnny's truck, a little grass, maybe, but a bullet, huh?"

Justin nodded. "Did the old man, Mr. Walker, come by and fill out a statement? He didn't mention anything about having heard a shot, but it's not something I asked him either since he was gone by the time I noticed it. He said there was no one else on the road when he came up on the wreck. He didn't hear the crash, though, but he thinks he arrived no more than a few minutes after it happened."

Chief McFarlane shook his head. "I was out until about half an hour ago, so he could have come in. Sheila will have it, but if that's Louis Walker you're talking about, he isn't likely to have heard anything if he was driving. He's getting on up there age wise and his hearing isn't what it used to be."

Justin thought back on the wrinkles etched into the man's face wizened by age. "I think that was him."

The chief pointed to the camera. "You want to download those and print out a couple? You look around for the bullet?"

"Yeah, but it could be anywhere," Justin said, taking the camera.

"Probably smashed up if you did find it," the chief agreed. "Give me the ones of the tire and the front."

The task took only a few minutes and the chief was in front of his desk when Justin brought four photographs in and laid them down. They studied them in silence, the chief's face neutral. He tapped his forefinger on one of the tires. "Yeah, not much question about it," he said. "Not the best time of day to be out hunting."

"I thought about that myself," Justin said as the chief propped against the corner of the desk. Justin recognized the look as one of concentration and he stepped to the other end of the desk where he could comfortably lean, waiting for the chief to speak.

"You know Dealy Road?"

"Not really," Justin said. "Haven't had any calls out there that I can remember."

"Not much reason that you would have," the chief said. "Used to be a lot of logging when we had the pulpwood yard in town, but that's been closed for better than ten years now. Logging trucks are part of why the road's in such bad shape. Should have been repaved after they quit running." He ran a hand through his hair. "Dealy Road Ts into the highway and into Turner Road about three miles past Walker's place. Unless they've moved, the Barbers and Shepards are the only other houses that are occupied, but the Nelson and Ratford places have been vacant for well over a year, probably closer to two."

Justin tilted his head. "What are you thinking, boss?"

The chief exhaled. "Like I said, most folks don't go hunting in the middle of the afternoon, but there's plenty of people who could be out shooting. There are enough guys around that have nothing better to do than to be wandering the woods taking pot shots, but the Nelson place is between Walker's and the highway. The Ratford Place is closer to Turner Road. If somebody has something to hide, it follows there are guns included."

Justin nodded in understanding. "Are you thinking about the meth lab rumors we keep hearing?"

Chief McFarlane shrugged. "Plenty of other possibilities.

Stills, marijuana, squatters, and who knows what else? Since no one knows what Johnny was doing out there, it could be he was nosing around for purposes of his own, and whoever's supposed to be keeping watch fired a warning shot. Or, if someone's supposed to be keeping a watch, it could be a matter of getting bored and firing off a couple of rounds for the heck of it."

"You want me to take Dave and check it out, or let the night shift have it?"

The chief shook his head. "Sun's about down and if there's something set up, it likely didn't start today. It'll be there in the morning. I'm not leaning either way on this one, but you and Dave head out that way first thing tomorrow and take a look, okay?"

"Sure thing," Justin said, glad it wouldn't be a trip in the dark for what could be either a wasted trip or coming up on a trigger-happy lookout.

The chief stood. "It's my house for poker night, so I've got to run by for beer and ice. You need me for anything else?"

"I'm good," Justin said, taking the photos for the file. He could catch Sheila about Mr. Walker's statement before she left for the evening, do the initial report, and call Tricia to see if she wanted him to pick something up for dinner. He hadn't recalled her saying today was early dismissal. Even if she had, it was probably one of the workshop days, and it would have been the students who got out early, not the faculty. Thoughts of dinner made him think they hadn't had barbecue for a couple of weeks. If Tricia wasn't having problems with heartburn, she loved the little sweet potato soufflés that Smokin' Good BBQ had introduced as a new side dish. Their slow cooked beans were hard to beat, too, and he wouldn't mind a slab of ribs now that he was running their menu through his mind. He was as good with grilling steaks, chops, burgers, sausage, and chicken as anyone he knew, but he was convinced ribs were a meat that needed to be slow cooked the right way with the right wood. He knew people that did them at home, and while they were okay, he had yet to find anyone who could match the professional rigs when it came to getting that fall-off-the-bone kind of tenderness. As for dry rub versus wet technique, he didn't have a firm opinion, having had great ribs done both ways. The image of a pile of ribs was firmly fixed in his mind as he hit the speed dial for the house.

"Hi, sweetheart," Tricia said, after the second ring. "How was your day? Were you on the call with Johnny Jenkins?"

"Uh, yeah, Dave and I caught it," he said. "Is he one of your students?"

"No, Johnny isn't on the college track," Tricia said. She had mostly advanced placement classes this year. "Is he going to be okay? I took them keeping him here as a good sign."

"I don't really know more than what Sheila told me," he said. "He hadn't regained consciousness when Dave left the hospital, from what I understand."

"Well, Mamma called with them starting a prayer circle, so I imagine Mrs. Turner will be on top of any changes in his condition."

Justin, who still hadn't quite figured out what a prayer circle was, did know that Mrs. Turner was in charge. "I'm sure she will," he said, ready to get back to the idea of dinner. "Listen, I was wondering if you'd like me to go by Smokin' Good for pick up."

"Are you the sweetest thing," Tricia said immediately. "I was looking at what we had in the refrigerator and you were on the way to a tuna casserole. Pulled pork and sweet potato soufflé sounds better. And cole slaw," she added.

Yes! He was going to get ribs and husband points for being thoughtful, not to mention that Smokin' Good gave the police, firefighters, and seniors a discount. What more could you ask?

CHAPTER THIRTEEN

—◦—

"Well, isn't she just completely adorable?" Tricia said, ruffling Tawny's ears as Helen held her up for inspection.

Tawny delivered rapid laps when Tricia lowered her hand, smiling warmly. "How is it going with you two?"

"Good," Helen said, setting the dog on the floor. She thoroughly sniffed Tricia's feet and proceeded to the water bowl after the inspection. Helen had taken the advice of Tim at the store, having the feeling they would soon be on a first-name basis. He'd suggested the stand-style food and water bowls, explaining some people genuinely thought it was better for the dog and he knew for certain it was easier to clean up around. Helen liked that idea.

Introductions to the dog completed, Tricia sank onto a chair. "Lord, what a hectic day! The kids have all been buzzing about Johnny's wreck, Baby Kendall here has been squirming like crazy since this morning, and I have to replace one of the judges for the science fair next month."

Helen pushed the plates of lemon squares toward her. The

teapot was nestled in a quilted cozy that Tricia had made her for Christmas one year and Helen smiled as she reached out to touch it. It was a bright blue fabric sprinkled with daisies that Tricia had found somewhere. That was when the old kitchen had been predominantly yellow and Helen was discovering herbal teas.

"I didn't know you still had this," she said, putting a lemon square on her napkin.

Helen poured the tea. "I have every single piece you ever quilted for me and so does your grandmother." She glanced down at Tawny, who trotted up and placed her front legs on the edge of Helen's chair. Helen had been warned by Rita, Terri, and Tim at the store to give Tawny pats instead of treats. They assured her the dog would respond to affection and being on a regular feeding schedule was important. Helen stroked Tawny's head for a moment. Apparently satisfied, the dog made her way to the den where her bed sat next to Helen's easy chair.

Tricia nibbled a corner of the lemon square. "When are Mamaw and Papaw getting home? Have they had a good time?"

"Saturday. And we'll do lunch here after church on Sunday. They've loved the trip. Your Aunt Eloise introduced them to one of their new neighbors down the street, and small world that it is, the husband's roommate at college worked at the plant with your papaw for three or four years. Plus, the senior center in Lawrenceville has been running a series of big band concerts and old World War II movies." Helen sipped the hot tea, breathing in the scent of orange blossom. She knew that look of strain around Tricia's eyes.

"I know you said it was a bit of a rough day. Are you upset about the Jenkins boy?"

Tricia looked startled at the question, then half smiled. "You always know, don't you?" She rolled her shoulders back, forward, and back again. "Not Johnny, exactly. I mean, yes, anytime one of the kids is injured like that, you feel badly. It was a relief to hear he'd been moved from critical care, although I guess he's still fairly incoherent with the pain killers."

Helen didn't press her. She could tell Tricia was building up to something. "There are rumors, of course, that he'd been drinking or smoking a joint or whatever. With Johnny, well, he's not, well, let's say that I hope not and I wouldn't be terribly surprised to find out it was true."

"The boys have been in trouble more than once," Helen said quietly.

Tricia pressed her lips together before she commented. "Oh yes, and as we do, some of us were talking about the kids, you know, the ones who are the troublemakers, the ones that are on the verge of dropping out, and then the ones…" She paused for a sip of tea. "You know Albert Gilbert, don't you? Boyd's second cousin?"

Helen ran faces through her mind. "Albert? Yes, scrawny child, isn't he? Well, not a child, sixteen, I guess he is. Smart. Always has been. Do you have him in your class?"

"Last year," Tricia said, a note of affection slipping into her voice. "He's fifteen, by the way. Took biology a year early because he wanted to do chemistry this year. He's a slam dunk for a special program Georgia Tech has designed for students, but he wants to make his application stand out. I told you about that, didn't I?"

Helen shook her head. She didn't mind Tricia bouncing from subject to subject. Tricia would tie it all in together when she was ready.

Her eyes brightened. "I can't believe I forgot to tell you. We're one of three schools in the district getting this. The program will be for juniors and seniors and they will be allowed to take freshman level classes in engineering, math, and science—any of the non-lab classes offered. They're linked via a new type of videoconference and we had to dedicate a classroom to have it properly wired. That money came from a grant. The kids take the classes for credit, not just auditing. They can take one class per semester, which means if they max out, they get to start college with twelve credit hours." She paused for effect. "All of this is at no cost to them. Not a dime."

Helen raised her eyebrows. "No cost? My goodness, that's a huge help. Oh, does it only count if they attend Tech?"

Tricia picked up her mug. "No, it's fully transferable no matter which college they get accepted into. Isn't that great?"

"I would say so. Why hasn't this been in the *Gazette*? I should think they would see it as newsworthy."

"There were some final details to work out and, of course, we weren't entirely sure the grant would come through. Principal Taylor didn't want to get people's hopes up until it was confirmed."

"I can understand that," Helen said. "You were saying that young Albert is likely to be in the program?"

The strain in her eyes flickered again. "Yes, and I know he's excited about it, but lately, I can't quite put my finger on it. He seems troubled, not his usual self." She broke the remaining piece of lemon square in two, leaving the pieces on the napkin. "See, Albert is one of those kids who is a, well, a *nerd* is the only way to describe him. If he's not the smartest kid in school, then he's definitely in the top five and I don't mean in his class, I mean in the school."

"I didn't realize he was that brainy."

Tricia's tone was soft. "He is, and the truth is, from a genetics perspective, of the two Gilbert men, Boyd is, quite frankly, the really smart one in the family. Albert's father is no dummy, but there's a reason Boyd was the brother who went to law school. Albert's mother, well, she is very pretty." Tricia ate one of the pieces of lemon square. "Sadly, she didn't pass on any of her looks to him."

Helen refrained from commenting that Albert, at best, resembled a small scarecrow and she didn't think his appearance had improved since the last time she'd seen him, although she struggled to recall their last encounter.

Tricia finished the pastry and shook her head at the offer of another. "I genuinely don't think the family understands how intelligent Albert is. Sadly, there's no way he hasn't been teased all his life, but he gives the impression that he takes it philosophically. He grasps that all of this is temporary, that college is where he will shine, especially if he attends Georgia Tech or somewhere similar—a school that actively seeks and appreciates brains like his."

Helen heard the catch in Tricia's voice. "He's been having problems with other students? More than usual, you think?"

A line creased across Tricia's forehead. "We keep an eye out for bullying and take it seriously, but the staff can't be everywhere at once. There's a group of boys, mostly jocks, but not exclusively, led by Steve Hillman. We hear rumors we can't pin down that they've been making life hard on students like Albert for being too smart. They put students into categories and target them. I say *they* even though *they* is probably Steve." She narrowed her eyes and wrinkled her nose. "Is there not one decent member in the entire Hillman family? What makes them think they're so superior?"

Helen sighed. "I wish I had an answer to that other than the fact that as Daddy says, 'Some folks are just born mean.' As far as I'm concerned, Fred and Deborah both are mean through and through, and that's probably why they were attracted to each other. Carl was several years younger than Fred and not a bit better. He's got a kid in high school because after Rhonda finally couldn't stand being part of that family anymore and left him to go to Raleigh, I think it was, he married that woman who was half his age and she insisted on having a child. They fell right in line raising Steve the same way Tommy was with the idea that they're about the biggest fish you can be in this small pond of ours."

Tricia licked her finger and pressed up the few crumbs on the napkin. "You have that right. Neither Ethan or I could stand to be with Tommy when we were in school and I see it all over again in Steve."

Helen wondered if Tricia knew Tommy was why Ethan had chosen baseball over football. From the time the boys played peewee sports, Tommy mocked those with poor athleticism and constantly tried to exert his skills over the others. He had no talent for baseball and Ethan could enjoy a sport without being one of Tommy's teammates. Not that Tommy ever passed up the chance to remind Ethan he hadn't been "man enough" to stick with football.

"The problem is there isn't anything in the open—only accidental trippings, glasses knocked off and stepped on, both bicycle tires flat at the same time, or lockers glued shut."

Had she missed something Tricia said? No, apparently not. "So, have you noticed anything specific with Albert? Anything you can talk to him about?"

Tricia looked into her empty mug and raised her eyes. "No, and that goes back to the earlier conversation about Johnny."

"Johnny?"

Tricia raised one hand. "It's a bit circuitous, so bear with me. I'd like to say Albert at least has friends in the science club, but he doesn't, not really. I didn't know him before we moved back here, so maybe he tried to make friends and it didn't work or maybe he's always preferred to keep his nose in a book. He's literally the perfect student from a teacher's perspective. He excels at his work, always knows the answer, and keeps absolutely quiet until he's called on. He waits until the end of the class when no one else is in the room and then he asks questions that are at least a grade level above what you're teaching, or brings up some article that he wonders if you've read." She sighed again. "Unfortunately, he has no sense of humor and he is rather, well, dorky looking. He's the kid no one wants to sit with at lunch. I honestly don't know if the book he hides behind is because he's hiding or because he would just as soon not interact with anyone."

"It could be some of both," Helen murmured.

"True, and now I'll shift to Johnny. He and his group, if you want to call them that, are more troublesome than they are trouble makers, if you know what I mean."

"The kind that don't openly defy teachers, but make up names for them, skate by as close as they can to flunking, cut up in class, or jeer at the athletes?"

That brought a tiny smile to her lips. "I guess things haven't changed all that much since you were in school, have they?"

Helen would like that to not be true, but the stories she heard about some of what went on, especially in Atlanta, were definitely more serious than in her day.

"Anyway, I mentioned that Albert hasn't seemed like himself lately. He's missed some science club meetings with vague excuses about having other things to take care of, and it's as if he's nervous about something. I have asked if there is anything I could do, or help with, and he's told me no, that everything will be fine." Tricia paused and placed a hand on her belly, wincing slightly.

"Lower back or kicking?"

"Both, and I need to go to the bathroom, but let me finish this." She pushed her chair back. "The thing is, when we were talking about Johnny, I suddenly remembered I've seen him having lunch with Albert a couple of times and then talking in the hall."

"Do you think Johnny has been the one bullying him rather than Steve and his friends?"

Tricia awkwardly pushed herself from the chair. "I don't know. It doesn't really fit. Johnny has his faults, but I don't think bullying is one of them. It just struck me as odd, and Lord knows, if Albert has the chance to have friends, Johnny isn't the one I would choose even though I know I shouldn't say something like that."

"That doesn't mean you aren't correct," Helen said. "Another cup of tea?"

Tricia glanced at her watch. "Yes, please, and I've complained enough. You're right, maybe I'll sit down with Albert and tell him that I'm worried about him and see if he'll open up. Or, maybe my hormones are acting up and I'm imagining it."

Helen laughed. "I didn't say any of that."

"Okay, and you talked me into another lemon square." Tricia grinned, the worry gone from her face. "I needed a sounding board, and you were great at that, like always."

Helen stood to replenish their tea. Tricia stood as well and headed toward the bathroom. Helen's suppressed giggle at Tricia's waddling posture, something every woman went through at this stage of pregnancy, was overlaid with a surge of love at both her daughter's caring for Albert and her comment about feeling better just having talked to her. Their closeness as mother and daughter was a trait Helen knew was absent in many families. She was the same way with her mother. A friendship was able to emerge once the firmness of parenting was no longer required. Not that she or Eloise had required a great deal of discipline. Their sisterly squabbles had been routine and nothing overly dramatic. Neither had been caught up in the urge to rebel. Whether that was by virtue of personality or that they had no reason to do so was difficult to know. Family values were passed, expectations were clear, and any longing for material wealth had been put into perspective. Envy for a bigger house with a fancy playhouse or the long wish list for Christmas was met with the calm assertion that being rich did not guarantee happiness.

Helen understood she had led a sheltered life in one sense. Yet, that had not been the intent, just as she and Mitch had not sought to protect Ethan and Tricia from the world outside their own. When the children pondered why bad things happened to good people, they discussed it realistically. When faced with the truth of a friend who came from a "good family" where disturbing abuse was finally revealed, they provided as gentle an explanation as they could. And as Helen's and Mitch's parents had done with them, there was guidance for their future without pressure. Money was set aside for college, but Helen liked to think they would have been equally supportive had Ethan and Tricia chosen other paths.

"Okay, on to more pleasant topics," Tricia said, sitting at the table again and bringing Helen away from her thoughts. "We're closing in on names."

Helen hadn't lobbied for anything in particular. She knew how difficult a choice this could be. "I'm listening," she said instead.

Tricia stirred a spoon of honey into the steaming beverage. "We're ninety-nine percent sure it will be Russell Mitchell if it's a boy. Russell is Justin's paternal grandfather. And Kelly Elizabeth if it's a girl."

"My grandmother's name! That's a nice combination," Helen said, glad that they weren't going for something trendy.

"We think so," Tricia said, and reached out to touch the tea cozy with her fingertip. "And just like this Max Mayfield you were telling me about, we will see about passing on the love of quilting, whether it's a boy or a girl."

"Good for you," Helen said with a laugh. "Does Justin know that?"

Tricia nodded, a lemon square in her hand. "He's fine with the idea as long as I agree that Kelly, if there is a Kelly, gets a plastic ball and bat set, football, and soccer ball as soon as she can walk."

"That sounds fair. He realizes you were no stranger to sports though, doesn't he?"

"Oh, sure, and speaking of which, or related to sports, the band is having a bake sale next week. Can you and Mamaw commit to providing something?"

"Of course," Helen said. "They don't have another trip planned until spring. I suspect that has as much to do with wanting to be here for their first great-grandchild as anything."

Tricia grinned. "I can see it now. Papaw has probably already found the tiniest fishing rod they make and he's waiting for the right time."

"I think it's in the coat closet in the front hall," Helen laughed. "Do you remember the time Ethan tangled a hook in your braid when he was practicing his casting? Lord, I thought we were going to have to cut it out."

Tricia fingered the edges of her pageboy. "The way I remember it, removing the hook took second priority to you chewing him out for being so careless."

"He should have known better," Helen said. "However, I also seem to recall that once we got to the bottom of everything, there might have been a dare in there somewhere."

Tricia's eyes gleamed mischief. "Really? You mean like from his baby sister?"

"That's okay," Helen said and lifted her mug in a toast. "Your time is coming."

CHAPTER FOURTEEN

———⟨⟩⟨◆⟩⟨⟩———

While they were checking the Nelson property, Justin and Dave received word that Jenkins was coherent enough to respond to questions. They had been to the Ratford place first. That property had been devoid of any sign of recent activity, the sadness of shuttered houses, that if left much longer, would begin a deterioration that would be difficult to stem. There were some crisscrossed tire tracks here that indicated at least two vehicles recently, although the house seemed to be untouched. Even though someone carelessly firing shots into the woods was the most probable scenario for Jenkins's accident, they walked around with a careful eye rather than giving a cursory look. The barn, in better shape than the dwelling, had been silent, no evidence of human habitation.

"I'm supposed to take Mamma to a doctor's appointment this morning," Dave said, after acknowledging the hospital's notification about Jenkins.

"You go on," Justin assured him. "I'll get Jenkins and call you if he has anything important to say."

"Thanks," Dave said, as he squeezed his wide frame into the patrol car. He drove one of the department's two Explorers whenever possible since those accommodated his size better than the standard sedan.

Jenkins had been removed from critical care and Justin used the main entrance to the hospital, admiring the architecture of the 1922 red brick building. White scrolled millwork above the retrofitted automatic sliding glass doors surrounded a medallion of granite that depicted the bas-relief profile of George Wallington, the second generation of town founders. Maybe it was the third. Justin didn't have them memorized. What he liked about the building was the committee in charge of renovation had sought the help of a local architectural firm that specialized in restoration. They had correctly concluded the twenty original rooms on the first floor could be converted into administrative space while cleverly concealing modern necessities such as fiber optic wiring. The sorely needed medical equipment upgrades could be housed in additions that were connected to the original building. It was less expensive than constructing a completely new hospital and also preserved the history. The second and third floors towering above the entrance couldn't very well be torn down, but the exterior windows had been clad in replicas of the ones downstairs. The end result was a smooth blending of decades. Anyone entering through the emergency and outpatient sections stepped into a gleaming, modern hospital. Going through the front, however, were sealed, polished wood floors, beautiful crown molding, and walls covered with framed black-and-white photographs of the town at the time the original hospital was built.

Justin made his way to the third floor, stopping briefly at the nurse's station to verify Jenkins's room number. He was glad to see the bed next to Jenkins was empty. A woman rose as he stepped across the threshold. She was about Tricia's height with straight black hair cut short. Her brown eyes with dark circles underneath indicated she could use a good night's sleep. She was curvaceous in the way men appreciated and women always seemed to think meant they should be on a diet. She stood, extended her hand, and glanced at his name tag.

"Isabelle Jenkins. You're Helen Crowder's son-in-law?"

She had a pleasant voice. "Yes, ma'am," he said. He shifted his focus to the boy in the bed. "I need to get a statement from Johnny about what he remembers."

"Nothing," the boy mumbled. His swollen face would be going through multiple shades of green, black, and purple before returning to normal. His hair, which looked like his mother's, had been partially shaved to allow for stitches that angled from his forehead to his left temple. He was propped against two pillows with the bed cranked into a semireclining position. Broken ribs, a smashed face, a mild concussion, and a gashed head weren't the best news, but it could have been a lot worse.

Isabelle moved around the bed to stand on the opposite side, clearing the way for Justin to stand next to Jenkins. "I'm Justin Kendall, the officer who was first on the scene. Mr. Walker from down the road was the one who found you and called it in."

"That's what Dave told us," Isabelle said. "We're grateful to him."

"Don't remember nothing," Jenkins repeated in a stronger voice, the defiant lie in his brown eyes. Despite being in a hospital gown and under bedcovers, his muscled forearms indicated he was in good shape. The position of his feet put him at about five feet nine or ten.

Justin wished he had a dollar for every time he'd heard that come from the mouth of a surly teenager. He let his gaze linger on the boy's face communicating the message of, "I don't believe you for one second."

"Well, Johnny, Mrs. Jenkins," he said slowly. "The thing is that you lost control of the truck because your left front tire was shot."

"What?" Mrs. Jenkins' hand flew to her throat. "What do you mean?"

The boy's eyes flickered and then became hooded again; his intent was to reveal nothing obvious.

Justin wanted to play it out, his senses on alert, wondering if the boy was hiding something. Perhaps it was merely the resistance to authority that was the automatic reaction of the type of kid Jenkins had been described as being. It was that *didn't see nothing, hear nothing, know nothing* answer that had been the routine mantra on the streets of Baltimore when he patrolled the neighborhoods. He spoke directly to Mrs. Jenkins. "There was a bullet, probably a .30-06 that struck the rim as it penetrated the tire." He shifted his gaze to the boy. "We want to know if you saw anyone while you were driving—hunters, anyone."

"What fool's out hunting in the middle of the afternoon?"

"You mind your mouth," his mother snapped, her eyes angrily moving from Justin to her son. "God knows there are plenty of idiots out there with guns for no reason other than to be shooting for the heck of it," she said sharply. "Half of them don't have enough sense to come in out of the rain and shouldn't be wandering around armed. You saw anything, you tell Deputy Kendall, and I mean right now."

Jenkins shifted minutely, Justin empathizing with his memory of the stabbing pain of broken ribs. Respect for his mother, or maybe it was habit, edged out the hardness. "I didn't see anyone, Mamma. I was driving and next thing I know, I wake up in here, hurting like crazy."

"He did take that bad cut to his head," she said, placing her hand on his shoulder. "He was out for hours, then they had him on some pretty powerful pain killers. They want to run one more of those scans on him and he'll be going home in the morning."

Justin probed with another question. "Where were you heading from or to?"

The boy gave a semblance of a shrug. "Nowhere. Just out driving around."

A nurse entered the room, blood pressure cuff in one hand, pen and paper protruding from the pocket of her pale blue smock. "Time to check vitals," she said, in the tone nurses use that means, "I have work to do and I'd like you to get out of my way."

Justin inclined his head and passed a business card across the patient as he dutifully cleared a path for the nurse. "Thank you, Mrs. Jenkins. Johnny's memory might clear up in the next day or two, so if anything comes to mind, give me a call, okay?"

Johnny couldn't respond with the thermometer in his mouth.

"It's Isabelle, deputy," she said with a nod. "I'll be taking my maiden name back after the divorce is final. Johnny will be coming home with me for a few days to make sure he gets proper care."

Justin wasn't sure if that warranted a comment, so he smiled politely instead. He was halfway to the patrol car when his cell phone rang. "This is Alicia Johnson," the distressed voice said. "There isn't anyone here, and there's nothing wrong with me, but could you please come right away? There's something that I need to show you."

"I can be there in less than ten minutes," he said immediately.

The sigh of relief was unmistakable. "Thank you, I appreciate it."

Justin called his change of plans into the station. If Johnny Jenkins was lying for any reason other than stubborn habit, it would have to wait until he found out what had upset Alicia. She opened the front door as soon as he pulled in behind the Camry, noticing that the Highlander was not in the drive.

"I haven't called Hiram," she said, motioning him inside. "He has an important meeting this morning and I don't want to disturb him. It's in here." She led him up the steps to the living room where they'd met before. A spectacular bouquet in a pale yellow ceramic vase with a gauzy white bow tied around it was on the coffee table. Red, pink, yellow, and white roses were arranged among other flowers and greenery that Justin couldn't identify by name. A card was next to the vase, on top of an envelope.

"I found the e-mails this morning and then this showed up," Alicia said, the strain clouding her green eyes and tightening her face. She handed the card to him. It was typed, the way cards are when an order is taken by telephone or via the Internet. *Remember all those bouquets I used to send?* That was the only message.

"Your ex-husband?"

Alicia drew her bottom lip in, perhaps to keep it from trembling. "It has to be," she said. "I have the e-mails on the computer in the office. Oh, I've made fresh coffee, too, and I have muffins."

Of course she did. Why let the possibility of being stalked interfere with Southern hospitality? "Let me take a look," Justin said, "then we can sit down."

He was impressed when Alicia led him to the office. It was sparsely yet practically furnished with a large computer workstation and high-end black leather chair. There was a credenza underneath the single window. A metal pole lamp in a black matte finish was to the left of the desk and Justin almost whistled at the sight of two 21-inch LED monitors and a sleek trackball mouse.

"I need the extra high-speed connection and dual monitors with the work I do," Alicia said, pointing to the chair. "Have a seat. I left them up on the screen."

There were four e-mails, spaced approximately fifteen minutes apart, beginning at 6:00 a.m. that morning. The e-mail address was no more than xyz@cmail.com. *That's the guy you think you want to be with now? That's the house you're in? A Camry instead of a Mercedes? You've been stuck in Hicksville long enough.*

Alicia passed a hand across her eyes. "He's been here, hasn't he? That's the only possible explanation. It was him in our house that day."

Justin swiveled the chair and stood. "You could be correct about that. We don't have a computer technician on staff. I'd like to call in a county expert to see if we can trace the source of these."

Alicia's eyes misted and Justin resisted the urge to put her head on his shoulder, not sure how she would interpret the gesture.

"Okay, but wouldn't you think he sent them from a cyber café?"

"Quite possibly," he agreed. "The flowers were delivered from in town?"

"Forsythe's," she said. "Could we please go into the kitchen? I need a cup of coffee."

"Certainly," Justin said. "I'll call the people I need to from there. I'll let Chief McFarlane know, too." He clapped his cell phone to his ear as he followed Alicia into the eat-in kitchen off the dining room. He suspected her need for coffee was as much wanting an activity to keep her busy as it was to satisfy a craving for caffeine.

The kitchen was not much larger than theirs, in a neutral palette of browns, beiges, and white. It was a galley kitchen with a long island absent an overhang for stools. The stovetop was on the island, a wall oven and microwave on the end next to a narrow door that was probably a pantry. The refrigerator against the back wall had sections of granite counter to the left and right. The double sink was beneath the single window, and the dishwasher to the right. All the appliances were white instead of trendy stainless steel and there was a narrow table against the far wall of the kitchen with a bulletin board above. A portable telephone on its stand and a small rectangular wicker basket sat on the table that was otherwise clear of clutter.

Justin moved to the square, white painted kitchen table to make his telephone calls. Quilted placemats in a predominantly blue floral pattern were on the table. Two small plates and two mugs with spoons on the saucers rested on top of them. The solid blue cloth napkins almost blended into the placemats. A plate of muffins covered in plastic wrap was in the center of the table along with a sugar bowl, a bottle of liquid creamer, and the cream pitcher filled with packets of artificial sweetener. If his nose was accurate, the aroma permeating the kitchen was cinnamon.

Chief McFarlane said he would contact the county to request someone that afternoon. When Justin ended the call, Alicia was filling the mugs from a black ceramic coffee carafe, the plastic cover gone from the muffins.

"They're apple cinnamon," she said, taking the chair to his left. "I sometimes bake when I'm nervous. Please help yourself."

Injecting a social note was likely to help and he did love the flavors of apple and cinnamon. "You said you haven't told your husband yet."

Alicia took a muffin, although she didn't break off a bite to eat. "Hiram went in at his regular time and I took care of a few things after he left before I checked e-mail. I couldn't believe it and I sat there staring, not certain what to do. I thought about calling you then, and thought maybe I could try to trace the e-mails first. I have a friend who can help with that." She pulled the mug closer to her. "I came in to bake the muffins to clear my head a little bit. I literally pulled them out of the oven when the delivery came."

The muffin was excellent with a crumbled top and little chunks of apple inside. "You did the right thing," he said calmly, picking up his mug. The coffee smelled delicious, too. "The chief hopes to have a technician here right after lunch. Is there anything particularly significant about the flowers?"

Alicia exhaled a long breath. "The mix of roses. That was a bit symbolic, I guess. When Leo was sweeping me off my feet he used to frequently send me a dozen roses. Each time, the bouquet would be a different color. Having two roses of each color in this one was his way of wanting me to remember, I imagine."

Justin thought having another muffin would be supportive. "You haven't had any other telephone calls, signs of an intruder, or seen the black Cadillac again?"

"No, and we've been careful about setting the alarm system. I thought maybe it was over and that was part of why this came as a shock."

"That's completely understandable," Justin said gently. "This is an invasion of privacy."

Alicia's lower lip trembled and she covered it up by bringing the mug to her mouth.

The chief had reluctantly said that without proof that it was Rosso, or an actual threat, issuing an all points bulletin would be stretching the legal definition of what they could do. "We're going to increase patrols around here and you can call me at any hour, no matter how small a thing it is," Justin said. "If you or your husband see the Cadillac, or anyone who remotely resembles your ex-husband, I want you to call immediately, okay?"

Alicia smiled tentatively. "I promise and I'll tell Hiram as soon as he comes home." Making the statement seemed to have triggered relief as she glanced at her plate. "The muffins are from my grandmother's recipe. It was one of the first things I learned to bake."

"She was obviously a good teacher," Justin said, finishing the second one. "The adjustment in the patrol route will have a car by here about every two hours."

Alicia's smile became warmer. "Can you do one more thing for me? Will you take the flowers? I hate to throw them out, but I certainly don't want them in the house."

"I'm going by Forsythe's from here. I'm sure Lisa will have an idea of what to do with them."

He left Alicia in a much better frame of mind, running different scenarios through his mind. One of the telephone calls he'd made was to leave a message for Sergeant Robbichaut in New Orleans to see if he could get the report on Leo Rosso by the end of the day. They might get lucky and find out he was the subject of some kind of investigation. If so, that could give them the excuse they needed to issue a bulletin and have him picked up for questioning. That is, if he was in the area. Alicia was correct that the e-mails were most likely sent from a cyber café, the kind where you could rent time on a computer that was used by many different people. It would be impossible to trace him to it. He expected to find the same at Forsythe's. It was most likely an e-mail order that came in the middle of the night. There would have been a credit card, but probably a prepaid that would also be untraceable. He didn't know how smart Rosso was, but he did know if he thought they were just dumb cops in the Hicksville he'd referred to in his e-mail, he was likely to be in for an unpleasant surprise.

CHAPTER FIFTEEN

Helen learned that Max drove a red Ford Explorer, but with three of those in the parking lot, she wasn't sure if he had arrived before her. Clara Tipton, one of the newer residents, had mentioned to Edith, Max's mother, that she wanted to try her hand at appliqué. Max called Helen to see if she could join them to provide a lesson. It had been almost a month since Helen had been to The Arbors and she was glad to help.

People who had grown up in Wallington still referred to the entire complex of Wallington Memorial Center as "the hospital," even though it was actually a campus setting, thanks to Wanda's husband's foresight and understanding of the changing patterns of eldercare. The nursing home had been built adjacent to the hospital in the 1960s, a time when many families still chose to move their aging parents into their own home for their final years. Seniors, who required 24-hour care or suffered paralyzing debilitating conditions, be they physical or otherwise, were the ones who were entered into the "old folks home." As more women took jobs outside of being traditional homemakers and de facto caregivers, and as people began to live longer, Wanda's husband, Randy, recognized that Wallington had need of the assisted-and-independent living approach that a number of places in the country had already adopted.

He began with a complete renovation of the nursing home to transform it into two L-shaped wings. A skilled nursing facility, central kitchen, chapel, and laundry were in the center. The wing closest to the hospital remained as the long-term care area to include a special section for dementia patients. The wing to the far side was assisted living for patients who required some level of care, yet who were neither bedridden nor unable to comprehend where they were. Large windows provided natural light throughout the building. While there was a pleasant main room and dining room on the long-term care side, the fact was that most of those residents rarely left their rooms.

The assisted-living wing was designed specifically to give residents the opportunity to engage in as many activities as they wished. The main room was an open space divided with furniture to designate sections. The large, flat-panel television with DVD player was positioned against the wall without windows and was surrounded with sectionals on casters. Naturally, there were spaces for wheelchairs. It was easy to move the seating out of the way for exercise classes that were tailored to accommodate a variety of limitations. The "Walker Workout" was always a popular choice. Four sets of bookcases, also on casters, were to the right of the television area with six Queen Anne-style chairs with firm cushions that were easy to lower into and rise from. A small table was next to each chair. Floor lamps were behind the chairs for those who might require extra lighting and half of the library was devoted to large-print books and audiobooks.

The back portion of the room had two rows of folding tables with padded folding metal chairs on either side. With a total of four tables, there was seating for card games, board games, crafts, puzzles, and twice-weekly bingo. Additional tables and chairs were stored close by. The shorter section of the room to the right of the wide opening that connected to the dining room had four computer stations set up with head-high dividers between them to provide a modicum of privacy.

Randy had not neglected the landscaping. Residents enjoyed a beautiful courtyard accessible from both wings with a wide path that linked the newly named The Arbors to The Oaks, the Independent Living/Active Retirement Community that was added later. He had also concluded that privacy was an important factor in allowing residents to retain their dignity, so the rooms in the Arbors were not large, but were all singles. Having only the hospital-type bed and one chest of drawers with one bedside table allowed enough space for each room to have a sitting area with a window that looked onto the courtyard. Residents had the option to bring their own furniture if they wished to do so.

The philosophy of The Arbors was that canes, walkers, and wheelchairs, impaired eyesight or hearing, and the need for medication to be monitored did not mean that an individual was an invalid. The activities director, with responsibility for both facilities, ensured a range of options that were more sedentary and slower paced at The Arbors while still being mentally stimulating.

Helen and her mamma were frequent visitors, knowing the staff by name, and also the names of most of the residents. Quilts were in high demand because many of the residents chilled easily and a quilt gave a greater personal touch than did a blanket. Lap quilts and bed quilts could be found in virtually every room. Quilted bed jackets were a common sight as well, lovely pieces that retained their color despite multiple washings. Helen was by no means the only outside quilter who contributed to the facility, but she did have a 1000 Hour Club certificate, honoring her for her volunteer hours. She hadn't bothered to keep count, although it had been a nice gesture, with a little ceremony for her and the three other recipients. Despite the enjoyment she received from her work, and no matter how rationally she understood the inevitability of residents relocating to the continuing care wing or passing away, Helen experienced a pang of sadness each time she received the news. That was inevitably followed by a sense of gratitude that her parents were a lively seventy-nine and eighty. The day might come when they, too, entered either The Oaks or The Arbors, but that was not a subject on which she chose to dwell.

"Hi there," Max's voice broke into her thoughts as she climbed from her car. He'd parked two slots down without her noticing. "Need me to take anything?"

"Oh, I've got it," Helen said, black leather purse over one shoulder and quilting tote in her other hand. "Maybe I should make the same offer."

"I'm balanced," he said, coming next to her, carrying three quilts and a red backpack on his back. She suspected that was his equivalent of a tote.

"I don't think I know Mrs. Tipton," he said, falling into step with her.

"She's Russell Tipton's mother, as in Sheila Tipton's mother-in-law. Sheila is the one who really runs the police department, or at least keeps it organized. I suppose her official title is administrative something or other. She started work there as a clerk right out of high school and is on her fourth chief. Lord only knows how many deputies she's broken in."

Max allowed Helen to enter in front of him. "She sounds like a good woman to know."

"That she is. Hello, Sally, Maggie." Helen greeted the nurses at the front desk.

They exchanged brief pleasantries, Helen making sure they knew who Max was. They then moved down the hall to the activity center. The walls were painted a warm yellow on the bottom half and off-white above the oak chair rail. Bulletin boards with photographs of events and different notices were interspersed among beautiful landscape prints and commemorative quilts. There was the one celebrating the town's bicentennial, another of the hospital itself, and two that had the images of all the local churches that had been built in the 1920s or earlier. It spoke to the importance of churches that it required two quilts to portray them. Then again, that was when churches were the social centers of the town as well as the primary means of social assistance. Even though most of them had been renovated, they all chose to retain the original structures in some form to preserve the architecture. Well, sadly, not the Methodist church that had to be completely rebuilt after a blazing fire.

"There you two are." Edith Mayfield was standing with her walker, a quilt draped across the front. A pocketed black mesh bag beneath held her supplies. Max had always resembled his father rather than Edith who barely topped five feet. She had a delicate build that belied the muscle tone she worked to maintain. She was a regular at the beauty parlor that was available three days a week and her white hair was softly curled in an attractive cut that framed her face. It was her gray eyes that sometimes looked blue that Max had inherited. She was one of the few residents her age that didn't wear glasses.

Like most of the women, she was dressed in comfortable velour pants and a pull-on top with sneakers on her feet. Today's color was teal and Clara Tipton's similar outfit was a deep rose that set off her dark skin.

Clara, not much taller than Edith, leaned on her cane, her head turned in the way of someone who has difficulty hearing. Her heart-shaped face was remarkably devoid of wrinkles; her gold wire-rimmed glasses slipped halfway down her nose. She waved a bony hand toward the tables. "I've got my things over there already."

"Let me get that for you, Mamma," Max said, reaching for the quilt.

She gently pushed his hand away. "I have my system that you don't need to be messing with. You give Clara a hand."

The other woman inclined her head, her hair a mass of black curls that reminded Helen of a style from the 1940s. "I can move just fine on my own with this cane. What did you bring us?"

They began to slowly move toward the table, no one hurrying.

"Three quilts for whomever might need one," Max said cheerfully. "Nothing fancy about them."

"Don't need fancy unless you're hanging them on a wall," Clara said. "Everything gets washed a lot around here and we need things that can hold up."

They reached the table to the far left and Helen saw there were four people in the reading chairs and two at the computer. A small stack of quilting squares sat on the table and a tote leaned against the leg. Edith deftly maneuvered her walker to the opposite side. Max and Helen stood back to let the ladies get settled as other residents moved about.

"I'll go deliver these to the office and be right back," Max said, unloading items from his backpack onto the table. "Just move any of this however you need to," he added with a smile.

"No rush. Myrtle and Agatha were going to come along and they decided to watch that movie, *The African Queen*, instead," Clara said tartly. "Myrtle's son installed one of those small flat-screen televisions on the wall in her room and she can't get enough of it yet."

"Well now, Clara, let's see what you have," Helen said quickly as Max winked at her.

Clara hooked her cane to the back of the chair and motioned for the tote that Helen handed to her. She lifted out a bulging envelope and a folded piece of cream-colored chintz. "You'd think that I would have tried this before, but I never have, and I've got a four-year-old great-granddaughter who loves rabbits. Her mamma found these in a store and asked if I could do up a quilt for the child using them."

There were a dozen cute embroidered bunnies of two by three inches in different poses and colors. The colors were blue, pink, purple, and yellow. "It will be a twin-size quilt and I found a pattern I like for making those. I was thinking that the chintz would be good for the bunny squares."

"The chintz is good because you'll have that extra thickness with the appliqués to take into account," Helen said, "and I like to leave a big one inch seam allowance, although others don't do more than a quarter."

"More is better for my first time, I think," Clara said. They looked up as Max took a seat next to Edith.

They worked companionably for over an hour. Clara's stitches were steady and she nodded as Helen offered to do a square for her and discussed her favorite techniques. Max, too, was working with Edith on her project that needed another twenty squares. They were what she fondly referred to as "one of my garden quilts" that she planned to contribute to the long-term care side. She sometimes focused on one type of flower, but in this case, there was a mix of floral fabrics that people had brought her.

Sounds from the dining room had elevated as tables were set

in preparation for lunch. Roasted chicken, meatloaf, and spinach quiche had been listed on the bulletin board.

Helen often enjoyed staying for the meal, but she'd called Alicia, thinking that an outing would be good for her. She wasn't trying to pry about what was going on, merely recognizing that it was a stressful time for Alicia and she'd sounded grateful for the offer. They were supposed to meet at Bess's Place at noon.

Max also begged off, promising he'd return for dinner. The departure ritual required the usual ten minutes or so of chatting, and as they exited the main room, the hall was filling with the slow progress of residents moving in their direction. Helen had come to understand the way the staff kept a watchful eye while never hurrying the men and women who might be shuffling instead of stepping. It was one of many small things Helen now viewed from a different perspective, her awareness heightened as she observed the staff's respect for their elderly charges. Tripping was a danger that was not perceived by younger people who often broadcast their impatience with body language or outright urging.

"I'm so glad they have a place like this," Max said when they were alone again in the parking lot. "Once Mamma couldn't drive anymore, it made it really hard on Angela. She was trying to find a way for Mamma to move in with them, but their bedrooms are all upstairs and their property isn't large enough for an addition. After she moved here, we finally discovered how much Mamma had given up in trying to stay in her house. She hardly ate because she was tired of cooking and she hadn't had a decent shower in months because she couldn't get in and out of the tub. She'd been giving herself sponge baths in the bathroom sink and we didn't know that."

"It isn't an easy decision to make," Helen agreed, rummaging in her purse for keys. "And sad to say, a place as nice as this isn't affordable for a lot of people."

Max glanced toward the building. "I know. Mamma and Daddy worked hard all their lives and had decent savings, but they never could have imagined that care was going to cost what it does these days. Mamma was worried about not leaving us an inheritance and we both told her if that was the reason she was reluctant to sell the house, then she needed to get rid of that notion. Her being taken care of properly was what mattered."

He laughed and turned toward his Explorer. "Lillian has given Wanda fair warning. I'm not sure what all she has planned."

"I'll check with her when I come in," Helen said, sliding into the car, setting her tote onto the passenger side floorboard, and waving her fingers.

Max was a great guy. She hated to admit she was still having a little difficulty accepting him as a quilter, even though she knew that idea was foolish. Old habits did die hard, and she imagined that the first circle meeting or two could have some awkward moments—that was assuming Max wanted to join the circle. Maybe he would decide not being a member of one particular circle was a better approach.

Helen cranked the car, her thoughts shifting to Alicia. She hadn't asked Justin about his conversation with them and hadn't expected him to divulge it. He wasn't like that, and although she was on the receiving end of a lot of gossip, people came to her because they knew she could be trusted to keep confidences and not pick up the telephone to spread a story. Lord, the pleasure some people took in passing rumors around like candy on Halloween. No, her kitchen table had absorbed plenty of secrets and she'd handed out plenty of tissues. She might not have an official role like Father Singletary, but she wasn't sure which of them had heard more confessions.

CHAPTER SIXTEEN

⬅◆➡

Chief McFarlane had called Wayne Dickinson, the District Attorney, for one of the hypothetical discussions between police and prosecutors when the police are well aware of the guilt of an individual and the prosecutor reels off multiple reasons why the law views their evidence as purely circumstantial. In other words, if they took any action against Mr. Leonardo Rosso at this point, it would be worse than useless. He would no doubt have a very expensive attorney who might choose to bring legal action against them for harassment. Justin was certainly not anti-technology, yet the ability to use public computers for sending e-mail and ordering flowers all while using untraceable prepaid credit cards was frustrating when trying to track down the sort of evidence that would hold up. They were able to spread the word about the black Cadillac and they also assumed Rosso had enough sense to have changed cars if he happened to be using a rental.

His intent was the puzzle and what really mattered. Did he want to simply harass the Johnsons? Was he planning to try to reconcile with Alicia? Was he plotting to take some kind of vengeance? Justin had called for Sergeant Robbichaut, hoping to impress a sense of urgency, only to be told he was out for a couple of days. He was promised that someone else would send them information the next day, or by the following one for sure. Tired of the delay, he'd called his New York contact that was not available, and yes, they would pass the message, but they didn't know when he might get it. That, in all likelihood, meant he was on a case and might be gone for days.

Justin was trying to soothe his frustration with one of the coconut chocolate almond bar cookies Lisa Forsythe had dropped off at the station. Dave Mabry and the chief's part in discovering that Lisa's husband had been stealing from her and ultimately helping save her fledging business had occurred well before Justin joined the department. He had, however, been in the office when Chief McFarlane had attempted to explain to Lisa that whatever debt she felt she owed to them had long been paid. She'd told him she would decide for herself when the debt was settled, and in the meantime, he was to enjoy the pastries she brought and shut up about it.

"I think you'll want to be speaking with Mr. Walker," Sheila said, crossing the otherwise empty bay. "He has something to tell you and the chief." Her voice was pitched louder than usual, and then Justin remembered the chief had mentioned Mr. Walker was hard of hearing.

Louis Walker, the man who'd possibly saved Johnny Jenkins's life by coming upon the wreck as soon as he did, was one step behind Sheila, twisting a black ball cap in his hands. They stopped at the side of the desk where the single chair was, Mr. Walker ducking his head in a type of greeting. His narrow shoulders were slightly rounded, his mostly white hair cropped close to his head. He was wearing the same type of clothes as he had been the day of the wreck. He wore a pair of khaki work pants, a cracked brown leather belt, and a long sleeve dark green cotton shirt with an open collar and a white tee shirt underneath.

Like his work boots that were scuffed yet clean, everything about Mr. Walker had an aged look. His eyes darted around the room before coming to rest on Justin. "Deputy," he said, his voice hesitant.

Justin rose and extended his hand. "Mr. Walker, a pleasure to see you, sir."

Mr. Walker's voice strengthened, his deep brown eyes steady. "You seem like a nice enough fellow and I don't have anything against this sheriff."

Justin wasn't sure if he was supposed to respond to that and Sheila gave an almost imperceptible shake of her head before she touched Mr. Walker on his arm. "Louis, you're doing the right thing. Officer Kendall will take you in to see the chief so you can talk to them both at the same time."

Justin turned to see Chief McFarlane standing behind his desk and Justin gestured toward the office. "If you'll follow me, sir." What was going on?

"Mr. Walker," the chief said, offering his hand while nodding toward the two chairs in front of his desk. "What can we do for you today? Can I ask Sheila to get you a Coke or anything?"

As he had done with Justin, the old man looked hard at the chief before he took the second chair and rested his cap on his knee. Carlton Feed Store was printed in faded gold lettering.

"I'm fine," he said as Justin sat next to him. "I hear y'all been asking about empty properties off the back roads."

"We have," the chief said. "Matter of fact, Officers Kendall and Mabry were out at the Nelson and Ratford places."

"Got an idea that someone's cooking up shine or some of those drugs they show on TV?"

"There's been some talk around the county and the Jenkins boy's tire was shot out. That was what caused the wreck," the chief said evenly. Justin didn't understand the obvious undercurrent

145

surrounding Mr. Walker and he sensed it was better to let the chief carry the conversation unless he was asked to speak.

"Can't say I saw or heard anything that day, but I got to thinking about the old Birch property off the end of Turner Road. Got a cousin lives out that way and she'd been complaining six ways to Sunday about too much traffic out there."

Chief McFarlane shot a quick look at Justin. "This is recent?"

Mr. Walker furrowed his brow. "I'd have to say coming up on a month, maybe. No more than that. Yvette, that's my cousin, lost her husband two years back and she ought to be selling her place and move in with her oldest daughter. She can't keep up that kind of property at her age, you know."

"It is hard work," the chief said patiently.

"Where was I? Oh yes, the Birch house. Well, house, barn, and got a meadow that used to be nice. Pretty much overgrown now with no livestock and nobody taking a bush hog to it like they ought to. Not even sure which of the Birch's are still alive." He wagged his head, perhaps at a memory. "Mind you, I haven't seen anything myself, but Yvette says there's been trucks going by, specially late afternoon, music blaring, interrupts her dinner and then worse, coming back at night when she's reading her Bible at bedtime. I was over to see her yesterday and she said she's getting mighty tired of it."

Justin raised his voice to be sure he was heard. "How close does your cousin live to the Birch property, sir?"

Mr. Walker turned his head slowly. "I'm not deaf, son, just a little hard of hearing. Yvette is about two miles away." He inclined his head to the chief. "She's out almost to where Turner meets Big Creek Road. The Birch place is set back from where lightening took out that tall pine. There's a gate across the driveway."

Mr. Walker looked at Justin again, a smile playing around his mouth. "Like I said, I don't know if it's anything to get in a fuss about because Yvette can get herself in an uproar over not much of anything, but I thought I'd come by and pass on the information." He slowly rose to his feet. "Y'all have a nice day, now."

"Thank you for coming in, sir," Justin said, standing, as did the chief. "We'll check it out."

The old man paused and Justin couldn't define the look that Mr. Walker passed between him and the chief. "You do that and I'll go make my good-byes to Sheila." He ambled from the office as the chief gave Justin a signal to stay, not speaking until Mr. Walker was nearly at the open double doors leading to the front desk.

"You must have made an impression on him the other day," Chief McFarlane said, propping on the edge of the desk. "Mr. Walker, like most of his kin and neighbors, don't usually bring matters to the police."

Justin shrugged. "Had a lot of that in Baltimore, too."

"Can't say that I blame him," the chief said. "His uncle was lynched when Louis was maybe twelve years old and his daddy was nearly beat to death trying to stop it. Case was never solved, if you want to call it a case to begin with. For what it's worth, that was the last lynching in the area's history. We've had a lot of changes for the better over the last forty years, but it's hard to get rid of memories."

"I got that," Justin said, thinking of a pastor who'd once told a group of at-risk youth that holding on to hate would hold them down and letting go of it didn't mean they weren't tough. He pushed the thought away. "You want us to go check now, or wait until later in the afternoon?"

"No reason to wait, if there's something to be had. Ask Sheila to get Dave and Lenny in. Y'all might as well take both Explorers." He moved behind his desk and held up a finger. "Oh, and get a twenty from Sheila from petty cash. Take the bolt cutters with you and run by the hardware store for a new padlock. If this is a dead end, we'll need to replace the lock you're likely to have to cut off."

Justin chose to drive by himself, trailing Dave and Lenny, who knew the area. He wasn't in the mood for what he was sure would have been a drawn-out story about why the Birch property was abandoned. He wanted to give the situation with Rosso some more thought. Had seeing Alicia in Atlanta been a coincidence that set a chain of events into motion? Had he possibly been looking for her? That didn't seem logical based on her version of their marriage, unless he was the type of guy that didn't appreciate something until he lost it.

Justin, Dave, and Lenny had discussed their plan for approaching the Birch property. Justin would hold back to let Dave and Lenny arrive first and basically draw fire, if that was going to happen. That would allow Justin to call the chief for backup as Dave and Lenny withdrew and circled behind the property on foot, both familiar with moving quietly through the woods. The taillights of the lead vehicle disappeared around a curve, and within two or three minutes, Dave's voice came through the radio. He hadn't heard a shot or observed movement. "It's quiet, but there's a brand-new lock on this gate. Come on up and we'll see what we've got."

Justin felt a surge of excitement at the unspoken understanding. You didn't put a new lock on an old gate without a reason. It could be something as simple as the absent owners were planning to move in again, or they had engaged a realtor who had been showing the property. That wouldn't fit with their understanding of Mr. Walker's cousin's complaints. They had also discussed interviewing her and decided against it. There would be time enough for that if they discovered anything of note.

The driveway was dirt, no gravel, with too many trees and too much underbrush to see beyond the slight bend. The mailbox sitting to the left of the gate was almost rusted through, the post listing at an angle as if it had been hit by a vehicle. When Justin bumped to a stop next to Dave and Lenny at the rusty metal gate sporting both a new chain and padlock, he saw they were both wearing vests, standing on either side of the Explorer behind the opened doors. He grabbed his vest from the passenger seat, and moved next to Dave, listening for any sounds that seemed out of place.

"Got a fire of some kind in there," Dave's voice was low, not quite a whisper. "House and barn should be about a hundred yards in."

Wood smoke carried distinctly in the still air. The day was warm enough, but the temperatures dropped at night. If a wood burning fire was the only source of heat though, someone might bank a fire during the day, keeping the coals warm for faster lighting.

"Doesn't have the smell of a still," Dave continued, not describing what that would be. "I say, we cut the lock, roll in real quiet, and if we're in the wrong, we apologize and give him or her the new lock. Lenny will have the window down with the 12-gauge and you can be right behind us."

"Works for me," Justin said, as Dave nodded to Lenny who was able to see Dave holding the bolt cutters.

He sliced through the lock quickly. Justin and Dave looked outward for signs of movement. It was silent, their presence apparently quieting birds and other animals. Dave stepped up and swung the gate that was still sturdy despite its appearance and opened with the silence of the hinges having been oiled. Lenny was already in the passenger seat, shotgun in hand.

Justin waited a fraction of a second to crank his engine, and then they crept forward, seeing nothing until they came onto the house, tendrils of smoke curling from the chimney. The once white frame house hadn't seen a coat of paint in a long time. One shutter had fallen to the porch; another was hanging only by the lower hinge.

Patches of dead weeds and dirt were all that were left of what had been flower beds along either side of the steps. The meadow that Mr. Walker had spoken of did need a good cutting, for the weeds and grass were waist high. No light showed through what would be a dim interior with all the shades pulled down. The edge of the barn that was visible from this angle didn't look to be in much better shape.

There were no vehicles in sight, but the flattened grass, crisscrossed with ruts and littered with beer cans, was obviously a makeshift parking lot. The three men eased out, Dave and Justin now with their Glocks unholstered, Lenny moving around to the rear of the house. They looked at the steps closely as they mounted, the wood giving slightly under the pressure of their feet, Dave going to the left, Justin pulling the dilapidated screen door open as he rapped sharply on the interior door. "Wallington police," he called loudly. "Need to talk to you, please."

There was no sound or movement. Lenny's voice came in just above a whisper. "The barn, guys."

Justin and Dave, pistols at the ready, saw Lenny crouched behind an old black Ram truck outfitted with big tires. Dents, dings, and scrapes attested to its off-road use. Justin almost coughed at a smell he didn't recognize.

Dave wrinkled his nose and grinned at Lenny. "Twenty bucks says it's the Lamberts." He turned his head to Justin. "Cock fighting. George and Bruce Lambert are cousins. We busted their ring about three years ago and thought they'd left the county."

"Bruce been drinking or is high, he's liable to start shooting," Lenny said calmly. "I'll take the back." He slipped from the truck, signaling when he was in position.

Unlike the house, one of the wide doors on the end closest to them was open. Strains of a country song come from inside.

Dave looked at Justin, "You ready?" He nodded once and they

moved rapidly, the stench strong when they crossed into the barn, calling out their identification.

"Don't be stupid," Dave barked at the taller of the two men who whirled, lunging for the rifle leaning against a stall door.

The first man stopped, the second one only now turning, squinting as if the light was brighter than it was. Roosters started to cackle, moving in their cages that filled the four stalls, two on either side of the barn.

The man close to the rifle sneered. "What the hell you doing here, Mabry, bothering decent folk with no cause?" He was half a head taller than Dave, but not as broad through the shoulders and with a paunch straining the buttons of his chambray shirt. His scraggly brown hair hung limp tucked behind his ears, and his beard and moustache could use a trim. He was flexing his hands as though trying to decide if he could reach the rifle.

Dave motioned with his pistol for the man to move further from the rifle. "Bruce, decent ain't the word comes to mind when describing you two. Should we add trespassing to cock-fighting?"

"You don't see no fight going on, now do you?" The second man moved alongside the first, not as tall and with a bigger belly on a frame that wasn't built for it. The stubble on his narrow face might be laziness or the beginnings of a beard. The dirty red Braves ball cap he was wearing hid his hair if he had any. Now that he was closer, the faint scent of marijuana reached Justin's nose.

Justin saw that Lenny had slipped in from the back, shotgun held on both men. They turned briefly to see him nod an acknowledgement.

"Fighting roosters would make for some expensive barbecue," Dave said, and reached for his handcuffs. "You two know the position, so move on over to the wall there."

The one named Bruce stared hard, his watery blue eyes not

flinching. "Grounds of what, Mabry? Like George says, you got nothing to see. We're renting this place from Nate Birch. He's over near Macon. He's got himself a big rig he drives. You can ask him yourself."

Dave sighed, shaking his head sadly. "Why do you want to waste our time like this? You want to play it this way, we'll all sit and wait for your customers to start showing up, and I'll guarantee there'll be one or two willing to testify against you. Not to mention that based on that smell coming from George, it won't take us long to find his stash. This will be a whole lot simpler for all of us if you just come on and let's get it over with."

Despite an even tone, Justin noticed that neither Dave nor Lenny had dropped their guns, and he could see the smoldering anger play across Bruce's face. It was George who spoke in a whine.

"Don't go making trouble, Bruce. It ain't worth it."

"One of these days, Mabry, it's gonna be me and you without that gun and badge," Bruce said darkly.

Dave dangled the cuffs. "That could well be, but it ain't going to be today."

It took almost two hours to gather the small arsenal of guns on the property, find the stash of marijuana that didn't look to be more than for personal use, notify the proper channels concerning the caged roosters, and gather bits of evidence of who had been attending the fights.

"Dave, if you want to ride with Justin, I'll stop in to see Mrs. Thompson to let her know what we've got and that she shouldn't be having any more problems," Lenny volunteered.

Dave nodded and Justin helped secure the men in the patrol car, ready to return to the station. He didn't understood the attraction of cockfighting and while busting up the ring wasn't anywhere near as satisfying as if they'd found a meth lab, it wasn't a bad day's work.

CHAPTER SEVENTEEN

———◆———

Helen felt the prick of anxiety that mothers know never goes away, no matter the age of your children. That was doubly true when it was your daughter carrying your first grandchild. Tricia's face that had been in almost a constant glow was not only lacking that animation, but there was a tightness around her eyes that spoke of fatigue.

"You were saying?" Helen didn't want to nag, although she was tempted. Tricia would explain when she was ready.

"I was up way too early this morning." Tricia lightly bounced her hand off her stomach. "I am convinced that Russell Mitchell is what we have in here and Justin has been whispering about football to him. If it's Kelly Elizabeth, she's going to be a dancer, gymnast, or something along those lines."

"You couldn't get to sleep or couldn't get back to sleep?"

Tricia yawned. "Both, I think. I finally got up around four thirty. There were a couple of articles I wanted to read and haven't had the energy for lately." She ran her finger around the top of the mug. "One of them was about bullying in school. How the staff and rules could only get you so far. That providing the students with the awareness of what true bullying is, the means they have to stop it, and maybe mostly importantly, trying to understand why a bully is a bully in the first place are the actual keys."

Helen bit back her initial response of, "Because some folks are plain mean," and said instead, "Were there any practical ideas?"

Tricia smiled, but it seemed to be an effort. "One or two, but you know it did make me think of the situation with Albert, Boyd's second cousin, that I was telling you about."

"Who enjoys chemistry more than biology? I was listening the other day," Helen said, watching a grimace pull Trisha's mouth downward. That was enough. "Honey, are you all right? I mean seriously, do you feel okay?"

She arched forward, her voice strained. "Actually, I'm not sure."

Helen shot out her hand. "Tell me what it is. The pain, I mean."

Tricia gripped her mother's hand and used her other to brace against the edge of the table. "It's different, it was sharp, and now it's like a pressure in my stomach, but not the kind of pressure of needing to go to the bathroom."

Helen kept an even tone. "Okay, I'm going to walk over to call Dr. Fraiser."

"I hate to bother him if it's nothing," Tricia said. "I'm scheduled for a check-up day after tomorrow." Another flash of pain played across her face as she completed the sentence. "Well, maybe calling is a good idea."

The conversation was brief as she put Tricia on the telephone. She answered a few questions, the most important of which was that there was no bleeding. "Yes, yes, we'll meet you there," she said. She handed the telephone to Helen to switch it off. "He'd like us to come to the emergency room, but he said it's a precaution and for me not to worry."

As if that was going to happen. It was important to stay calm, though. At this stage of Tricia's pregnancy, there were a number of things that could be causing the pain and not all were reason for alarm. Helen was trying to shake the idea of premature labor, knowing that false labor was more likely.

Helen offered a steadying arm as Tricia struggled up from the chair. "Do you want to call Justin?"

Tricia shook her head rapidly. "No, this could be the simplest thing in the world and he acts like he's cool with all of this, but I don't want him speeding to the hospital with sirens blaring."

Helen managed a laugh at the image. "I'm not sure he'd go that far. Okay, good, walk as slowly as you need to," she said, hearing Tricia grunt with the first step. She looked down as Tawny had suddenly appeared at their feet, giving a soft whimper as she bumped against Helen's leg.

"It's okay, girl," Tricia said. "Everything is fine." She looked at Helen. "Isn't it?"

"Of course," Helen said, blowing a kiss to the dog. "We'll be back before time for your dinner." The dog, whether understanding or not, followed them to the door, but made no attempt to run out and jump in the car.

The drive to the hospital seemed longer than usual as Tricia closed her eyes. She seemed to be concentrating more on squeezing them shut as a means to deal with the pain. Helen thought that she, too, must be wondering about the possibility of premature delivery. The adage that the first child always came late was more often true than not, the "more often" meaning that was "not always." Helen was running the math through her head, thinking this would actually make the baby only three weeks early.

"I can walk on my own," Tricia said when Helen swung into

the parking lot. "Why don't you let me out at the entrance, then join me inside? I imagine that we beat Dr. Fraiser here."

Helen swung as close to the automatic sliding doors as she could, setting the emergency brake and coming around to help Tricia up from the seat.

"My purse. I'll need my insurance card," Tricia said, pointing to the floorboard.

Betty Wallington stepped through the doors, a clipboard in her hand. "Ah, Helen, Tricia, I was coming off break when I saw you pull up. Can I help?" Her round face was calm, a trait she would have developed from years of working the emergency room.

"We're supposed to meet Dr. Fraiser and I need to park the car," Helen said quickly.

"You go right ahead. Tricia, lean on my arm and we'll take it nice and slow," Betty said firmly after her green eyes appraised Tricia. "Let's get you inside."

Relieved that Betty was on duty, Helen relinquished Tricia's purse. It wasn't that she didn't trust the other nurses. Wallington Memorial was an excellent hospital. It was more comforting, though, to have someone they'd known for years. Betty, one of the sixth generation of Wallingtons and Wanda's granddaughter, was in her late thirties. She'd begun her nursing career as a candy striper volunteer and never wavered from the profession. While she hadn't inherited the doll-like delicacy of many of the Wallington women, her astuteness and business sense matched that of any of her ancestors. There had been talk of medical school since doctor was one of the few titles not held by a Wallington. Betty, however, preferred nursing, and if what Phyllis had passed on to Helen proved true, Betty was quietly closing in on a master's degree in hospital administration to add to the master's degree in nursing she'd already completed. Helen could easily see Betty sitting in a big office before too long.

Helen was glad to see the emergency room was in a relatively quiet state when she entered. There were only five chairs occupied in the bright fluorescence of the tiled room. The armless chairs with padded vinyl seats, some in green, some in blue, were in four rows of four. There was a table on each end of the row, a magazine rack and a small bookcase with paperbacks and volumes of *Reader's Digest Condensed Books* to one side. No one was holding makeshift bandages to wounds. One young woman was stroking the head of a little boy who looked to be six or seven, his eyes closed, leaning across her lap. A man in dark blue work clothes was back two rows, with a copy of *Field and Stream* hiding his face. The woman in the second row had a tote next to her chair, a skein of yellow yarn poking out of it as she manipulated crochet needles, her head bent to her task. A youngish man close to her was supporting his left arm with his right, eyes closed.

"We have Tricia in the third cubicle," Betty said. "They're taking her vitals."

"Thanks." Helen slipped behind the curtain, the nurse looking up to see if she needed to admonish someone for being in the wrong place. "Hi, Helen, how are you?"

"Good, thanks, and you?" she said, grateful that the young woman was wearing a name tag: Forsythe. One of Lisa's cousins— Anna? Abby? No, Arianna.

"Your blood pressure is a little elevated, but it's probably the circumstances," she said, removing the cuff from Tricia's arm. She quickly ran through a short checklist and almost bumped into Doctor Frasier when she pulled the curtain aside to leave. They did the I'll go to the right, you go to the left dance with smiles that Helen found reassuring. She'd learned the body language of emergency room staff during the many trips with Ethan and didn't think they had changed that much. No matter how soothing their voices might be, there was an expression of gravity they wore and urgent moves they made when a situation was serious.

"Well now, let's see what we have," Dr. Fraiser said cheerfully. At age sixty-six, Tricia had been one of the first babies he'd delivered. He'd been talking about finally taking on a partner with the idea of phasing into retirement. His six-foot frame seemed to have shrunk a bit, but his blue eyes sparkled behind his round, silver wire-rimmed glasses and his posture was as erect as ever. Maybe it was his full head of thick hair with minimal gray that made most people think he was barely sixty.

"No, you stay right where you are," he said when Tricia tried vainly to bring herself to a sitting position. "I need to feel around a bit." He turned his head to Helen. "And how is the Mamaw-to-Be holding up? Or will it be Granny? Grandmother?"

"I think we'll stick to Mamaw for me, GG for my mother, and I'm not sure about Justin's side," she replied, glad for the absence of worry in his voice.

"Gram and Grandpa are the terms I've been hearing," Tricia said with a small gasp as the doctor gently pressed on her lower belly.

Helen snapped her head around and exhaled when he smiled broadly.

"Okay, give me a hand with getting her upright," he said, placing his hands to support Tricia's back. "I'm glad you called and there's nothing for you to be concerned about other than your Thanksgiving plans may be in jeopardy."

Helen was helping lift as they brought Tricia to a sitting position, her legs dangling from the examination table. "What is that supposed to mean?"

Dr. Fraiser took his smart phone from the holder clipped to his belt and began to scroll on it, looking for something. "At the moment, we have the new generation expected November 30, and that could still be true." He returned the telephone to his holder.

"What you have going on, however, is that the baby has turned head down and dropped. All the moving around is what you've been experiencing today and the new position is what's causing the discomfort. That shouldn't last for more than another hour or so as he, or she, settles down."

"The baby's head has dropped?" Tricia repeated. "So, you're telling us the baby will be early?"

Doctor Fraiser held up a hand to slow her down. "Not necessarily. If it's one thing you learn about babies it's that they have their own schedule, despite our predictions. Unless you set a date for a Caesarian procedure, the best we can do is estimate. Having the baby in this position is a good sign, though. In fact, we'll use this as your checkup. The baby is well developed and I suggest you and your husband review everything you've been learning in the birthing classes."

Helen wondered if the transformation of relief on Tricia's face was reflected on her own. Goodness, the baby might come early, or if not, at least everything was fine. "How about continuing to work?" she heard herself ask.

He patted Tricia's stomach once more. "That's up to Mamma here, but honestly, you and the baby are healthy. I don't recall the school's exact policy on maternity leave and my personal advice is that you keep working as long as you feel well and use the days off for after the baby is born." He grinned at Helen before looking at Tricia again. "You don't have to cut it quite as close as your mamma did, though."

"I'll do my best," Tricia laughed. "Maybe I'll go ahead and pack the suitcase and get registered on the ward."

The story of Helen delaying so long to get to the hospital with her second child that she nearly delivered in the car on the way in had been told on many occasions. It had truly been inadvertent. The baby wasn't due for three days and she'd made an early trip to the grocery store. She had ice cream and other frozen items in the car and didn't want them to melt, but when she'd pulled into the driveway, she realized the labor pains were coming closer together. She still insisted that Mitch put away at least the perishables before they left.

Poor little Ethan had to come with them because they didn't have time to get her parents to the house, as had been the plan. They'd met them at the hospital, explaining to Ethan that yes, Mamma's tummy was hurting, but she would be fine, and why didn't they go to the cafeteria while the doctor made her feel all better? And you know what else? When they finished, he might have a new baby brother or sister waiting for him. Did he get to choose which one? Well, no, but in either case, he would be the big brother.

"Not a bad idea and don't hesitate to call if you have any concerns," Doctor Fraiser was saying as he pushed the curtain open. "It really is difficult to be precise with natural childbirth, so pay attention to what your body is telling you. You might have false labor, and then again, the baby might come early. It's always better to let us check if there's any question about it."

"We'll do that," Tricia said, smiling at Helen and reaching for help to get off the examination table. "It's a good thing I didn't call Justin. I'm not sure he's ready for this."

"It sounds as if he needs to get that way," Helen said, taking Tricia's purse so she could sign the release papers and prepare to leave.

Helen pulled out of the parking lot and paused at the stop sign, looking carefully both ways. "Do you need to stop anywhere for anything?"

Tricia expelled a long breath and shifted the seatbelt to as comfortable a position as she could. "I don't think so. Even though I logically knew everything was okay, I was a little apprehensive, I guess. A nap might be the best thing for me."

Helen glanced at her daughter. "Don't try to be so logical," she said warmly. "I was anxious myself. It's perfectly normal. And here's what I suggest. Let's go home, you call Justin and tell him y'all are having dinner with me tonight, and you lie down in the guestroom for a nap."

"Should I protest and tell you I don't want you to go to any trouble?"

"Not for a minute," Helen said. "The only question you need to answer is if you want chicken or Swiss-style steak."

Tricia didn't bother to hide a yawn. "Oh, I haven't had Swiss-style steak in forever. Let's do that."

Helen slowed to let one of The Arbors vans turn in front of her. "Good, that was my preference, too."

Tawny greeted them with wiggles and Helen lifted her up to provide laps all around. "Oh, that reminds me," Helen said, setting her on the floor. "I read somewhere that we should take a small towel and put it in with the baby while he or she is in the hospital, then bring that home for Tawny to smell before she sees the baby for the first time."

Tricia took her cell phone from her purse and pressed the contact number for Justin. "That makes sense, although I can't imagine her having a problem with the baby, as precious and gentle as Tawny is to everyone. Hi, sweetheart, do you have a minute?"

Helen went to double check the guestroom as well as to give Tricia a moment of privacy. Ethan's old room had become the home office once all the quilting equipment and supplies had been moved. Tricia's old room, a few steps closer to the second bathroom, was painted a pale yellow and depicted a garden theme, although it was not overly floral. The quilt atop the double bed was the centerpiece with a basket motif with different floral patterned squares that alternated to give balance to the design. This was one of the last quilts

CHARLIE HUDSON

Helen's grandmother had worked on. The soft yellow and moss green fabric for the sashing and binding suddenly made Helen think about how similar this was to the quilt Rita was working on currently.

The two lampshades on the bedside tables were an antique ivory, and the floor length drapes with a matching swag were moss green with tiebacks made from one of the fabrics in the quilt. Helen felt a glimmer of emotion, as she often did when she gazed at the fine crafting of the quilt, representing the hours that had been shared between three generations of women. In actuality, there had been a number of afternoons that Tricia was also with Mamaw Pierce in the small apartment that had been created from Helen's parents' garage. Tricia, too young for quilting, however, loved to play with her great-grandmother's thimbles, sometimes decorating all her fingers at one time. That was probably stretching the concept of having four generations quilting together.

"Mamma, are you back here?"

"Yes, how is Justin?" Helen stepped into the short hallway to let Tricia pass into the room.

"I guess they had some excitement today, too. They found a cockfighting ring off Turner Road. Or, maybe, they just thought it was. He was in kind of a hurry, but he agrees that dinner over here is a great idea."

"Cockfighting is a brutal practice," Helen said angrily. "No excuse for men behaving like that." She shook the thought away. "I'm glad they found it. Now you get out of those shoes and relax. You sleep, and if you nap all the way until dinner, we'll wake you up."

Tricia turned and opened her arms for a hug. "Thanks, Mamma, thank you for everything."

"Of course," Helen said, and patted her back. "You just slide under that quilt and rest. It will bring you pleasant dreams."

162

CHAPTER EIGHTEEN

"Kind of a cute thing, isn't she? For a little dog, I mean."
Helen smothered a giggle at the sight of Tawny on Helen's daddy's lap attempting to go for his chin and settling for her tongue on his hands. "She is, and she's a sweetie, too. No problems at all."

"Well, I suppose it's nice, you having a dog here," he said, making as if to stand. "You sure that fence is sturdy all the way around? It's been there for years. I think we'll go out and check it."

"Daddy, it's fine," Helen started, and then saw the look from her mother. "Oh. Sure. It wouldn't hurt to check."

"You want your jacket, Frank?"

At five feet nine and a trim weight around 170 pounds, he easily cradled Tawny under his right arm, her bright eyes happily trusting this man she'd just met. "At my age, I ought to know if I need a jacket or not." He patted Tawny's head. "Come on, pup. Let's explore."

"And who will you complain to if you get a cold?" Joy's words were wrapped in affection as Frank blew her a kiss. His gray eyes crinkled with good humor, his glasses the old-fashioned black frames that he refused to change. That sort of loving exchange was what Helen had grown up with, not understanding at the time that not all parents cared deeply for each other.

"You know your daddy hates to sit still," she said when he left the den, jacketless. "So, Tricia is fine, and we need to talk about Thanksgiving."

Helen was on the love seat with her mamma, having relinquished the chair to her daddy. "Ethan said they would stay in Augusta this year and pop down for Christmas instead. That means we're only talking about just us if we don't go looking for orphans."

"Who have you invited?" Both Joy and Helen were sensitive to people who were alone at the holidays and they preferred cooking for a crowd. Having a large group around the table seemed more in keeping with the spirit. Between the two of them, they usually located half a dozen singles or childless couples that didn't have plans.

"Well, the Johnsons don't really know anyone and I'm not sure that the Raneys do either. With Steve working at the plant, that would give Daddy the chance to talk about the good old days when it was a textile mill instead of making carpet squares. How about you?"

"Sam Goodman usually goes to his daughter's in Macon, but when I saw him yesterday, he mentioned he wasn't feeling up to the trip. He said he was just going to get a TV dinner and watch football."

"We can't have that," Helen said. "Besides, there's no way of knowing if the baby will come early. On the other hand, I'd hate to get everyone here and have Tricia go into labor the day before."

"Let's plan for our house, then. Since the Johnsons and Raneys know each other and we know Sam, no one should feel awkward if you, Justin, and Tricia aren't there the whole time. I mean, the truth is that unless there are complications, Tricia won't be in the hospital for more than a day or two. She'll be home and the last thing either of them will need to worry about is what to do for Thanksgiving. We'll have dinner at our house and you and Justin can swap off being with her and the baby and whoever comes first can take food back for Tricia."

"The whole point of having Thanksgiving here is to keep you from doing all the work," Helen pointed out.

"And I have appreciated that for the past six years," her mamma smiled. "That doesn't mean, however, that I'm no longer capable of putting it all together. If it will make you feel better, I'll call Bess's Place and have them fry the turkey, and I'll get a pie and cake from Lisa. Then, all I'm doing are the sides. Lord, I can set the table a week in advance no more often than we use the dining room. I usually serve our plates right from the stove now and we eat off TV trays half the time like a couple of old people."

Helen couldn't hold back a laugh. If ever a couple at eighty and seventy-nine didn't seem old, it was her mamma and daddy. "How about a compromise? Bess's does do a fine fried turkey, and I never mind giving Lisa business, so we'll agree to that. We'll plan for here and keep the sides to dressing, gravy, green bean casserole, sweet potatoes, cranberry relish, and rolls. I'll get all the ingredients, and if we need to, we'll swap to your place and just transfer everything."

Her mamma's sable-brown eyes that she and Tricia had inherited were merry. "When was the last time I let you make the dressing? Besides, if we don't roast the turkey, there won't be pan drippings for gravy and I have frozen turkey stock on hand. That gives you sweet potatoes, the green bean casserole, relish, and rolls to take care of."

Helen raised her hands in surrender. "Deal, but I'll order the desserts from Lisa, and we'll keep our fingers crossed to get through this on the schedule for the baby after Thanksgiving."

Her mamma reached down for the stuffed tote she'd carried inside. "Speaking of babies being delivered, I have a present for you."

"For me? Tricia is the one who's pregnant, remember?"

"Yes, and this is your first time to be a grandmother," she said, unfolding the cloth and spreading it across the love seat. "A new lap quilt will be perfect for rocking."

"Oh, it's beautiful," Helen said, lifting it for a full view. The pastel bindings were blue on the top, pink on the bottom, green to the left, and yellow to the right. The center square in white, twice as large as the others, was embroidered lettering in silver thread saying, "Grandmothers sprinkle stardust over children's lives." Alternating squares in the same fabric as the bindings made up the quilt, a dozen appliquéd white full moons and stars scattered across the surface.

"The design is from Ruth, by the way. She and I were talking about it before we went to see Eloise and I thought it was a wonderful idea."

Helen pressed the quilt to her chest and leaned into her mother's arms. "It's gorgeous."

They each sniffed, not wanting the tears to fall. "It's true, you know," her mamma said when they both composed themselves. "You love your children, you do, yet there is something so very special about grandchildren that it's difficult to describe. I honestly don't think anyone understands it fully until the very moment when you hold the baby and realize that you are now a grandmother."

"How about great-grandmother?"

"Oh, I imagine that will be special, too, but you know, one of these days, we're going to be slowing down and corralling a youngster will be more difficult for us."

Helen carefully refolded the quilt, thinking she would keep it across the back of the rocker. "You're both in wonderful shape," she protested. "You walk almost every day and take Silver Aerobics and Daddy still does his own yard work and has that stationary bike that he likes."

Joy nodded. "Thank the good Lord, but you have to be realistic about this, too. His right knee is giving him more trouble than he lets on, and while I think all of us have become accustomed to the idea that we'll have at least one artificial joint, that sort of thing does have an impact."

Helen wondered if she'd registered alarm at perhaps a condition her mamma was keeping secret because Joy burst into laughter. "Goodness, girl, don't look worried. We are fine, and couldn't be happier about it. All I meant was that it doesn't last forever. That's why we're traveling as much as we are right now. The day will come when long bus trips and getting around in airports aren't things we want to mess with anymore."

Helen joined in the laughter. "Okay, I won't nag you. By the way, have the church and the bank put out the trip schedule for the coming year?"

"Yes, and the only problem is they're repeating some of the most popular ones and I'm not sure we want to go to Charleston or Washington, DC, again this soon. There is a nice one up into Minnesota in July we're thinking about, and there is the one to the Grand Canyon we haven't done yet."

Helen snapped her fingers. "Oh, I can't remember if I told you about Wanda's big news and Max Mayfield. All that happened while y'all were at Eloise's."

Joy looked bemused. "Max Mayfield and Wanda? No, I can't say that's ringing a bell."

"I don't mean them together. Well, not in that kind of way. It's a great story. Let's go in the kitchen so I can tell you all about it. I'm sure Daddy will be ready for a cup of coffee when he comes in."

When Helen hugged them both good-bye later that afternoon, her daddy planted a kiss on top of her head. "I think the little dog was a good idea. She's doesn't seem to be the yappy type." Tawny dutifully pressed up against his leg and he bent down to give her a final pat.

"That's high praise, coming from him," Helen said, going to the pantry to get her a dog treat. "Hunting dogs were what he grew up with and they definitely didn't come into the house."

She wandered into the kitchen, her mother's words about becoming a grandmother taking her back to her own childhood, and to the joy of going to their grandparents' farm. In actuality, both sets of grandparents had once been farmers, although her paternal grandfather had sold his place the year after his daddy and mamma died. Like her daddy, he'd started working the fields as early as he could hold a hoe and had helped milk cows and care for the chickens even before that. He hadn't enjoyed the constant cycle of worrying about too much or too little rain or about bug infestations that could wipe out a crop within days. Family farming was a hard life with a lot of worry unless you had enough land to spread out your risk. The more land, though, the more help you needed, and unless it was a lifestyle that you embraced, it could wear you down. Helen had seen the photographs of the small frame house with no indoor plumbing or electricity. The way her daddy told it, a man who wanted to expand his farm had offered a fair price and her grandparents moved into town where her papaw was able to find work at the bank. Papaw valued schooling and urged his only son to take to books and to be the first one in the family to attend college. And after Daddy returned from Europe, his college was funded by the GI Bill like so many men of what was called "the greatest generation." He rarely spoke of his time in World War II, and Helen thought that perhaps it was because he'd been assigned to desk jobs and felt that didn't put him in the same category as the men who fought on the front lines. His head for numbers had been noted. He had an ease with figures that later drew him to a career in accounting.

Helen understood that the rural upbringing of her daddy had been harsher than that of her mamma, and while she didn't glamorize the farm of her maternal grandparents, it had simply been more fun to visit them as a child. A farm with cows, pigs, chickens, rabbits, cats and dogs, and a gentle plow horse that could be saddled for ambles around the pasture made for fun Sunday afternoons and summer visits. Later, it was the chance for quilting with the three generations of them in her mamaw's parlor, a craft for which Eloise had no patience. She preferred the kitchen, and although Helen took deserved praise for her cooking, she couldn't compare to her sister when it came to baking. Eloise had the perfect touch for pastry and bread from scratch and the ability to turn out pies and tarts that could grace the cover of any food magazine. Her cinnamon rolls were practically family legend and no one was surprised when she chose to major in home economics.

Helen emptied the coffeepot, thoughts of Eloise now nudging out her grandparents. With the closeness of sisters, she'd understood Eloise's attraction to Eddie, despite the fact that there was something about him that she hadn't liked, but neither had she been able to define her hesitancy. On the surface, he was everything a girl could ask for. He was nice-looking without being jaw-dropping handsome and landed a good sales job his senior year of college. Perhaps Helen had sensed an undercurrent of what was to be his chronic infidelity. Helen had reluctantly supported Eloise's decision to forgive him for the first incident. She'd doubted the sincerity of his apology, trying obliquely to tell Eloise that she personally didn't believe him. That, however, was not what Eloise wanted to hear, although when she discovered the second affair, she'd asked Helen point blank about why she'd been such a fool. That question was not precisely answered, but did involve the two of them going away for a "girls' weekend" to Savannah in an effort to soothe Eloise's pain.

While Eddie had been a jerk as a husband, he was a weak man more than bad, and had been fair in the settlement and conscientious about child support. Eloise wisely made providing capital for a partnership in a catering company as a provision of the divorce rather than accepting alimony. *We'll Do the Cooking* catering began modestly, building cautiously as their reputation grew. When it became apparent Eddie was going to routinely disappoint Danny and Sean on the weekends when he was supposed to have custody, Eloise struck on the idea of introducing them to the business as a distraction. She'd let them come into the kitchen, see the well-stocked van, and be in the background when they served a banquet for almost two hundred people. They had been fascinated with all the behind-the-scenes details, that when performed correctly, were invisible to the clients. To Eloise's delight, they had branched into the perfect combination when Danny majored in business and Sean graduated from the Culinary Institute of Charleston. Eloise's partner made a reasonable offer to sell her share and the business became a family venture.

The click of Tawny's toenails on the tile floor drew Helen's attention. She sat, her eyes communicating that thinking of people food was all fine and good, but perhaps Mamma should be looking at the clock.

Helen smiled and reached for the dog, whose tongue found her favorite spot of Helen's chin. "My, it is coming up on dinnertime for you, isn't it?"

She would take care of Tawny, then give Tricia a call to fill her in about the Thanksgiving plans. In fact, she had turkey cutlets in the refrigerator. Turkey tetrazzini sounded like a good idea.

CHAPTER NINETEEN

———⟨≫•◇•≪⟩———

Justin's hand lingered on the receiver as he thought about the last part of the conversation with Sergeant Robbichaut of the New Orleans Police Department. "You do understand that a man like Mr. Rosso never being arrested doesn't necessarily mean that he shouldn't have been?"

"So this report is less than complete?"

The chuckle was deep. "I didn't say that. What I would say is that Mr. Rosso is one of those men that the department does not bring in unless there is a very solid reason to do so. Some guys, you can haul in for questioning every day, for all anyone cares. Others, you do not. In fact, we had a double homicide several weeks back. It seems that a detective in the department would have very much liked to have discussed it with Mr. Rosso." There was a pause for emphasis. "However, word was that Mr. Rosso was out of town for an extended period with no means of contact and no idea of when he might return. Since there were other homicides to investigate, the matter was not pursued. You see what I mean?"

"Got it," Justin said and felt frustration beginning to bubble to the surface as he mentally replayed the preferential treatment that had been afforded to Rosso by at least someone in the New Orleans Police Department. He jumped when the telephone rang.

"An Agent Bell for you on line two. Atlanta number," Sheila said crisply.

"Officer Kendall? This is Agent Tony Bell calling from the Atlanta DEA Office. It's my understanding that you have an interest in a gentleman named Leonardo Rosso."

"Uh, yeah, yeah, we've been asking a few questions around," Justin said immediately. The Drug Enforcement Administration? That was interesting. He knew there would be no use in asking how Agent Bell came to have his number and it wasn't particularly important.

"Are you at liberty to speak?"

Justin looked over at the chief, telephone to his ear. If a DEA agent was initiating contact, the odds were he wanted something and it would be better if the chief heard it at the same time.

"May I call you back in five minutes? My boss, Chief Norman McFarlane, is here and I think he'll want to be in on this."

"That's fine. I have half an hour until my next meeting."

"Be right back with you," Justin said, scribbling the number that showed on caller ID. He hurried into the office, the chief giving him a puzzled look as he rang off.

"I had a somewhat enlightening conversation with Sergeant Robbichaut and now a DEA agent that wants to know why we're interested in Rosso." Justin handed over the slip of paper.

"Close the door, will you?" The chief was already punching in numbers.

"Agent Bell? This is Chief McFarlane over in Wallington, west of you. I have Officer Justin Kendall with me and would like to put you on speaker. We have the door to the office closed."

Justin moved the chair as close to the desk as he could and the chief pushed the telephone toward the center.

Bell's voice came through crisply. "I don't see any need to waste time with small talk. A contact in New Orleans indicated you were making inquiries into Rosso and I was wondering if you would be willing to discuss your interest."

"Be glad to," the chief said. "I'll ask Officer Kendall to fill you in since he's been handling it."

Justin gave the basic information, as well as the names of people he had interviewed. There were no confidences at stake with what he'd learned up to this point.

There was a slight pause. "Are you gentlemen having problems with meth labs?"

Chief McFarlane raised his eyebrows. "Rumors, and we've carried out a couple of searches, but nothing to show for it."

"I would ordinarily ask for a face-to-face meeting, but I have a timing problem at the moment," Bell said. "So no one has actually seen Mr. Rosso in town?"

"Not that we know of," Justin replied.

"Okay. The situation is that his name has popped up repeatedly during the past two months and recurring names tend to rouse our curiosity. Apparently, there was a double homicide in New Orleans in which Mr. Rosso was a person of interest, except he has been unavailable for questioning."

"Because he's been out of the state?"

"Indeed. He is friends, or at least business acquaintances, with other gentlemen over whom we maintain an active watch. According to what we know, Mr. Rosso enjoys a very pleasant lifestyle, but maintains a low enough profile so as not to ordinarily arouse too much attention."

Chief McFarlane silently tapped his finger on top of the desk.

"He's come to your attention, though?"

"In a peripheral manner. We have reason to believe a fairly major operation is gearing up that will have a meth production and distribution network along I-20. The idea is to have multiple mobile labs that can fit in something like a barn, run production for a period, then clear out for a while, and return. It makes it harder to pin down. That's what you've been hearing about. The problem with multiple locations, though, is you then have to have someone you can trust to keep an eye on them, coordinate product with pickup, that sort of thing."

"You think Rosso is in for a piece of the action or maybe just keeping himself busy until he goes back to New Orleans?"

"Temporary help would be cost effective," Bell said. "Someone competent and fewer ultimate fingers in the pie, so to speak."

Chief McFarlane looked knowingly at Justin. "Any chance you have enough for us to make this official?"

"No, but if he's causing other problems and you brought him in for questioning, I would think a little road trip from our end would be in order."

Justin sighed. While this definitely whetted his curiosity, it wasn't what he'd been hoping for.

"I can't say that we do at the moment, but it is useful information," the chief said. "How about we leave the line open for more communication?"

"I can do that. I'll give you my mobile number, too, where you can reach me directly in case anything comes up."

All three exchanged numbers and Justin waited for the chief to speak first. "I have my own notion, but I'd like to hear yours. It seems to me we have several pieces of the puzzle."

Justin's mind had been working through different combinations. "Let's start with what we know. The rumors about meth labs are fairly recent. Alicia Johnson saw Rosso in Atlanta. We have every reason to believe he has been in town. Johnny Jenkins has no known drug connections, but he's no angel either. His tire was shot. We checked the most likely places that would house a meth lab near where he was shot and found no signs. We did not check every possible place, and if they have a trailer of some type that's self-contained, that could have been hauled away. There were some tracks on the Nelson property, although nothing else to indicate people had been around for any length of time."

The chief had his head cocked as if listening for a particular sound. "That seems right."

Justin ran his hand through his hair. "Let's set aside whether or not Rosso knew his ex-wife was in Georgia. There are too many ways you can get that information these days. Let's focus instead on the fact that he needed to leave New Orleans and he picked Atlanta because he has friends here, likes the town, whatever. He's here, he's bored, and he has the connections and know-how to help get this operation going. By coincidence, he sees Alicia in the hotel and it would be simple to find out the group she was with if he didn't already know where she lived. Maybe he was already scheduled to work this area and maybe seeing, or wanting to see her, caused him to ask for this area. What he has planned about her is an unknown."

"You're tracking with my thinking," the chief said, leaning into the desk, his hands laced together on top of it. "Jenkins?"

"They're going to have to have locals as guides and maybe lookouts, if nothing else."

The chief nodded once. "This is the kind of situation that Jared, Johnny's older brother, could be mixed up in, and it would be a shame, but reasonable to see him getting Johnny involved. We don't know where Jared went off to and Atlanta's as good a place as any. Why Johnny would have been shot at is another question, though."

Justin shrugged. "He might not be involved after all, and it could be that he just saw something he wasn't supposed to see. I'd lay money on the fact that he was lying to me. What I don't know is what he was lying about."

The chief chuckled and unlaced his hands. "Being a Jenkins boy, he's likely to lie to one of us about the time of day. They have issues with authority figures, I believe the term is."

Justin knew that term well. You sit someone like Jenkins from Wallington down with kids from the big city neighborhoods of Baltimore and their view of the police would probably be identical despite the geographic and cultural distances. "What do we do now?"

Chief McFarlane smiled a slow smile, as much daring as humor in it. "I understand the lawyer's reluctance for us to be seen as possibly harassing Mr. Rosso, however, I would say that our new information changes that equation."

Justin sat up straighter as the chief continued. "I do not believe we need to involve the Johnsons at this stage, but we do have one of our good citizens, well, one of our citizens, injured in a suspicious manner. A person of interest can be brought in for questioning as say, a potential material witness." His eyes held a sign of mischief Justin had come to appreciate in the time he'd been working in the department. "If we should happen to locate Mr. Rosso and bring him in and he feels we have unduly targeted him, perhaps he will merely view us as small town hicks that don't know any better. You do have a photograph of the gentleman?"

Justin grinned. "I can get one pretty quickly. As soon as I have it, can Sheila put out an all points bulletin?"

The chief picked up the telephone. "I'll take care of this. I suggest you go see our boy Johnny. If he's at Isabelle's house instead of with his daddy, she may be able to exert some influence over him."

Justin stood, glad of the chief's decision. He called Isabelle

Jenkins, her voice hesitant at his request, but she gave him the address and asked if he could come right away since they had a follow-up appointment with the doctor. As promised, he was parked at her curb in less than fifteen minutes. It was a small white frame house in an older neighborhood that had probably once held an element of charm that could be seen in half the houses where literal white picket fences stood separating neatly trimmed lawns from the street. Other houses showed the wear and tear of transients, or of residents who had no interest in maintenance. Yards pockmarked with dead grass, toys in stages of decay left at odd angles, and peeling paint were the sorts of thing that would make a realtor cringe when trying to write a sales description.

Justin reminded himself not to refer to her as Mrs. Jenkins and found Isabelle standing on the postage stamp-size concrete stoop that while topped with an overhang, could hardly be called a porch. The house itself looked to be in decent shape, the grass mowed and devoid of trash. It was due a coat of paint, although the blue house next door looked worse. She wore a black cardigan over a pair of gray slacks and some sort of lighter gray top that was mostly covered by the sweater. Her jewelry was only a pair of black ball earrings and a silver watch. She wore no wedding band.

She had her arms crossed as he approached. It was not in a defensive manner, but more in a self hug as if chilled. "Hi, deputy. Could we have a minute before we go in?"

He had seen that look more times than he could count. The mother of a child, no matter the age, who knew her son or daughter had either crossed or was preparing to cross a dangerous line. Isabelle struggled with a mother's love and desire to protect her offspring, torn between trying to decide if the way to protect them was to admit there could be wrongdoing involved or fiercely deny the possibility. Justin recognized the struggle and sympathized with it in marked contrast to the anger that stirred when he was confronted with contempt for the law that was passed from generation to generation. He stood, one foot on the short, cracked sidewalk and one on the bottom step. "Yes, ma'am, is there something you'd like to tell me?"

Her smile was wan and she waved a hand around the yard. "First, you'll have to forgive the place. It's all I can afford until we get through the divorce."

He nodded once, allowing this inconsequential lead up as she drew in a breath and exhaled. "You know, my mamma tried to warn me back when I married Roger that it wouldn't work and I thought she was just being snooty. I'm not saying that wasn't part of it, but I guess she saw something I didn't want to see. I tried when the boys were little, I did, but Roger, as far as he was concerned, thought settling something with your fists was the manly approach."

"Yes, ma'am, that can happen."

"Jared's too much like his daddy and Johnny, well, Johnny isn't quite as stubborn, but he doesn't want to be thought of as a mamma's boy either. It's not that I'm giving up on my sons. I wouldn't do that. It's that I felt I could do more for them and for me by getting out of the constant fighting. They need to understand that's not how a marriage is supposed to work."

Her face reflected the emotions she was expressing and Justin didn't try to hurry her. She inclined her head to the closed front door. "Johnny's in the living room and his story hasn't changed since you talked to him. I've known when those boys were lying since they were old enough to put words together. I tried to get him to tell me what really happened, and he wasn't disrespectful, he just won't budge. I'm thinking you might want to be with him alone, man-to-man like."

Her voice wavered slightly and Justin was cautious. "I appreciate this, ma'am, and I'm not looking to get him into trouble. I need you to understand that he is a minor and he does have the right to have a parent or even a lawyer around."

She gestured to the door. "You promise you'll be straight with him and not try any tricks of any kind and you have my permission. Do you need me to sign a piece of paper?"

"No, ma'am, I don't think that will be necessary," Justin said and stepped past her with a questioning look.

"Go ahead in. I'm going around to the side door into the kitchen. I'll be able to hear voices, but not what's said."

Johnny was on the couch in the minimally furnished room, his legs stretched out on the coffee table, sneakers tucked underneath. Two mismatched easy chairs were on the other side and there was a single end table with a cheap-looking lamp on it. The look brought to mind a grouping at a yard sale, the dappled brown wall-to-wall carpet well beyond the date when it should have been ripped out and changed. The bare walls were perhaps the most telling mark of the temporary nature of the inhabitants and Justin briefly wondered where Isabelle was planning to move after the divorce was final.

Justin thought Johnny's face was average looking underneath the mottled bruising. The stitches were still clearly visible. He didn't bother to rise or extend his hand and his brown eyes were no less hostile than at the hospital. Justin took the chair directly across from him and perched on the edge where he could move quickly if necessary. Not that he was expecting a problem, but he'd learned long ago that teenage hormones were unpredictable. "Ribs causing you a lot of pain?"

"Nothing I can't handle. Been hurt worse than this lots of times."

"Your mother is concerned about you."

His eyes flashed. "That's what mammas do, isn't it? Worry a lot?"

"They do," Justin agreed, his hands on his knees, fingers splayed. "I thought I'd see how your memory was coming along— where you'd been that afternoon, who you'd talked to, if you saw anyone right before the crash."

"Like I said, we had the afternoon off. It was a nice day, so I went driving in the woods. Didn't see nothing or nobody and next thing I know, I wake up hurting in the hospital."

Justin grinned. "Man, I can't tell you how many times I've heard that. Well, not the woods part, but the same story."

Johnny shrugged without comment.

Justin leaned forward. "So if I ask about a mobile meth lab, your brother Jared, or a man named Leo Rosso, none of that will mean a thing to you?"

Johnny no doubt thought he was keeping a poker face, that his eyes didn't register surprise, and that he was maintaining his cool. "Why would it? Haven't seen Jared since school started and the rest of that crap, well, that's what it is."

Justin slipped the cell phone from his holder, tapped the screen and returned it. "I have the number for a DEA agent in here. That's Drug Enforcement Administration, in case you don't know it. They keep track of all kinds of interesting people in Atlanta and other places. I hear what you're saying and I got it. I do. You're a tough kid and your brother is tougher, and what I'm telling you is that this is not something you want to be messed up in. Whoever took that shot at you would have taken another one if he hadn't heard Mr. Walker coming. You talk to me, to us, and we can probably find a way out of it for you. You keep going the way you are and there's no telling what will happen. The odds are, though, that you aren't going to like it and it will break your mother's heart."

Johnny slowly moved his feet to the floor, leaning forward with his curled hands pressed into his knees. "I reckon you can think what you want and I'd ask you to leave my mamma out of this."

He couldn't have heard the note of bravado in his voice. He wasn't skilled enough to recognize he'd basically confirmed

Justin's suspicions. Not in the legal sense that a lawyer would support, rather in the unspoken confession that every experienced cop would have heard.

Justin rose from the chair and placed his card on the coffee table, Johnny's eyes following him. "That's the number to my cell phone that I leave on all the time and the station can reach me at any hour. I'd say you have three to four days before things start getting real complicated. You want to talk to me before then, I'll be glad to. You wait until it starts breaking loose and that will be too late. I'll go out through the kitchen to let your mother know we're done." He moved toward the arch that connected the hallway he assumed led to the kitchen.

Johnny painfully got to his feet, not picking the card up, his jaw set. "Don't be upsetting Mamma with what you've got to say."

Justin shook his head sadly. "I'm not the one doing this, Johnny. That's something for you to think about."

He didn't look back at the boy as he found Isabelle. She was staring out of the small window over the sink into the empty back yard. She turned, her hands grasping the sink behind her. "It's bad, isn't it, deputy? Whatever this is?"

Justin almost flinched from the worry in her eyes. "I've left another card, ma'am, and told him to call no matter what time it is if he wants to talk. I hope I gave him a lot to think about."

"Thank you," she said softly. "I'll do what I can to get through to him that he's in over his head."

"Yes, ma'am," Justin said and let himself out, closing the door gently behind him. Well, he'd said all he could. Maybe one of them could get through to Johnny.

CHAPTER TWENTY

—⫸◆⫷—

I get you as a customer today? Should I bother to ask if I can help you find something?" Max smiled broadly, coming into the main quilting section of the store.

Helen looked up at the sound of his voice. "We all run out of things occasionally," she said with a laugh. "I need more graph paper and my marking pencil is wearing down. I like to keep extras on hand in case one of the ladies has forgotten something. You are coming tonight, aren't you?"

"I have been looking forward to it for days. In fact, I've been told by a very reliable source that your quilting room and stash of supplies almost rivals this place."

"On a much smaller scale, but it is amazing what you build up over the years, isn't it? A neighbor finally clears out some things and gives you fabric, you hit a great sale somewhere, and yard sales can be a bonanza." Max was obviously settling in, getting to know customers and products. The peacock-green cotton sweater he was wearing was a good color for him and he evidently was finding ways to keep fit. The YMCA had a good facility three streets south of the town square, although Helen didn't know what sort of exercise Max enjoyed. She couldn't imagine him as the type of guy who didn't have a regular routine.

"Ah, that's the difference between having a house and being somewhat of a nomad." Max tilted his head. "Well, I suppose nomad is incorrect since I have maintained my condo in Raleigh. Road warrior was actually the right term for me." He pointed his hand over his shoulder. "I know I'll be seeing you later, but do you have a few minutes? I'd like to ask you about something I'd rather not bring up for group discussion until I've thought about it some more."

Helen was intrigued. "Oh, sure. I have what I need right here."

Max's gray eyes were warm, and she couldn't help but notice his thick lashes. "The classroom and a cup of coffee? I'm sure we have cookies, too."

"Just coffee is fine," she said. "You'll understand when you see the sort of spread we have at circle. Let me go ahead and check out and I'll meet you in the classroom."

"Black, one sugar, right?"

"Uh, yes, that's the way I take my coffee," Helen said, surprised he remembered.

Max was sitting at the front table by the white board when she came in, the chair across from him pushed back, a blue mug on a patchwork quilt motif paper napkin waiting for her.

"Honduran today," he said as she took an appreciative sip. "I don't indulge often, and I refuse to shop the high-end coffee stores that jack the price up for the privilege of entering their doors, but I do like robust coffees. I hope it's not too strong for you. Lillian is mostly a tea drinker so she doesn't care what I brew."

"This is fine," Helen said. "I have to confess that while I have nothing against the brands we all grew up with, when the grocery

store started carrying the new line, that's pretty much all I drink."
She grinned. "I suppose we'll be getting one of the specialty coffee
places before too long."

Max's eyes glinted amusement. "It is hard to believe there's a town
left in the country that doesn't have at least one." Two beginner quilting
books were on the table next to him. He waved his hand across them.
"You know, I was watching Susanna finishing up a vintage-replica
shawl she was doing the other day. She's very talented, isn't she?"

Helen nodded. "Oh, my. Yes. Most quilters do one or two
other creative things, needlework, beading, scrapbooking, but
Susanna is a true fabric artist. She knits, crochets, knows all sorts
of needlework, does costuming, and makes some of the cutest
stuffed animals and dolls you've ever seen. She quilts, of course,
and makes beautiful wraps. Have you been on her web site?"

"Yes, and I was really impressed with her entrepreneurship. I
mean, she's what? Twenty-five?"

Helen thought for a moment. "Yes, but she's been at this since she was
old enough to thread a needle. I'm so glad she has the Internet business
going. She's a perfect example of how that has made all the difference for
someone like her. As good as she is, she simply wouldn't have had enough
of a market here. Now she sells all over the country, and if I understood
correctly, she got an order from some lady in England a few months ago.
I guess that makes her international." She wasn't sure where he was going
with this. "You want Susanna to do something new for the store? Increase
the number of classes she's teaching?"

Max hesitated. "Well, not exactly. Your daughter Tricia is at
the high school, right? I know they've done a lot of technology
upgrades to support Wi-Fi and that kind of thing, and they want
to apply for magnet status."

Helen was impressed. "Yes, one of the new council members
we elected has an education background and she ran on pledging

to work with, or I should say hound, the county about bringing improvements to our schools. She's done a lot of research about cost-effective things that can be done within our authority and she's very tenacious."

Max lifted his mug. "I think that's great. Anyway, I've been checking the classes that Wanda has here and I started wondering if maybe we could expand into the high school with quilting as an after-school activity. Approach it as a unique American art form as well as a useful skill."

Helen set her mug down and felt a little pucker across her forehead. "Uh, well, I can't say I've given that any thought. I mean kids are mostly into computer games and electronic gadgets, aren't they?"

"No question about that," Max said. "That's part of my idea. I'm all for technology and I get impatient if a network outage lasts longer than half an hour. It seems, though, that quilting is something that could help bring a balance. It's tactile, visual, you have a product at the end, and for those who aren't artistic, it's following a pattern. Those that are artistic, they can get into design."

"It's certainly an interesting idea. Have you discussed it with Susanna? She is, after all, closer to their age and I'm sure she knows everyone you would need to approach."

He shook his head once. "Actually, you're the first person I've told. I wanted to get another perspective before I said anything to either Wanda or Susanna."

"I would say it's certainly worth checking into. I mean it can't hurt to raise the subject and see what kind of response you get."

His smile was grateful. "I'll work out a few more details and run it by Wanda before she leaves. More coffee?"

Helen drank the last swallow. "I would love to if I didn't have more errands to run to get ready for this evening."

He stood, taking the empty mug. "Then I'll see you at circle.

I'm planning to bring baked Brie in pastry, if that's okay. I noticed they have it at the grocery store and when you slice it, it fits the one-two bite criteria Phyllis told me about."

"That will be fine," Helen said. "We usually have a nice mix of savory and sweet foods."

She gathered her package and Max walked her to the door, empty mugs in his left hand. "Oh, before I forget, I won't be staying long tonight. Phyllis said the after-quilting part is fun, too, but I have a conference call with some people in Hawaii at ten our time so I'll need to get back for that."

Helen offered her cheek for a kiss. "The after-quilting group is usually small, so no one will think you're running off prematurely if you don't stay. See you this evening." She waved hello to Lucy Morgan and Sharon Gleason as they pulled into the parking lot, another car signaling to enter. She loved to see customers coming into Collectibles. As much as women liked Wanda and Lillian, she was willing to bet that having Max around wouldn't hurt business one bit.

The day flew past and she'd barely gotten the final touches in place before Phyllis breezed in, followed by Katie and Deirdre. Alicia had called earlier, explaining Justin had been wonderful with keeping them informed and Hiram was asking her to please not drive alone at night. As much as she hated to miss quilting, she'd accepted a complicated project that would require her attention and take about two weeks to complete. They both hoped life would return to normal by that time. Helen promised to pass the word about her project in exchange for Alicia promising she would call if she needed anything at all. Sarah would be the other no show. She had a church committee meeting she couldn't gracefully get out of without lying, and that was bound to be a special kind of sin.

Max arrived in the middle of the group. Introductions were made to the few who didn't know him. Helen wasn't the least bit surprised that Phyllis patted the spot next to her on the sofa as the place for him to sit. Since he'd brought squares to work on and his own quilting hoop, he didn't need the table surface. What she wasn't sure about was how the dynamics of the evening would progress. Would the women, well, not Phyllis, of course, be somewhat stifled by his presence?

Deirdre led off quickly though. "Max, let me say it's a real nice thing you're doing for Angela. Not that Kevin isn't a good man. It's just that it wouldn't be the same thing with him going to see your mamma every day as one of her own children."

Max seemed almost reluctant to accept her praise. "I've spent my life jetting to a lot of places around the world. While that kind of travel has some drawbacks, it's been mostly fun. I wanted Angela to have the chance to go on this trip and I knew no matter how hard she tried, she would feel a little guilty about being gone for a long time. Me being right here in town takes care of that." He glanced around the circle. "It's been great too, seeing old friends and getting caught up. The situation with Wanda has made it that much better."

"I think what Wanda is doing is wonderful," Carolyn said, tying off a thread. "I told her we expected all the details after her first week and then I think we should plan a cruise for this group."

Katie grinned. "Sunsets over the Caribbean, rum drinks with little umbrellas, and quilting. I can promise you that was not a combination that our grandmothers ever imagined."

Phyllis hooted. "I'm pretty sure that my mamaw was no stranger to doctoring that hot tea they drank when quilting, but I do know what you mean. I'm ready to sign up whenever we decide to go."

"Max, I'm a little unclear about what you're doing," Carolyn chimed in. "I mean, I understand about you at Collectibles, but are you also still with Click for Quilting?"

"Yes, strictly in a part-time capacity. The lady who was with me in the booth—I don't think any of you met her—is taking over the show circuit. I'm mostly doing a little web site content and an article every week or so."

Becky removed pins from a square she'd finished basting. "Have you spent any time in Asheville? They say that museum is a real must for quilters."

"It is impressive," Max said. "As a matter of fact, I was there when they opened the current exhibit of *Waiting for You*. The Sheppard daughters contributed not only twenty-seven quilts that had been made by four generations of family, they had a couple of sketch books, their great-grandmother's notions box, a number of the letters their grandparents exchanged during World War II, and the ledger Teresa used when making the famous quilt. She would draw a sketch of the square she'd made that week as part of the letter. Her husband kept as many of them as he could. He would always remark on it in the letters he sent her."

Rita was sitting at the table with Helen and she looked puzzled. "I'm sorry. Everyone here seems to know what you're talking about, but I don't."

"Oh, it's a wonderful story," Deirdre said. "Back during World War II, when the men shipped out, it was for what they called the *duration*. They went to Europe or the Pacific and from battle to battle until the war was over, or they were wounded so badly they were sent home, or well, didn't come home at all." She paused, heads nodding. "Teresa Sheppard, from this little town in North Carolina, was a ribbon-winning quilter and she had an eye for design. She and her husband, Reggie, I think was his name, hadn't been married for more than a few months when off he went to Europe. He was in some nasty ones, Africa, Sicily, Normandy, all the way through until the war ended. They didn't see each other for three years, was it?"

"Three years and four months," Max said.

"And so she made a special quilt?"

Deirdre held up a thimble-clad finger. "Yes, although it was more than that. What she did was make a square for every week he was gone from the time she said good-bye to him leaving for the troop ship. The square depicted something around the house or the town and she had this special chest she kept the squares in as she completed them. She insisted she wouldn't start putting them together into a quilt until he came back home."

There was poignancy to Deirdre's voice that Helen understood. It was a heartwarming story no matter how often it was heard.

"As I said, it was a small town, more a village, and all sorts of people got in on it by bringing pieces of fabric that would have a special meaning to Reggie. A high school football jersey that got torn up—someone saved a piece and gave it to Teresa, a leftover scrap from one of his niece's Easter dress, that kind of thing. Teresa knew he was going to be gone a long time, and she kept a ledger to record the squares and made notes about them. When she looked back later, every single family in town had contributed something."

Rita did the math. "If it was three years and four months, that would be one hundred and sixty squares. How big was this quilt and how long did it take her once she started?"

"Very big and a long time," Max said. "As you can imagine, what it became was like a tapestry. It really is something to see and they did a great job with the exhibit. I do recommend a trip to the museum when you get the chance."

As the talk flowed, the only absence was ribald remarks from Phyllis who had apparently decided to tone her behavior down for the evening. The fact that Max was a man didn't seem to impede the conversations. Their usual break for eating was relaxed as it always was and when the group began to break up, Max was among the first to leave. "I had fun, ladies, and come on by the store anytime whether to buy something or just have a chat. That part won't be a bit different than having Wanda here."

Everyone told Max how pleased they were he had joined them, although no one issued an invitation to return the next week. That would be done after Helen spoke with them all individually. Although they had their share of differences of opinions occasionally, their personalities blended well and no one wanted to disrupt that pleasantness. Bringing a new member in was not something to be done casually, and Helen couldn't recall the last time they'd brought in three members in one year. Well, Max would only be temporary, so she wasn't sure if that counted.

"You know that I'm ready for Max to join the circle," Phyllis said, locating the top to the container that had held the few remaining chicken salad finger sandwiches she'd brought. "I can't stay tonight. I've gotten behind on the quarterly taxes and if I don't finish them up, the rest of the week will be totally out of whack."

"I'm voting for Max, too," Carolyn said, with a good night kiss thrown in the air as she held the door open for Phyllis.

Deirdre and Mary Lou exited with the same enthusiasm for Max and Katie looked at Helen when she realized it was only the two of them left. "I'd say Max was a hit."

"So it would seem," Helen said, inclining her head toward the kitchen. "How about something to drink? There's still coffee and tea, of course."

Katie sucked her lower lip in and then released it. "Actually, if you don't mind, there's something I'd like to talk to you about. I was sort of hoping that Carolyn would stay, to let me pick her brain, but then again, once I tell you what I have in mind, you might tell me it's one of the dumbest ideas you've ever heard and I should come to my senses."

Helen laughed. "That certainly sounds like a conversation best had over a glass of something. Let's go in the kitchen."

CHAPTER TWENTY-ONE

⟨⟩⟨⟩

I think you getting a dog was a great idea. She's sweet as she can be," Katie said, and delighted Tawny by picking her up for a snuggle. "It's not that I don't love Buster, it's just that at sixty-plus pounds, he's not the same kind of cuddly."

"I called Rita a day or two after I brought Tawny home and admitted how right she was to save her from the I-told-you-so routine," Helen said, carrying both glasses to the table. Katie had transferred the rest of the cheese ball covered in walnuts and the multigrain crackers she had brought, as well as Helen's miniature quiches.

Katie put Tawny down and the dog turned to Helen for more attention. "Off you go," Helen said fondly, scratching her behind the ear. That was apparently adequate as she padded into the den with no further demands.

Helen spread a cracker, holding it over the napkin before she popped it into her mouth. "This cheese ball is great, by the way," she said. "It's a blend, right? Homemade?" Katie was one of those women, who despite working full-time, rarely brought anything to circle that didn't come from her own kitchen.

Katie took a quiche. "Thanks. And yes, Cheddar, cream cheese, some smoky Gouda, cracked black pepper, a couple of roasted cloves of garlic mashed in, and a little cayenne. It doesn't take more than a few minutes in the food processor." She lifted the quiche. "I love these, too. In fact, that's related to what I want to talk about as soon as I eat this."

"My recipe? It's a basic one and I use the mini muffin tin," Helen said, and Katie held up her hand to indicate that Helen had misunderstood.

"Not recipes per se." She smiled shyly, not an ordinary expression for her. "There are several parts to this, but you know the Farley house on Third Street?"

Helen was curious as to where the conversation was going. "Sure, it's been sitting there on that corner going from bad to worse since Lynette died. It is a pity the way that all happened. I can't remember how many people tried to help her and she wouldn't hear of it. Starting on her eightieth birthday, every single day of the week, rain or shine, cold or hot, she would sit in that rocking chair on the porch from noon until sunset, reading her Bible waiting for the Second Coming. Why, if she'd have died inside the house instead of out front, there's no telling how long it would have been before someone found her. Did Boyd ever locate an heir?"

Katie lifted her glass. "Finally. It turns out there is a niece. Do you remember how we were told they kicked Lottie out of the house and no one knew where she went off to? Well, of all places, it was up somewhere in Minnesota, not far from Minneapolis. She died almost five years ago, and apparently she never did get married. She had a daughter, Heather, who's still there, and raised her with absolutely no contact with the family—never, not so much as an acknowledgment that either of them existed. Needless to say, the niece doesn't want to have anything to do with down here other than to get the estate settled as quickly as she can. She's sent down power of attorney and said she has no intention of setting foot inside the state, much less this town."

The Farleys had been the kind of religious people that were commonly known as stiff-necked and raised their two daughters, Lynette and Lottie, the same way. The girls were actually contemporaries of Helen's parents, but after Lynette became a borderline public nuisance, old tales of the family had circulated to explain Lynette's eccentricity. No social contact outside of church and no activities in school other than classes were permitted. Technically with church twice on Sunday, once on Wednesday, and twice a day during revival week that the church held three times a year, that was a fair amount of social interaction. Of course, all of that reinforced their own strict beliefs. Lottie, though, had managed to slip the constraints, found herself pregnant within days of graduating from high school, and refused to name the father. That had precipitated her being put out of the house with one suitcase and no more than a hundred dollars to her name. She was forbidden to return unless she was willing to renounce her sins and beg forgiveness for the shame she'd brought on the family. The way Helen had heard it, Lynette was as unyielding as her parents, declaring Lottie was dead as far as they were concerned.

Lynette's physical appearance matched her sour, rigid personality. She never married, continuing to live in the house, caring for her parents until they passed away, the town changing around them. That stretch of street became a mixed-use zone with an accountant's office, a childcare center, and a beauty parlor, until Lynette's frame house inside the fenced yard was the only remaining residence that hadn't been fully or partially converted.

Katie handled Lynette's modest accounts at the bank and the

woman's increasingly bizarre behavior included constant worry that someone was trying to steal her money. She would appear at the bank at least one morning a week, march into Katie's office, and demand an explanation as to how they were protecting her from potential thieves. Like Katie, Boyd Gilbert had not sought out Lynette as a client, and when the mailman found her on the porch dead from a heart attack, there was nothing in writing that indicated the next of kin. The church arranged a service and burial and Boyd felt an obligation to try to track down Lottie. Katie's intimate familiarity with Lynette's finances was why she was involved with Boyd's efforts.

Helen couldn't blame the truly long-lost relative for how she felt. "She wants to sell the house, I assume?"

Katie nodded. "And she wants it done fast. She told Boyd she didn't care what kind of price she got for it as long as it would cover whatever it cost to get rid of everything Lynette owned. Her instructions were to hire someone to donate what they could and have the rest hauled off." She paused and took a sip. "That's a very long way around to what I'm thinking. I want to buy the house and turn it into a specialty catering business."

"Oh," was all Helen could think to say. "You mean quit your job at the bank?" She was careful not to express surprise since that might have interpreted as skepticism.

Katie set her glass aside and placed her forearms on the table, leaning in. "Yes. The truth is that I've been doing that same job for years now and I've been with the bank my whole adult life. It's a good place to work, but realistically, there's no upward mobility for me. Scott's doing well with the business and the boys, bless them, are old enough and involved in so many activities that they don't need me the way they used to."

"This isn't a midlife crisis, is it?"

Katie's lips twitched toward a smile. "I wouldn't call it a crisis as much as I would a re-thinking of priorities. I've checked the market value of the house, and quite frankly, Lynette missed the best time to sell. I can make Heather a decent offer, we can close the deal quickly, and both come away happy. Granted, if I didn't have a husband in the construction business, making the renovations would be a major additional cost, but I don't have to worry about that. Do you want to hear the rest?"

"Of course," Helen said immediately, watching the animation rising in Katie's face.

The other woman unfolded her arms, her fingers resting on the table almost as if she was playing the piano. "Okay, I started in the kitchen when I was eight or nine years old and the idea was planted last year when Mamma said she was tired of cooking. I think I was over there and put something in the freezer and saw all those prepackaged frozen meals. I asked her what that was all about and she said it made sense for them because the portions were sized correctly and there was enough variety to eat them three or four days a week. She picked up a roasted chicken for another couple of meals, they eat out, and they've been coming to our place for Sunday dinner for years now. They have soup or sandwiches for lunch, and add a salad. She doesn't spend hardly any time in the kitchen anymore. I was stunned and she almost fell out of her chair laughing. She said the look on my face was priceless."

Helen had to admit she would have felt the same way to hear that her mamma wasn't cooking any longer. Well, actually, now that she thought about it, for all she knew, it was true for her, too. No, that couldn't be. "Really? Huh, I wouldn't have thought that."

Katie nodded vigorously. "Mamma and Daddy aren't that old. I mean, she's coming up on her sixty-eighth birthday and he's seventy-one. They're in good shape, though, so it isn't like she has problems getting around. She told me it simply got to the point that the whole grocery shopping, cooking, and cleaning was more than she wanted to mess with." Katie grinned. "Daddy has never known his way around a kitchen, and quite frankly, Mamma wouldn't have won any blue ribbons for her culinary skills. It was Mamaw Pickett on my Daddy's side that was the great cook in the family."

Helen was absorbing the information. "When you said *specialty catering*, this is what you have in mind?"

"Yes, as part of it. I've been researching the local demographics. While we know the town just by virtue of having grown up here, if you actually look at the numbers, we do have an aging population, but also a fair number of young couples. Telecommuting and home-based businesses mean that people aren't having to go off somewhere to find work as much as they did even ten years ago."

Helen thought of Alicia and Susanna as examples.

"Now, the point is that even though a woman, or a guy, I suppose, is working at home, that doesn't mean she, or he, has that much extra time on their hands. And don't get me wrong, between the factory expanding and a number of storefront businesses opening up, there aren't as many stay-at-home moms as there used to be." Katie paused to finish her drink. "Even though the grocery store has expanded their line of prepared foods, it isn't that extensive. What I have in mind is pick up or delivery within the town limits, and it can be one meal or a whole week's worth, proportioned depending on your family—smaller portions for seniors or dieters for that matter, larger for growing boys like ours, or to have leftovers. Everything will be either for the microwave or in the oven for no more than an hour with no preparation needed. Just turn the oven on and pop it in."

"I like it," she said. "Do you think Wallington is ready for this?"

Katie spread her left hand, ticking points off, using her fingers. "Think about it. Right there close to the Farley house is a childcare center and a beauty parlor. Pick dinner up when you pick the kids up or after having your hair done. The Farley house is on the edge between the town square and one of the larger residential areas, with a lot of older homes. The real key will be to keep the costs under control, because in the cities, people don't mind paying extra for convenience, but that will be a consideration here, especially for seniors on a fixed income."

"True," Helen said thoughtfully. "Although, I could see someone like Phyllis paying for her parents rather than them doing so."

Katie smiled. "Oh, absolutely. I'll have gift certificates exactly for that reason, and..." she hesitated. "I, well, I'm close to completing an associate's degree in nutrition through the community college. It's actually called a dietetic technician degree, but that doesn't sound very appetizing, does it?"

"Why, look at you," Helen said with a laugh, "all this preparation."

Katie smiled, no doubt glad to be sharing the secret. "This will be something big for me if I take the final step and that's one of the reasons I wanted to get your perspective. Scott has been incredibly supportive, of course, but you've seen what your sister has gone through and you worked with so many different small businesses on their insurance. If it's one thing I've learned, bankers, lawyers, doctors, insurance companies, and beauticians are the ones that really know what goes on in a person's life."

Helen was reminded of her conversation with Wanda about knowing an owner's secrets. She reached out and touched her glass to Katie's despite the fact they were both empty. "Any new business is risky, but I like the idea and it sounds as if you've done the research. What are you looking at in terms of time?"

Katie's eyes reflected her appreciation of Helen's comments. "Buying the house has to be done quickly or I'll lose the opportunity. Fortunately, we're in a position to do that. It's the commitment to the business and the renovations that are in question. The truth is, if we decided not to move forward, we could do a little work, turn the property, and at least break even. Once we start the renovation, it's a different story. I won't be quitting the bank immediately, of course. I imagine it will be around six months before we're ready."

Helen tapped her forefinger to the table. "You should talk to Lisa Forsythe. She went through something very similar getting the bakery going and then adding the florist shop next door."

Katie clapped her hands together. "You're right and I don't know why I didn't think of that. I'll give her a call in the morning and see if I can meet with her tomorrow. I'll change my lunch hour and go later after she gets through the midday rush." She pushed her chair from the table, as if to stand. "Uh, if it wouldn't be a problem for you, would you mind going with me?"

Helen was startled. "I'm available tomorrow, but isn't this something you'd rather discuss with her privately?"

Katie grinned. "Considering the kind of secrets we've all shared in the past, how could this possibly be more private? The only reason I haven't told the rest of the circle is because I didn't need a dozen pieces of advice. Besides, you might think to ask something that I don't."

Helen returned the smile, realizing her friend was correct. By the time you'd been in a circle for years, there weren't too many details of one's life that hadn't emerged to at least some degree. That special bond was part of why the makeup of the circle was important. Most nights were routine chatter, but collectively, they had suffered emotional crises of death, divorce, a medical scare, loss of a job, a child out of control, and the loving support among them could be counted on without hesitation. It was a spirit of sisterhood that was stitched together as surely as any of the quilts they produced.

"I don't have anything scheduled, so give me a call as soon as you get it set up and I'll be glad to join you," Helen said.

They parted a few minutes later and Helen thought through the evening's events as she waited for her nightly cup of herbal tea to steep. Goodness, having Max there was interesting enough. Katie's news was certainly unexpected. She could see her point, though. Katie was originally from Conyers, a star forward on the girls' basketball team who accepted a scholarship to Augusta State University. There was no thought of continuing to play beyond that since it was before professional women's basketball became popular. She'd met Scott and married him between graduation and when he left for basic training. His only assignment while in the Army had been to Fort Riley, Kansas, where their oldest son was born. His intent had always been to return to Wallington and enter into partnership in the construction business where he'd worked summers during high school. Although Katie took on the job in the office, it was one of those situations where they quickly discovered they did not work well together, and she began at the bank as a teller. She was correct that in a family bank, there were only so many upper-level positions and being the senior loan officer was a good job, but with no potential for advancement.

Helen didn't know how much of a market there would be for what Katie envisioned, but she thought back to when she was working full-time with two children and frequently one or more of their friends stayed for dinner. She would have gladly paid not to have dealt with that a couple of nights a week. Now that she thought more about it, losing the desire to cook was something several of the women at The Arbors had mentioned. They'd described how they reached the stage where they were tired of thinking about it, planning meals, shopping, and cleaning up, and that frozen meals and cans of soup were easier. Katie just might be on to a really good idea after all.

CHAPTER TWENTY-TWO

———>◦<———

Helen and Katie arrived at Forsythe Bakery within minutes of each other, Lisa ushering them to a table in the back corner where she could keep an eye on the room. At two inches shorter than Helen, decidedly plump with short, almost frizzy black hair and brown eyes, Lisa could not have looked less like Katie. She was, however, the proverbial bundle of energy who had overcome a lying, cheating husband who very nearly put her out of business when she'd first started. Notwithstanding her talent for pastries, the real reason the town had rallied behind her was because she was a decent person and someone who hadn't deserved the treatment she'd received. Lisa, aware of how close she came to being destroyed financially, didn't give enough credit to her own personality as to why she'd been supported, but then, no one had expected that of her. In Lisa's version of the story, a number of people were responsible for her ability to pick up the pieces and come back stronger than ever. Other people, like Helen, remarked how Lisa had proved resilient, working sixteen to eighteen hours a day to get back on her feet. She had shrugged off the heartbreak of her own husband taking out a second mortgage without her knowledge, then setting the original store on fire in a plan to claim the insurance money. All that didn't take into account the fact that he was messing around on her to boot.

"I love the new paint scheme," Katie said, laying a black leather portfolio at the empty space next to her.

"Thanks, it was Cheryl's color design and we lucked out on getting a great deal with adding seat covers to the chairs. As soon as we get through the holiday rush, well, that's assuming we have as good a holiday season as we did last year, we're calling Scott to put in those French doors. Won't that be nice?"

Forsythe Bakery was the end red brick building in a row of four. The front rectangular room that held fifteen tables had been repainted right after Halloween, the original white replaced by a Venetian-plaster effect with three walls done in coral and the back one in terra cotta. Open shelves held antique bakeware and kitchen items, and framed prints of bakery-related still life provided most of the decorations. The ordinary black metal-frame chairs at the wooden tables had been perked up with stain-resistant fabric cushions in muted coral and gold, the colors being alternated rather than having all coral or all gold at one table. The wide front windows allowed plenty of light with simple, unruffled valances done in an Impressionist-type print that blended the colors of the décor.

The two-shelf glass display cabinets were filled with individual cookies and pastries on the right hand side and cakes, tarts, pies, breads, and rolls were on the left. The counter section in between the two cabinets held the cash register. A counter against the wall behind the cabinets was devoted to hot beverages on the right. Coffee, tea, and chocolate were all served in old-fashioned thick brown ceramic mugs or in to-go cups that came in only two sizes. Juices, milk, bottled water, and limited Coca-Cola products were in the refrigerated cabinet on the left. Lisa made the decision to remain strictly a bakery. The idea of branching out into soups, sandwiches, and salads was always a possibility. Despite that, there tended to be a steady flow of customers in the afternoon.

When Nancy Smith decided it was time to retire from the florist business next door, Lisa, who had always admired the woman, quickly leased the property and turned it over Cheryl Sullivan who she'd grown up with. The two women had a sister-like relationship and they made sure samples of Lisa's cookies were always available in the florist shop and there was a bud vase with a fresh flower on all the tables in the bakery. Installing French doors to give easy passage between the two stores did make sense.

A couple Helen didn't know and three young women were the sole customers at this hour and Rhonda, Lisa's only full-time employee, was managing the counter. Helen breathed in the aroma of cinnamon and pastry crust. "Did you take an apple pie out of the oven right before we got here?"

Lisa grinned. "Turnovers actually. It's a pick-up order, but I've got others in the case I could warm up."

Helen and Katie simultaneously held out their hands in a "no" signal. "Not today. We had circle last night," Helen said. "When we finish here, I do need to put an order in, though."

"Always happy to oblige," Lisa said, and looked at Katie's notebook. "You sounded a little mysterious over the telephone and I'm dying to know what this is about."

The women spent almost an hour outlining Katie's plan and sharing ideas. Lisa was cautiously enthusiastic, pointing out potential pitfalls that Katie had researched. "As much as I would love to extend this into an afternoon coffee break, I need to get back to the bank," Katie said with a smile. "I appreciate both of you taking the time and being honest with me." She turned to Lisa. "Like I was telling Helen, I'm not trying to keep this a big secret, I just didn't want to talk to a lot of people in case I decided to not to move forward."

Lisa waved her hand around the room. "I totally understand. It is a huge step and the excitement of being a small business owner can wear off very quickly when you realize you're the one making all the decisions, handling the mountains of paperwork, coping with employees, and in our case, making the products, too. It sounds as if you've got a handle on all the important pieces and please don't hesitate to ask if there's anything that I can do for you."

"Be careful about making that gesture," Katie laughed. "I may need more hand holding than I think."

They stood to exchange hugs and Lisa waited until Katie left. She tilted her head and looked at Helen. "Well, I wasn't at all sure what this was going to be about. I'm in the bank every day and I never would have guessed Katie was considering something like this. Did you know before last night?"

"No, it took me by surprise, too, but the more I thought about it, the more sense it made. Katie is a strong woman and you're too young, but when you get to middle age, you do tend to start to take stock of where you are in life. This will be quite a change for her, although I believe it has real possibility."

"Oh, I agree," Lisa said. "I know you must be ready for coffee, tea, water, or something unless you have to head out, too."

"Coffee would be nice," Helen said, rolling her shoulders after having been hunched over the table as tends to happen when talking the way they were.

"Shall I tempt you with a teensy, teensy slice of cake—chocolate, carrot, praline, or lemon pound?" Her smile was mischievous.

"You know how I love the carrot cake," Helen said, remembering she did have a salad topped with roasted chicken for lunch and was planning a light dinner. "Teensy, promise?"

"Coming right up," Lisa said.

"Give me a minute to pop into the ladies' room," Helen said, thinking she should probably run by Collectibles when she finished with Lisa to see how Max had viewed his first time at circle.

Lisa had the order form, two cups of coffee, and the thin slice of cake waiting when she slipped into the chair again. Helen savored a bite of cake before she sipped her coffee. It was superb, as always, the complex flavors coming together perfectly, moist, and not overly sweet.

"This is delicious," she said, seeing gratitude on Lisa's face for the compliment. "Anyway, about the order. Mamma has convinced me we shouldn't try to handle Thanksgiving all by ourselves this year. Tricia isn't due until the end of the month, but as you know, that first baby can be unpredictable. Ethan and his family are going to wait and come at Christmas so it will probably be only ten of us. Two pies and a cake, do you think? That's a little much, but Daddy has to have apple and I do love your pumpkin chiffon. Tricia will want chocolate whether she's with us or we're taking Thanksgiving dinner to the hospital."

"How about that chocolate raspberry? It's the dark chocolate cake with a layer of raspberry filling, a thin layer of shaved milk chocolate, and white chocolate buttercream frosting with dark chocolate rosettes."

"Perfect," Helen said. "That should make everyone happy. We'll send leftovers home with people, or I suppose if it comes to Tricia being in the hospital, we'll take some in to the nurses."

"Maybe making these arrangements will mean everything will be normal with no interference," Lisa said, and looked over as the door opened. "Not that having a baby, especially your first, should be called an interference."

Helen laughed, stood to gather the dishes, and noticed that the customer who came in was Albert Gilbert.

"Be right there, Albert," Lisa called while handing the Helen the order form. "I'll get the dishes and you double-check this."

Albert was of more interest than the form, considering what Tricia had been telling her about him. She took the opportunity to stroll to the front cases as she read over the form that was of course, correct. The other patrons were gone and Albert gave her a studied look.

"Hello, Mrs. Crowder. How are you, ma'am?"

His voice was sadly squeaky, exacerbating his image as a stereotypical nerd who, had slide rulers still been in use, would have one protruding from his front pocket. With his thin build, short stature, unruly brown hair, an overbite, and thick black glasses, he was saved only from severe acne. His too-pale skin was fairly clear and had no scarring.

"I'm fine, Albert. And you?"

"Uh, okay, I guess," he said, and seemed relieved that Lisa appeared with a box.

"That's one dozen chocolate chip, one dozen oatmeal, no raisins, and one dozen caramel toffee. Did your mamma want anything else?"

Albert took a twenty from his left pocket and another one from his right pocket and laid them both on the counter. "No ma'am, but could you please use this twenty for those and then let me have three brownies, a bottle of milk, and a Coke from the other twenty?"

He turned and looked solemnly at Helen. "I don't want to mix up my money and Mamma's."

"Good idea," Helen said, and when Albert completed his transactions, he politely said good-bye and pushed the door open with his back, his hands full. As he did so, Helen saw someone get out of an old, mud splattered green truck. Why, it was Johnny Jenkins.

"Huh, that's surprising," she said aloud before she could stop herself.

Lisa looked out the big window and nodded once. "Oh yes, Johnny and Albert. As strange a pair as you could ask for. Johnny's moving pretty slowly, and if we were closer, I imagine his face is still a mess. Thank the good Lord he wasn't hurt any worse. That's Roger's old truck they're in. Albert's bicycle is probably in the bed. That's what they usually do."

"I don't mean the two boys shouldn't be friends," Helen said, making sure Rhonda was out of hearing distance. She didn't want her remarks to be misunderstood and she could trust that Lisa would put them in the proper perspective.

"Oh, believe me, you could have knocked me over with a feather the first time they came in here," she said cheerfully. "It was, I don't know, three months ago, maybe? Right after school started. Most of the after-school kids hang out at the drive-in, but Albert comes in here a lot where it's quiet, sits at that table close to where we were with a brownie, milk, and his computer." She giggled. "He can be the funniest little thing. Do you know he helped me work out the recipe for that new lighter pound cake I'm doing?"

Helen leaned against the counter, pushing the form toward Lisa. "Really?"

Lisa pressed a finger to her lips. "I was talking to Rhonda about it, had taken a couple of tries at it, and couldn't get the taste I wanted without that famous pound of butter, pound of sugar, etc. Albert, his nose in that computer, must have been listening after all and he piped up asking if I would like a suggestion."

She smiled fondly. "I said sure, and he proceeded to go into this long explanation about how baking was closer to chemistry than almost any other form of cooking and why my goal of a lighter pound cake was difficult."

"I've had that cake and you obviously solved the problem," Helen said. "It's terrific."

Lisa giggled again. "Thank you, and that little scamp is part of the reason. He took a look at my latest recipe, suggested two changes and, by golly, he was right. I just wish he wasn't so hopeless when it came to making friends." She waved her hand toward the window and lowered her voice. "The deal with Johnny is, I think, maybe not as odd as it seems when you see first them together. I get the impression maybe Albert is helping Johnny with something in school."

"Ah," Helen said, waiting for the next part.

"Yeah, like I said, this is sort of new and they come in once, sometimes twice a week and you can tell Johnny is actually listening to Albert and he's usually showing him something on the computer or in a notebook." She paused and picked up the form. "My guess would be they come here because it's away from the school and isn't where the other kids hang out."

"You could be right," Helen said, insisting on fully prepaying the order. That would be one less task to deal with the day before Thanksgiving. She thought about Johnny and Albert on the drive to Collectibles.

As strangely matched as the two boys were, this wouldn't be the only time such a friendship existed, and it would fit Tricia's observations in a way that was nice rather than disturbing. There was no telling how it would have started, although probably more by accident than design. She didn't know Johnny, but considering what she'd heard, she doubted he would have sought assistance with his studies. Albert was well known as being smart despite not having any friends to speak of. If Tricia was correct about Albert being the target of bullying, Johnny probably knew about that, too. It was logical they could have had an encounter where Albert's need for someone to stand up for him and Johnny's need for help with part of school coincided. It would also be logical that Johnny wouldn't want to explain the friendship and so contact at school would be minimal.

She was going to call Tricia anyway to invite them to dinner. If they already had plans or didn't feel like coming over, she could at least pass on what she'd seen and what Lisa said. It was so like Tricia to be concerned about Albert, and with everything else she had to deal with, she would be glad to hear that the relationship was a positive one.

Helen's preference for optimism and wanting to believe the best about people didn't make her naïve or blind to human flaws. She didn't doubt that Roger Jenkins was probably a lousy father and husband and the older boy, Jared, might not be salvageable. It was perfectly reasonable for Johnny to want to emulate his brother and father. What boy didn't, up to a certain age? Isabelle would have had less influence as the boys grew older and how difficult it must have been for her to recognize what a mistake she'd made marrying Roger and watching her sons slip from her. No mother wanted to see her children getting into trouble and disdaining school. It was distinctly possible, though, that Johnny might be conflicted between the behavior his mamma urged and what his daddy and brother demonstrated. If he happened to be fundamentally a good kid at heart, Albert might have touched that cord within him even though she was sure Johnny would never say so. Albert, if he was as lacking in social skills as Tricia and Lisa indicated, might be equally unable to explain the friendship, although he might view it analytically. Helen had a sudden vision of him spouting cultural and anthropological statistics about unlikely pairings.

No matter how some people might view Johnny, her opinion was that he was much too young to be written off as some hopeless case of a bad boy who would be going to worse. His needing a stern lecture and maybe a little of that "scared straight" talk was an entirely different matter, and when she parked the car she had an uncontrollable desire to giggle as Lisa had. Watching scrawny little Albert huddled together with husky Johnny had to be quite a sight.

She swung out of her car and didn't see Max's Explorer among the cars in the lot. Was he not in or was he perhaps parking around the back now? If he wasn't in, she could catch up with Wanda and find out who was planning what kind of farewell. If Wanda thought she was going to be gone for nearly four months without some sort of festive send off, she might as well rid her of that notion right now.

CHAPTER TWENTY-THREE

W hy, there you are, stranger," Wanda said, coming from behind the counter where she was talking with Lillian.

"I'm not the one who hasn't been around," Helen said, giving her a hug. "I've come by a couple of times and you were nowhere to be found."

Wanda stepped out of the embrace and patted her hair. "I confess. I'm a fairly organized woman and have been truly amazed at all the different loose ends I've needed to take care of in order to be gone for this length of time." She rubbed her upper left arm. "I even had to get a tetanus shot, can you believe that?"

Helen laughed. "That's something most people overlook until they get hurt and it really can be serious. It's not a bad precaution to take whether you're traveling or not. How is Miss Ruth doing, by the way?"

Wanda smiled and gestured toward Lillian. "She couldn't be better, except I need to run some supplies over to her. She absolutely loves that hand cream Juanita makes and swears it's the best she's ever used. I think she's converted half the ladies and maybe some of the men to it."

"I've heard that and keep saying I'm going to give it a try," Helen said, always pleased to hear when one of the Lurley's products became popular.

"Oh, hi, Helen," Max said, guiding two ladies from the quilting room to the counter.

Helen didn't know either of them and their shopping baskets were filled with a variety of objects. The taller one, who looked to be in her mid-forties, had short black hair cut in a pageboy that helped soften her strong jaw and sharp chin. Her companion, who barely came to her shoulder, looked like a middle-aged pixie with ash-blonde hair in a short layered cut and a heart-shaped face.

"We heard about this place from Sharon Gleason and it is absolutely worth the drive," the taller one said. "We'll tell everyone we know and will definitely be back."

"That's always a pleasure to hear," Wanda said, and moved toward them, ready to lay on a little extra charm. "You found everything you need? And did you have a chance to see the other rooms?"

Max smilingly switched places with Wanda as she assured the newcomers they could leave their baskets right there while she gave them a special tour if they had time. "She has the touch for this," he said in a low voice.

"There's no doubt about that," Helen replied, tilting her head to the room he'd come from. "Are you busy?"

"The others are regulars," he said. "I'm glad you came by. I was going to call to tell you that I had a great time last night."

"Oh, how was your call to Hawaii?"

"Quite productive, thank you," he said and glanced over as the telephone rang. Lillian answered it and shook her head to indicate she didn't need him to take it. "Do you want to go into the classroom? Can I get you a cup of coffee, tea, whatever?"

"That's fine and I don't need a thing," Helen said. "I just came from Lisa Forsythe's bakery."

"That is a place I have to be careful about," Max said, one step behind her. "I insisted that I'm bringing dessert to Angela's for Thanksgiving so I have an excuse to buy from Lisa and I'm riding the bicycle as much as I can now. I can get to more than half the places I need to using that, and Phyllis was right about the fitness center at the YMCA. It's nice."

Helen thought about Max sitting next to Phyllis last night. "That's right, y'all have been out together a couple of times, haven't you?"

He gave her a mildly puzzled look as they went into the classroom and he switched on the lights. "Out together? Well, sort of, I guess. It's really just us meeting for dinner in a friendly kind of way. Phyllis is, well, was Phyllis always like that in school? I can't say I knew her then."

"You were a year ahead of me and she's a year younger, which made her a sophomore when you graduated. You wouldn't have had much contact and she actually was a bit shy in those days, if you can believe it."

They sat at the same table as before, side by side, facing the door in case Wanda or Lillian needed to get their attention.

He chuckled. "Shy is not a word that I would ever associate with Phyllis."

Helen smiled. "College was where she really cut loose. She went out of state to Auburn, and while you can hardly call that a hotbed of liberalism, I think it was more that she was away from home and people who knew her. She joined a sorority, had a makeover, got in with some of the older girls, and definitely dated some older boys. You could see the difference in her that first summer she came home." Phyllis's new outlook on life had been typified with the incident that involved a bottle of Jim Beam and skinny-dipping at the quarry that Helen wasn't about to reveal.

"She's fun, that's for sure," Max said, "a little, well, I'm not sure what the right word is."

"Outrageous?" Helen supplied. "High-spirited is the one we use most often."

"That's a good one," he agreed. "So the ladies last night. I genuinely enjoyed the group. It's a nice mix and I was glad to see the one younger girl—oops, I mean woman—there. Rita, right?"

"Yes, and Alicia is only a year older than her. I hope she'll be able to join us next week. She works from home as a copy editor and has been tied up with some complicated projects. She and Rita are fairly new in town and to the circle." Helen looked into his eyes, a sensation of warmth wrapped in mirth. "And speaking of joining the circle…"

"I would love to," he said and grinned. "Unless you were going to tell me that you didn't think I would fit in."

A bubble of laughter escaped her lips. "Heavens, no, or would that be yes? Yes, we want you to be a part of us and no, there was never any doubt you would be a good fit."

"Great. Now that we have that settled, and speaking of going out to dinner, when are you and I going to do that?"

Helen lifted her hands in a questioning pose. "It's been more hectic than I was expecting since you arrived. I had fully intended to have you over."

"Not you cooking for me, although I know that would be thoroughly enjoyable. I'm talking about in a restaurant so you don't have to go to any trouble."

Helen smiled. "I really don't consider it trouble to have people over. Oh, you will be having Thanksgiving with Angela and her family, won't you?"

He grinned. "Yes, that was the 'me bringing dessert from Lisa' part."

"Right. Anyway, the question of whether Tricia going to deliver early, on time, or late is having a bit of an impact so my scheduling has been somewhat erratic."

"I completely understand," he laughed. "Let's just say my time is yours and you let me know when it's convenient. I won't force you into a restaurant either, but that is what I'd like to do. In fact, I've heard the Magnolia Inn is really special and it isn't the kind of place I'd want to go by myself."

Helen was startled. "Oh, yes, they've made it a wonderful spot with lovely ambience and excellent food. That's more like a date place, though."

"Ah, well, that doesn't mean we shouldn't go," he said. He shifted his chair so he was face to face with her. "By the way, since we're on the subject of coming and going, aside from the fact that Wanda will be gone for close to four months, I guess in my short trips home, I'd been too busy to notice all the changes in Wallington, or maybe I've been to enough major cities now that I appreciate a slower pace."

His voice had dropped a note, sparking Helen's curiosity. "Does that mean you're considering staying longer, even after Wanda and Angela come back?"

His gaze was thoughtful. "The truth is that I like Raleigh, but as much as I traveled, I can't say I've made any close friends there." He grimaced. "While my ex-wife and I parted on relatively amicable terms, there were no strong relationships forged on that side either."

"You mean it wasn't one of those cases where her parents liked you so much they wanted to keep you no matter what she did?"

He laughed, as if at a joke. "It was more the case that if I had spent more time around my future mother-in-law I would have realized her daughter wasn't the woman I should be marrying."

Helen smiled at his response. "Phyllis, Sarah, Mary Lou, and Alicia are all divorced, so you have that in common. Mary Lou and Alicia remarried, Sarah is in a pretty serious relationship with Ross Perryman, who happens to be a good electrician if you need one, and Phyllis, well, you already know about her."

"She does speak her mind and doesn't hold anything back," he said. "Seriously though, Wallington seems to have managed steady growth without overdeveloping. That's not easy to do."

"The mayor and the council get a lot of credit for that," she said earnestly. "You remember when we had three textile factories and the pulp mill?"

Helen briefly wrinkled her nose. "Didn't they stink to high heavens at times? It was upsetting to people when they started folding and it was pretty rough for a year or two."

"Mamma and Daddy were worried," he said. "It's good to see low-impact manufacturing though. I mean, I know there's room for more to come in, but if I read the Gazette correctly, unemployment here is below the state and national average."

"It is, even though they aren't the kind of jobs where people get rich."

He shrugged. "Helps keep inflation down."

Helen nodded, still unsure as to what he was getting at and not sure this was the moment to ask more questions. "True, and…"

"Hey, Helen," Lillian said, sticking her head and upper body in the door. "I hate to interrupt, Max, but you have a call. It's Denise from the Gazette."

Helen rose and took her purse from where she'd draped it on the chair. "I've got to run anyway. I bet Denise wants to run a hometown boy back from world travels story. We'll talk soon and fix a night for dinner."

"Tell her I'm on the way," Max said to Lillian, stood, and

leaned down for a peck on the cheek.

Helen delivered the friendly kiss, breathing in the musky scent of his aftershave that for some reason she hadn't noticed earlier. She threw a kiss to Lillian, heard Wanda's voice in the quilting room talking to customers, and hurried to the car. She wanted to call Tricia before she made plans for dinner. Dinner with Max! She'd been serious about having intended to invite him over. She couldn't believe more than two weeks had passed since his arrival, and she wasn't entirely sure what to make of his comments about Phyllis. Her assumption that their second time to dine out was a date didn't seem to be correct and, in all honesty, she hadn't asked Phyllis the direct question. She'd certainly had a lot on her mind lately and well, when it came to men, she didn't always want to ask Phyllis direct questions. She was no prude. It was just that she wasn't into graphic details, particularly not in situations when she knew the man.

It was funny, in a way. Phyllis had been urging her to attend events where she might meet single men. She said it was past time she broadened her social scene from female friends and church. Phyllis would get that wicked look on her face and declare she would be more than happy to gather an array of suitable men and Helen could take her pick. It wasn't that Wallington was filled with single men their age as much as it was that Phyllis said expanding to a thirty-mile radius would include adequate territory, and if a man couldn't be bothered to travel thirty miles, he wouldn't be right for Helen anyway.

So far, Helen had declined Phyllis's offer and, if she was being honest about it, one of the biggest reasons was she simply wasn't sure how to behave on a date. The truth was she hadn't been on one since she and Mitch went to the junior high school fall festival dance, her first boy-girl event. That, of course, hadn't been a real date, but they'd both known they were meant to be together and were commonly discussed as boyfriend and girlfriend after that.

When the allowable date at age sixteen finally occurred, it was simply a ritual. Helen didn't know if it was luck or fate that allowed them to recognize each other so early in life. What she did know was having the strength of love they shared meant they knew they never wanted to settle for anything less. She was grateful to see both Ethan and Tricia seemed to have what she and Mitch had, and she felt like they had set a good example for the kids. It wasn't that life had been without squabbles and periodic disagreements; they were human after all. It was that they shared a balance with each other, a harmony that allowed them to work through their minor grievances with no major ones ever erupting. In her stunned grief over Mitch's death, a part of her had been torn away. There were moments when the four years that had passed seemed like no more than the blink of an eye and she was fully aware that everyone from her own parents to Tricia felt she shouldn't turn away from the idea of romance. The problem, although she didn't personally view it as a problem, was that with her family, friends, church, quilting, classes that she taught, and volunteering, she did have a full life.

When she'd spoken to Max earlier about Mary Lou and Alicia being remarried and Sarah in a serious relationship, that was different. Their marriages had been flawed. Alicia's had been frighteningly so, from her description. It was not until later that they found what Helen and Mitch had from the beginning. Although she cognitively understood she might meet a man she could fall in love with, it was emotionally difficult to grasp. It wasn't that she was putting Mitch on the proverbial pedestal as much as it was she had no reason to settle for anything less than what they'd had together. That seemed to be a tremendous amount of pressure to inject into the dating process. Why should she bother?

Her brain, branching from subject to subject, was marginally aware of the streets and cars, the route so familiar that she was on mental autopilot. She pulled into the carport, thinking how interesting the day had become with what she had anticipated as nothing more than half an hour or so spent with Katie and Lisa. That session had been fun and seeing Albert had been enlightening. She trusted both Lisa's skills of observation and judgment and hoped her assessment of the boys' friendship was accurate.

Then, to have Max hint at perhaps staying longer in town was a distinct surprise. His comments about Wallington weren't completely unexpected and there had been others who'd left for years and returned. There was a draw for someone who had roots, unless the lure of urban living trumped that lure. Helen had been to the big city, to several in fact, and it wasn't the kind of environment she wanted for any length of time. Of course, there were aggravations living in a town where most people knew other people's business and where it was tricky to avoid those you didn't like. The advent of the Internet and expansion of some of the nearby towns had, however, opened access to shopping that had previously meant more than two hours of driving time. The growth of small businesses like Memories and Collectibles and Always Fresh Farms was filling niches that hadn't existed previously. Increased goods and services were being balanced with steadfast small-town values that mattered more to Helen than having some mega hardware or super retail store. She wasn't fundamentally against those, she just didn't think the town was incomplete without them, and she wasn't keen on the population increase that would cause those national chains to view Wallington as a prime target.

She opened the car door, amused at her wanderings. She had tasks at hand and the first one was to call Tricia. She hoped they could come to dinner and she was absolutely going to find an evening to invite Max over as well.

CHAPTER TWENTY-FOUR

Helen could feel her brow pucker, certain she was hearing the thin, nervous voice correctly, her thoughts divided along two lines at the startling plea from Albert Gilbert.

"Mrs. Crowder, are you there? Can you help us?"

"Well, of course," she said hurriedly. "Wouldn't this be better to do at the police station?"

Helen had lost track of the number of "pleases" in the puzzling request for help. She took a deep breath. "It's okay, Albert. I'm going to call Justin and explain and I'm sure he will agree. When can you be here?"

"Thirty or forty minutes," he said, a tiny wheeze in his voice that she hoped didn't mean he was on the verge of suffering an asthma attack. "I promise I'll call if we're going to be later than that."

"All right," Helen said, wanting to add, "be careful, or let me call your parents, or your cousin, Boyd," but that would be repeating what she had already suggested.

She dialed Justin's cell phone to keep from going through

Sheila and was grateful to hear he was away from the station. "Justin, I have just had the strangest telephone call from Albert Gilbert. He and Johnny Jenkins will be here at the house in thirty to forty minutes."

"What? Did you say what I think you did?" She could imagine the look on his face.

"Yes," she sighed. "They want to talk with you, said it was urgent, but are afraid to go to the police station and want you to come here, and not in the police car, if possible."

His response was precisely what she anticipated. "Yes, I agree, and yes, I argued with him, but I will also tell you I think if we don't do it this way, Johnny is going to do something foolish. No, I don't know what this is about. You do? Oh, well, all right. No, he didn't give me the telephone number, although I'm sure it was a cell. No, I don't have caller ID on the phone and I have no idea if I have a call-back feature or not. No, I haven't spoken with Tricia. Under the circumstances though, I don't think she would forgive either of us if we don't tell her. You're going to go home and get the car and tell her? That's fine. Yes, I'll stay right here."

She realized her hand was almost numb from how tightly she'd gripped the receiver. She inhaled another deep breath and slowly exhaled it, focusing on what she should do to prepare. She had milk and Coke. Coffee and hot tea would probably be good. She didn't really have time to make brownies, but didn't she have a box of Girl Scout cookies in the pantry? She knew this was no social occasion, but good manners were good manners, after all.

She looked down as Tawny whimpered, perhaps picking up Helen's confusion as to what on earth young Albert and Johnny had gotten themselves into. Why they wanted to come to her was fairly easy to determine. Begging her not to tell their parents made her uncomfortable, but she could always do so after everyone was assembled.

The last of the coffee dripped into the carafe when Tawny perked her ears, the sound of her toenails clicking-clicking to the back door.

"Mamma, what on earth is going on?" Tricia's face was a mix of worry and bafflement. "It was only yesterday that it sounded like everything was fine."

"The boys haven't called again?" Justin was virtually on Tricia's heels, reaching his hand down to pat Tawny without taking his eyes from Helen.

"First, everyone come in, sit, and I will explain what I know," Helen said, having thought through the conversation after her initial surprise.

Tricia deposited her purse on the counter and lumbered to the chair on the opposite side of the table where she could sit and be facing the door.

"I think we have maybe ten minutes or so before the boys arrive. Yes, Tricia, what I told you on the telephone last night was good news as far as we were both concerned. I haven't seen Albert in ages and what I think must have happened is that when he saw me yesterday, it triggered this idea for him to call me as a way to get to Justin without going directly to the police station."

Justin was still standing, one hand on the back of Tricia's chair, the other on her shoulder. "That makes sense," he said. "I hadn't known Tricia was so worried about Albert. When she passed on what you told her, we could both see an odd couple kind of relationship between Albert and Johnny as a possibility." He exhaled a long breath. "I had enough time to call the chief and he wants me to handle this as quietly as we can until we know what's going on."

"I'm glad to hear that," Helen said, now looking pointedly at

Justin. "Could you kindly tell Tricia and me what you think this is about?"

Justin cleared his throat. "In a nutshell, it goes back to those rumors about drugs. There has been new information to indicate a portable meth lab may be moving around within a two-county radius. There's a chance Johnny, probably through his brother Jared, is involved in some way."

Tricia's voice was stricken. "Oh no, not that. And Albert? You're not saying Albert is involved?"

"Honey, I think whatever this is about, Albert is trying to help," Helen said quickly. "Now, how about…."

Tawny alerted them before they heard the car doors, well, truck, Helen assumed. Slam. Justin started to stride forward and Helen placed her hand on his arm. "Let me get this," she said with a half smile. "You sit at the head of the table instead of me and I'll be next to Tricia."

Justin's eyes were steady and he patted Tricia's shoulder once more before he moved to the head of the table.

Albert was in the lead, Johnny silently behind him as Tawny sniffed both their ankles and Helen motioned them into the kitchen.

"Thank you, Mrs. Crowder. Hello Mrs. Kendall and Officer Kendall," Albert said solemnly, nodding to each. "You all know Johnny."

His nod was curt, wariness stamped on his face. No one shook hands, although Tricia, like Helen, smiled encouragingly.

Justin spoke firmly. "Boys, before we sit, I think I am going to say thank you for coming, but as minors, we really should have your parents here, or at least a lawyer."

Johnny narrowed his eyes, and Albert shielded him in a way that otherwise would have been amusing. His voice was firm. "Office Kendall, please, we understand, but when you hear what we have to say, you will see why we didn't want to go to our parents for this first contact. We know you will have to call them and my cousin, Mr. Boyd Gilbert, will provide us with legal representation. We ask, however, that you hear us out first and we waive the opportunity to have either parents or counsel present. We will, of course, repeat everything later for a formal interview."

"Ah, well then, we can do that," Justin said drily, no doubt trying to not smile at Albert's earnest declaration.

Helen wanted to dispel the tension shimmering around Johnny. "Albert, Johnny, would you like to have a seat, please? I'll get everyone something to drink.

Johnny turned to her, the bruising on his face muted shades, the stitches on his head not yet removed, but the skin was no longer red around them. "Yes, thank you, Miz Crowder," he said cautiously and acknowledged Tricia. "Miz Kendall."

Justin waved to the chairs. "You're here about the meth lab."

Albert, who must have been practicing what he intended to say, sat closest to Justin with Johnny on his other side. "Yes, sir, and as you and probably Chief McFarlane have no doubt surmised, Jared is involved, but for the record, when there is to be one, Johnny has not been an active party to the production or distribution of methamphetamine. His role, to date..."

Johnny patted Albert's shoulder in the same way that Justin had Tricia's and sighed. "Bert, I got this," he said heavily. "What do you want to know, officer?"

Helen quietly slipped beverages in front of each person as the story began to unfold, Justin asking questions, Johnny answering reluctantly at first, then relaxing as Albert stalwartly supported his friend. The two of them sipped, listening intently.

Jared was indeed the connection, having fallen in with a man from Atlanta who was the one behind the scheme. The meth lab was set up in an old RV, nothing that would draw attention and Jared was to scout out the best spot for it and make arrangements for use of the property. He'd confided in Johnny because they didn't travel with the supplies, but rather purchased them in batches in multiple stores before coming together at the site. They would also need an extra lookout when they went into production.

"Jared's my brother and he's been in trouble before, but nothing like this," Johnny said. "Tried to tell him that maybe we didn't want to get mixed up in it, but sounded like he was too far gone to back out. We met with some Eyetalian fella out at the Nelson place couple of times and he made it pretty plain that Jared was into them for some stuff."

Justin flicked a look at Helen. "That would be a Mr. Rosso?"

Johnny shrugged. "Didn't get a name, but could be."

Justin looked at Albert. "How did you find out?"

Johnny intervened. "I went to Bert to ask him some questions about this whole thing. He's a smart little guy and I wasn't sure about carrying around some of the supplies Jared was telling me to get. I know some of that stuff can blow up when it isn't handled right."

"It wasn't difficult to draw the appropriate conclusion," Albert said seriously. "The production of methamphetamine is not complicated from a chemistry perspective, and considering what I know about his brother, I ascertained what Johnny was implying."

Tricia's voice broke in softly. "That's what you've been worried about? Trying to convince Jared to back out of this?"

"Yes, ma'am," Johnny said with a resigned look. "He's my brother, though."

Justin tilted his head. "The day your truck was shot, that was the second time you met the guy?"

Johnny ducked his head briefly and then met Justin's gaze directly. "Yeah, he called my brother afterwards and said if we didn't keep our mouths shut and do our jobs, it would be more than a tire next time."

"The RV is scheduled to arrive day after tomorrow," Albert said, reaching for the cookies. He put one on his napkin and one on Johnny's. "We don't know if this gentleman might be in town watching. Jared is due in tomorrow."

Johnny took a swallow of Coke and ignored the cookie. "You were right, officer, when you were telling me this was some serious stuff and Bert's been begging me to talk to you."

"Going into the station did pose a risk," Albert said. "So when I saw you yesterday, Mrs. Crowder, it seemed to be a fortuitous encounter and coming here would provide access to Officer Kendall while minimizing the chance of being seen."

"Yes, I'm glad to be able to help," Helen said, thanking the Lord if she had been the catalyst to bring the boys forward.

Johnny lifted the cookie and looked at Justin. "What now?"

"I'm going to need to make some calls," he said. "First to the chief, then we've got to talk to your parents, and Albert, you can let yours call Boyd. Johnny, you want both your father and mother contacted?"

Johnny lowered the cookie. "Best talk to Mamma and we'll decide about Daddy later. He'll be upset, for sure."

Justin stood. "Okay, I'm going into the other room. This will take me a few minutes to know exactly what we're doing next. I need the two of you to stay here, you understand?"

The boys nodded and Helen pushed the plate of cookies closer to them. Tricia moved her chair back so she could lean forward, her hands laced together on top of the table. "Albert, Johnny, what you're doing is incredibly brave. I know it's very difficult for you, Johnny, and we are here to help you in any way we can."

Helen felt a sting of tears at the surge of pride in her daughter.

"It's Bert's doing," Johnny said after a pause. "I didn't know what to do. It was too messed up, if you know what I mean."

"Of course it was confusing for you," Tricia continued. "You love your brother."

Johnny shrugged, his face set in an expression Helen couldn't read.

"Johnny," Tricia's voice was warm and coaxing. "You've been helping Albert with Steve Hillman and his friends, haven't you?"

The boy's upper lip curled. "You call them friends? They're all stupid jerks," he said. "Hillman's the leader all right, but the rest of them can't think for themselves. Want to pretend they're better than everybody else. Decide who they want to pick on and are only smart enough to do it in a way where they won't get caught."

"They do know how to conceal their actions," Albert said tremulously. "They'd stuck tiny nails into my bicycle tires so they wouldn't puncture until I started to ride and they'd coated the handlebars with some sort of pepper substance and it was all over my hands. They were waiting in the parking lot to laugh at me. I fell, not expecting both tires to go flat and my glasses came off. Then I had pepper on my face and in my eyes."

Johnny pushed gently against him with his upper arm. "Lucky thing I was there that day and saw it. Bert's a smart guy. So what that he's a nerd? Hillman and those guys are idiots. They scattered as soon as they saw it was someone who could stand up to them."

"Johnny had some water in his truck, got me cleaned off, gave me a ride home, and helped me fix my bike." Albert smiled. "I knew Johnny was having some problems with math, so I thought that maybe I could assist him in exchange for his help."

"Albert, I'm sorry that we, as teachers, haven't been able to do more," Tricia said, a catch in her voice.

"You can't be everywhere," Johnny said philosophically. "I had a talk with Hillman private like and told him to lay off Bert."

"Okay, here's what we're going to do," Justin said, standing behind the chair, pointing at the boys. "The three of us are going to Boyd Gilbert's office. The chief, Johnny's mom, and Albert's dad will meet us there. We'll get into more detail and talk about what happens next." He turned to Tricia. "I don't know how long this will take."

She gave him a poignant smile. "I'll stay here with Mamma and we can figure things out. Y'all go ahead. Albert, Johnny, thank you again for this decision. It's the right thing to do."

Johnny's look was less certain than Albert's. The boy who was determined to save his friend stood erect and gave a single nod. "Yes, ma'am, and may I again express my appreciation to you, Mrs. Crowder, for your assistance?"

"I was glad to help," Helen said, even more glad that she wouldn't be a part of the next discussion. That was going to be a doozy and her heart went out to Isabelle. This was going to be terribly hard on her. As for Roger, who knew how he would react?

The moment the door closed behind them, Tricia turned sideways in the chair and massaged her temples with her fingertips. "I swear, Mamma, I don't know whether to laugh or cry."

"It was certainly something," Helen said, with a shake of her head to clear her thoughts. "I think another cup of coffee would help. More tea?"

Tricia grimaced. "Give me a hand getting up and let me go to the bathroom first," she said. "How on earth could all this be happening and Justin not say so much as a word?"

Helen held out her arm for Tricia to hold onto as she pushed herself up. "Honey, you know better than to ask that. Justin doesn't run his mouth off about cases and people."

Tricia's mouth tugged down. "He and the chief are the only two who don't," she said. "And please leave the cookies out."

Helen laughed and called Tawny's name softly to let her know

227

she could join them. The dog trotted into the kitchen, wiggling for attention. Helen bent down and scratched her ears. "What a good girl you were. Let's get you one more treat as a reward."

Helen left the teakettle on low and poured her second mug of coffee while Tricia's tea was steeping.

"Thanks, Mamma," Tricia said, slowly lowering into the chair again. "I mean, for everything. For being someone Albert thought he could trust and for being willing to do this."

Helen waved her hand dismissively. "You would have done exactly the same thing." She cocked her head as a fleeting look of chagrin clouded Tricia's face. "I hope you're not feeling guilty because Albert didn't come directly to you."

Tricia wrapped her hands around the mug. "I don't think it's that as much as I wish we could be there for the kids. I don't mean to step in to solve all their problems. The bullying, though, and Johnny getting mixed up in something this dangerous."

"Honey," Helen said, able to reach out the comforting hand now. "You are a wonderful teacher and you care deeply for the kids, like so many of the others. The world is more complicated than it used to be, and while we have far fewer problems than somewhere like Atlanta, we aren't completely immune. The important point here is that Albert and Johnny did come forward. They did trust us to help."

She smiled softly, unwrapped her hands, and laid one on top of Helen's. "You're right, as always, and thank goodness for Chief McFarlane and Justin. They'll know how to handle this."

"Yes, they will," Helen said. "Now, how about we have one of those cookies?"

CHAPTER TWENTY-FIVE

⟨⧓⟩

Justin left the house thirty minutes earlier than usual, a full day ahead as they worked out the final details of planning the raid on the meth lab. The previous afternoon had stretched into late evening.

Chief McFarlane not only supported Justin's actions, he'd taken Isabelle, Dennis Gilbert, Albert's father, and Boyd Gilbert aside to assure them Justin had gone out of his way to keep the boys from talking. Not surprisingly, Albert had solemnly explained that Officer Kendall was in no way to be faulted for what the boys had chosen to tell him or the manner in which they had approached him.

The chief made the call to the Atlanta DEA office. Agent Bell hadn't been able to arrange for helicopter transport and had settled instead for everyone being on a speakerphone as he was driven from Atlanta. He agreed to kill the sirens and proceed at the speed limit when he was twenty miles out of Wallington. He'd sent the most recent surveillance photograph of Leo Rosso and Johnny identified him as "the Eyetalian guy in a fancy suit."

Isabelle held together with a strength that impressed Justin and she and Johnny agreed it was best not to let Roger in on the situation. Roger was too unpredictable and maintaining the information confidentially was critical. Johnny was still at Isabelle's pending his last check-up with the doctor and it wasn't as if his father had been dropping by to see how he was progressing. Boyd assured Isabelle he would be representing both her sons pro bono as they navigated through what could be some tricky legal territory. The chief debated about bringing in District Attorney Wayne Dickerson. As far as the chief was concerned, way too many people were already involved. He ultimately decided that small towns being what they were, it would not be a good idea to exclude the DA from what should be a major law enforcement coup. Justin suspected the chief also wanted the DA to see how much assistance Johnny was providing.

Agent Bell arrived at an opportune moment since another important issue about it being a small town was that Chief McFarlane had no one he could put into an undercover role that Jared didn't know. Asking Johnny to wear a wire was out of the question considering his age. Bell had apparently anticipated this problem and one of the three agents he'd brought with him was a scruffy-looking man whose youthful appearance had been quite useful in high school undercover operations.

The chief suggested reconvening the operational discussion at the station, leaving the civilians at Boyd's office to discuss whatever they needed to under attorney-client privilege. Justin called Tricia who said Helen had brought her home and they were in the process of making dinner. Chief McFarlane did order pizza to be brought in as they mapped out a general plan that was to be refined the next day.

The decision was made to meet Agent Bell and his team at the DA's office the next morning in case anyone was keeping a watch over the police station. When Justin arrived home, Tricia had taken him into her arms and whispered that she didn't want to know any details other than he promise to be careful and keep Johnny safe. He held her close, marveling as he did sometimes about his great fortune in having met this woman that he loved so deeply. Justin thought briefly how Tricia looked when she kissed him good-bye that morning, her eyes communicating the faith she had that everything would work out for the best.

He drove around to the back entrance as they'd agreed and saw the chief's car was there.

"They're in the conference room. Got donuts, coffee, and water in there, too. Y'all let me know if you need anything else," Delilah Carter said, motioning from her desk with a welcoming smile. If the name "Delilah" conjured images of a sultry temptress, that was shattered upon introduction to the DA's administrative assistant. Technically, she wouldn't have been eligible to be a linebacker, but she did have the build for it. However, just as everyone who knew anything understood that Sheila Tipton was the proverbial glue that held the police department together, "Dee" did the same for the DA. The other reason for the meeting location was that Dee, unlike Sheila, was known to be closemouthed about what went on within the office.

The three men exchanged greetings and Justin was only partway through a donut when the others arrived. After seeing them in, Dee closed the door with the promise that no one would be disturbed. They wanted to lay the plan out in detail before they met with Boyd, Isabelle, and Johnny to go over his role.

Bell, maybe a few years younger than the chief, looked every bit the former Marine that he'd been, a lean physique that spoke of a rigid exercise regimen rather than being desk-bound. Agent Nat Ronkowski, with his blonde hair and green eyes, was practically slender compared to Colby Morton who might well have made his way through college on a basketball scholarship. His hands could probably palm a ball and his shaved head gave him the appearance of a chunk of black granite. Ryan Gant, the baby-faced agent with shaggy, streaked blonde hair, was wearing an oversized blue Atlanta Braves jersey and baggy jeans, not breaking from the role of alleged high school student—the exact type that Johnny would bring into a situation like this.

It was closing in on lunch when they had argued through the details, making adjustments here and there, determining they didn't require county support, focusing on simplicity, and ensuring Johnny's safety.

"Okay," Chief McFarlane said. "Let's go over this one more time, then we'll break up and Agents Bell and Gant, Justin, and I will meet with Boyd, Isabelle, and Johnny."

Everyone nodded, the acknowledgement wrapped in the unspoken excitement that Justin knew from his own experience with scheduled busts. During his patrol days in Baltimore, it was almost always reacting to events, and since being in Wallington, their level of crime didn't require a heavy police response. Although this was a common occurrence for the DEA agents, there was still the thrill of outwitting the bad guys.

"Since Agent Gant will be undercover and they are providing those resources, Agent Bell is in charge. He and I will be in the van about half a mile down Dealy Road. The van has the electric company markings on it, so we should be okay with that. Dave, you and Lenny will be set up behind the barn into the wood line at 8:00 a.m. That's a full two hours before we expect them, but we can't have a lot of traffic moving around either. Justin, you'll be with Agents Ronkowsi and Morton, waiting between us and the turnoff into the Nelson property. There's a short section of an old logging road that will put you back far enough to not be seen. Same deal, we'll all be in place by eight."

There were more nods and no interruptions as they listened. "Johnny will get the supplies he's supposed to bring today and he'll pick up Agent Gant tomorrow. They will proceed to the Nelson place where the RV, Jared, Rosso, and, we assume, one to two more will arrive around ten o'clock. Agent Gant will be wired and will have a minicam embedded in his cap. We're not too concerned about him being challenged since Jared doesn't know all of Johnny's friends and he told Johnny they were looking for another guy." He pointed to Dave and Lenny, the two least familiar with this kind of raid. "In all likelihood, the RV will be tucked into the barn and that's where they'll unload the supplies. We anticipate the chemist, who'll be in charge of cooking the meth, will have some finished product on hand or have started a batch. The reaction to Agent Gant should be one of two things. Rosso and Jared will want him to stay to start with additional security, or they'll tell him when to come back. We're hoping for the latter because we'd rather have him with Johnny until we get the boy clear of the area."

Chief McFarlane grinned. "If luck goes our way, Agent Gant gets some good photos, great sound, and he and Johnny come back out in half an hour or less. Johnny drops him off with Agents Ronkowski and Morton and Justin, and Johnny then tucks out of sight. Agent Bell and I are right behind the lead vehicle and we go directly into the property. Dave and Lenny, as soon as you hear us, you close in, and grab whoever tries to get out the back. With no more time than that elapsing, the odds are that everyone will be in the barn. Any questions?"

Heads were shaking in agreement this time and Chief McFarlane tapped his watch. "We have less than twenty-four hours and I can't stress enough about keeping this quiet. The presumption is that Jared is somewhere around, maintaining a low profile, and that Rosso will drive in tomorrow, but he could be here as well. You all have photos, but if you see him, just report the sighting to me or Agent Bell and do not go anywhere near him. We all understand?"

"This is a solid plan," Agent Bell said, approval in his brown eyes. "That doesn't mean it will go the way we think, but we have a good team here."

"Okay," the chief said. "Dave, how about you and Lenny take Agents Ronkowski and Morton out for BBQ and then head to the firing range where y'all can talk about weapons for tomorrow." He turned to Agent Bell. "Unless you object, I thought we'd meet at my house. None of my neighbors are home during the day and we'll have time for a sandwich before Boyd brings Isabelle and Johnny over."

The afternoon went as smoothly as could be expected with few questions from Isabelle, Johnny, or Boyd. Then again, it was a good plan. Gant looked directly into Isabelle's face and promised he would protect Johnny. There was little to say after that. Justin lingered with the chief as everyone else trickled out. They were in the chief's living room, an older bungalow similar to Helen's, although on a smaller scale with an attached two-car garage instead of a carport. It had been built in the post-World War II boom as veterans returned home and the chief had bought the fixer-upper after his divorce. It had been a practical and economical move, but had also given him a work in progress that he was able to focus on instead of his failed marriage. At least that was Justin's conclusion, based on comments from Sheila.

"Remarkable," Chief McFarlane said, breaking the silence. "I've got to hand it to Isabelle and Johnny. They're holding together on this."

"It's hard to believe this is the same kid I saw in the hospital that wouldn't give me the time of day," Justin said, then remembered the look on Isabelle's face the afternoon he was at her house. Maybe it had been the combination of her loving concern, Justin's warning of being in over his head, and Albert's faith that his friend would do the right thing that had come together to bring Johnny back from the dangerous edge he'd been approaching. "Breaking the news to her husband won't be easier either."

"Not much we can do about that. You know, though, I suspect Albert was what really made the difference. Funny how things turn out sometimes." He shook his head once, as though dislodging some thought. "We'd better get back to the station. You call me if you think of anything and we'll be at this early in the morning. Get some rest tonight. In fact, you head on home if you want."

Justin started to protest and then understood the chief's offer. It was a good plan and they had discussed everything that needed to be discussed. Being with Tricia and getting more sleep than the previous night was the best thing he could do to be prepared for the morning. He thought about asking if she wanted to go out for dinner and felt that might be a bit much for her. No, a trip to the grocery store for roasted chicken and her favorite sides was a better idea. No fuss with cooking and very little clean up, which he would do, would allow her to relax. As he left the chief's house, he fleetingly wondered how Isabelle and Johnny might be spending their evening. He and the chief had both insisted Isabelle and Johnny should call if either of them wanted to talk. Somehow, he doubted they would.

CHAPTER TWENTY-SIX

Justin tensed involuntarily when they heard the code phrase passed to them from the van. "The party should be a good one."

Agents Morton and Ronkowski grinned as Justin cranked the SUV and almost lurched forward out of the stand of trees that screened them from the road. They hadn't been wired to hear what was happening between Agent Gant and Johnny or what was said on the Nelson property, but there either hadn't been problems or Gant had answered any questions correctly. The code phrase was the signal that he and Johnny were on the way out together and all the suspects were still on site. Justin and Agents Morton and Ronkowski had quietly agreed that sitting semiblind, waiting to see if the trap would be sprung or turn into a disaster, was not the fun part of the job.

Justin drove the Explorer as fast as he could, intercepting Johnny and Gant within a few minutes. Gant was out of Johnny's truck almost before it stopped and Johnny had the window rolled down.

"You did good, kid. No, you did great," Gant said, and slapped the frame of the door with his open hand when he slammed it.

Justin saw a range of emotions flash across the boy's face. Betraying your brother, even if he did deserve it, couldn't be easy. Justin didn't try to pretend he genuinely understood what the boy was feeling. "You okay?"

"Yeah, I guess," he said, turning to look at Justin, the words barely getting through his clenched jaw.

"If they're smart, no one will get hurt," Justin said, watching Gant scramble into the Explorer's back seat, gun drawn. "You go straight ahead to your mother's and stay there. I imagine your brother will call her or your dad as soon as he's allowed and you'll know. If she hasn't heard anything within about four hours, she can call my cell."

Johnny nodded once, raised the window, and drove away without looking back. They had modified that single part of the plan, preferring to have him completely out of the area before they moved in.

Justin spotted the chief's car closing in on them and knew that Dave and Lenny would be poised, maintaining radio silence.

"I'll tell you guys all about it later," Gant said, as the chief halted by them. "It was as smooth as you could ask for and we have audiotape and video. The kid's got nerve, for sure."

All six of them quickly donned vests, Agents Morton and Ronkowski with their M4 carbines. That was the same weapon Dave preferred, Lenny sticking with the 12-gauge shotgun he liked. Since Justin and the chief were driving and couldn't draw their Glocks, they chambered a round to be ready as soon as they stopped. Agent Bell pointed his hand forward with no further discussion.

The short piece of road was not wide enough for two vehicles to pass, but they wanted to be in sight of the house before they hit their lights and sirens. Gant told them there were only four men total and their timing could not have been better. The entire crew was in and around the barn that had both end doors wide open. The RV was inside and a black Lincoln Town Car was parked between the barn and the house. Rosso had changed vehicles, just as they'd expected.

Gun in one hand, bullhorn in the other, Agent Bell blared instructions to lay down their weapons as both vehicles angled in to block the front exit. The figure that took off out the back ran almost directly into the muzzle of Dave's rifle. Lenny was posted with his shotgun aimed at the doors.

Morton quickly had Jared on his knees, hands locked behind his head. Jared was cursing. The chief stood to the side of the RV door, whacked the butt of his pistol against it, and yelled for them to throw any weapons out first, then come out slowly. Justin, Bell, Ronkowski, and Gant were in a shooting stance, positioned where they wouldn't catch each other in crossfire if it came to that.

"No reason to shoot," a voice called out, the door swinging open, the toe of an expensive black leather wingtip visible. "There are two of us, one pistol."

Ronkowski, to the right, yanked the door fully open. A man framed in the doorway and a Sig Sauer 220 was offered butt first.

The chief took it, motioning him to come down. "Mr. Rosso," Agent Bell said formally. "This is exactly the way I hoped to make your acquaintance."

The dark-haired man in the black designer suit, blood red shirt and black tie gave him a sardonic smile and looked at Gant. "Well, well, I might have known."

"Don't blame the kid," Gant said. "These guys aren't exactly sophisticated when it comes to things like this. He's not the first one I've fooled."

"You can continue on down," Agent Bell said, handcuffs ready.

The man behind him was as nervous as Rosso was nonchalant. He was average height, soft in the middle, balding, with a dismayed expression on his lined face. A stench wafted from the RV.

Dave and Lenny escorted the fourth man in, hands cuffed, and tattoos on the side of his neck, indicating that he's probably done prison or at least jail time.

"Let's all move out in front," Chief McFarlane said, pointing his chin at the RV. "I assume there are enough chemicals in there that being outside is better."

Justin saw several cardboard boxes and jugs of liquids stacked against the side of the barn, the supplies Johnny and Gant had brought. The danger of explosions was minimized if no meth was actually in the "cooking" process, but he wasn't entirely sure what was going on in the RV, so the chief's precaution was probably a good idea.

Bell stepped to the chief's side, not taking his eyes off Rosso. "I'll call the techs to come in," he said. Gant can stay with them and they'll bring him in when they're done here. You want to go ahead and get these guys to the station?"

"Works for me," the chief said. "Dave, you and Lenny take Jared and the other guy. Justin, you take Mr.— I didn't catch you name," he said, looking at the man who was obviously the chemist responsible for creating the methamphetamine.

"Mr. Nesbitt," Rosso said with a mocking bow. "A gentleman who won't have anything to say until we have an attorney present." He shrugged. "I'm not certain if we'll have one or two, but I'll let you know after I make my telephone call."

"Justin, you have Mr. Nesbitt along with Agents Ronkowski and Morton, and Agent Bell and I will take Mr. Rosso."

Bell inclined his head to Morton. "I need to stay for a while with the techs. Colby will ride with you and I'll be along as soon as I can."

There was no question the group that trooped into the Wallington police station was the most exciting that had happened in no telling how long and Justin could only imagine the stories that were flying around town. Four suspects at a time were unusual enough, adding the DEA agents nearly strained their physical capacity, and that was before the lawyers and a bellowing Roger Jenkins showed up. Dave Mabry took him outside and whatever he said had the impact of shifting the angry denials to sullen reality and a huddled conference with Boyd Gilbert. Who knew? Maybe Jenkins was finally going to recognize the kind of trouble his son was in. The senior writer for the *Gazette* made his appearance and coaxed a joint statement from the chief and Agent Bell with the promise of a more detailed interview the next morning.

During the almost four hours before the suspects were completely processed and a level of calm restored, Justin made a fast call to Isabelle to check on Johnny and one to Tricia to let her know everything was all right. Agent Gant filled them in on trying to maintain the fiction they designed about how the authorities had somehow gotten word about Jared, had targeted Johnny as a link to his brother, and perpetuated the undercover deception on him. It was a plausible lie that might allow Johnny to be viewed as a dupe by his brother rather than a snitch. Sheila, in her element of handling multiple ringing telephones and being in the know regarding what was happening, managed to order lunch brought in from the Sandwich Shoppe. With the official actions under control, Agent Bell and his men exchanged handshakes and congratulations for a successful operation before they departed for Atlanta.

Chief McFarlane squeezed Justin, Dave, and Lenny into his office with their coffee mugs to hold the double fingers of bourbon he poured from the bottle he kept in the bottom desk drawer.

"Here's to the good guys winning," he said with a slow smile. He lifted his mug in a toast. He cocked his head at Justin and the smile became a grin. "Did I notice you and Dave having a heart-to-heart talk with Mr. Rosso at one point?"

Justin threw a glance at Dave who shrugged. He smiled at the chief. "Yes, well, what with his lawyer being on the way, we figured we should have a little discussion with him about how things work in Hicksville. I think we got across that we didn't really care about his troubles with the DEA or the New Orleans police, but it would be in his best interest to never show up here again or have any further contact with the Johnsons."

"Seems he might be on his way back to New York," Dave drawled, holding out his mug. "Or maybe it was out to Las Vegas. Either way, he said there were plenty of pretty women in the world and he decided his ex-wife wasn't worth any more of his time."

"That would seem to take care of that problem," the chief said. "Okay, I would say that today should about fill our excitement quota for the year. We can go back to worrying about lawn mowers being stolen and guys firing off rounds in the parking lot at Herb's."

"Amen to that," Lenny said and drained his mug. "In fact, speaking of Herb, he's got a T-bone special on tonight. Y'all want to go out there?"

Justin rose, thinking how many questions Tricia must have. "Thanks guys, but I'd better pass. I think I'll swing by the Johnsons on the way home and let them know everything should be back to normal."

They chuckled and half rose with nods of farewell. What a day it had been, and now, he could look forward to taking good news to the Johnsons and relieving the worry Tricia had been masking. As for the Jenkins' family, well, that was something they would have to sort out. Boyd Gilbert promised he would help in every way he could, and from what he'd seen of Isabelle and Johnny, they would find a way to get through this.

CHAPTER TWENTY-SEVEN

Helen opened the front door and reached to take something from Alicia.

"It's okay, I'm balanced," the young woman laughed, her face only partially visible behind the bouquet.

"I'll take these carefully," Helen said, lifting the mass of yellow and dark red chrysanthemums, orange lilies, sunflowers, daisies, and greenery. "They're gorgeous."

"They should last you all the way through Thanksgiving," Alicia said, a relaxed smile still in place. "I know flowers were hardly appropriate for Justin, but I sent a bouquet thinking that Tricia would enjoy them."

"That was incredibly sweet and completely unnecessary." Helen waved her free hand to the quilting room. "Unload in there and I'll put these in a vase." She looked down at Tawny turning circles. "Yes, it's okay, Alicia doesn't mind."

"Of course not," she said, her voice following Helen into the dining room. "She's adorable, and as far as the flowers are concerned, they don't remotely compare to us getting our lives back."

When Helen entered the quilting room, the bouquet safely ensconced on the dining room table, Alicia was standing next to the sofa where Tawny was perched, enjoying having her ears scratched. Alicia's tote was on top of the quilting table. Helen had folded her project and draped it on the back of a chair to make room.

Alicia, looking like her old self for the first time in weeks, was wearing a pair of sage lightweight wool blend slacks and a forest-green V-neck sweater that was probably merino wool. Tiny beads, the same shade of her slacks, outlined the V and a beaded necklace alternating the two greens with matching earrings made it the perfect ensemble for her hair and eye color.

"Yes, it's a brand new outfit and yes, it's from Carolyn's shop. I felt like celebrating."

"You look terrific," Helen said, taking both hands that Alicia offered. "I am so happy for you—for y'all, I mean. I assume this takes a load off Hiram's mind, too."

Alicia's laugh was delightful to hear. "Does it ever. By the way, we are most happy to accept your invitation to Thanksgiving, if it's still open. Are you sure, though, with Tricia being so close to her due date?"

Helen released Alicia's hands with an affectionate squeeze and stepped to the quilting table. "Y'all are absolutely invited and we've decided we'll just all be flexible about the baby. Mamma has the logistics worked out and quite frankly, making sure we're prepared in case the baby comes early means he or she will probably be late."

"I'm not sure I wouldn't have wanted to know the sex beforehand either," Alicia said, reaching for the materials in her tote. "Although I think the whole pink and blue thing isn't as popular as it used to be, not with all the fabulous colors available out there."

Helen watched as she withdrew a magazine and a stack of fabric. "You're probably right about that, and as much as I appreciate modern medical technology, Tricia is showing all the signs of carrying a boy and that's the way I'm betting. Okay, what have you got here?"

Alicia opened the magazine to a bookmarked page and set her tote onto the floor. "This whole unsettling experience with Leo has had the benefit of reminding me what a wonderful man Hiram is. Even though Hiram doesn't really understand the quilt thing, I want to make a very special one to commemorate—oh, I don't know—I suppose you could call it my celebration of our marriage." She gave Helen a fond look. "That's the thing with quilting, though, isn't it? We can identify the story behind the special ones?"

"Indeed," Helen said, recognizing the pattern in the magazine. It was one of Max's beginner's designs, one that might be a bit basic for Alicia, but also fairly quick to put together. "I like this one."

There were six squares across and seven down with the sashing and binding the same solid color, which was blue in the pattern. There was a small square of solid fabric in dark red between each of the squares except for the top and bottom rows. There were also slightly larger red squares, one in each corner. The absence of small squares on the top and bottom rows provided an unbroken line of binding to frame the quilt.

"Me, too, and here's what I've done for fabric." Alicia grinned. "As you know, I've spent a lot of extra time in the house lately so I cleaned out all the linen closets and went through other stuff in storage. I found all sorts of things tucked away I'd forgotten about and that's what inspired the idea. A set of curtains from the apartment where I was living when I met Hiram, a tablecloth I used the first time he came to dinner that got a stain on it I could never remove, and a little red satin heart pillow that was in the first Valentine's Day bouquet he gave me."

Helen nodded. "Bits and pieces from the very beginning of your relationship."

Alicia touched the page of the magazine. "The fact that Max did this design just makes it that much more fun, don't you think?

What I want to do, though, is lay out all these fabrics and get your opinion about the binding and sashing. I don't really have a dominant color in mind right now. Our master bedroom is fairly neutral with a lot of green accents, but quite frankly, I've been considering a makeover anyway. My inclination is to do the quilt and use it to select the color palette for the room."

"I like that idea," Helen said. "Unless you are are planning to move soon, you can go with whatever colors you want for the walls and not worry about the realtor admonition of staying neutral for resale purposes."

"No, we're in the house for the long term. We bought with four bedrooms in mind and a fenced-in backyard so we would be ready when the time came for a family." Alicia said as she gave a quick smile. "I was talking with Rita and it seems all of us have been considering that we're settled to the point where children could be the next thing, and pretty soon."

"I can't say I'm surprised, but of course, there are couples who choose to do otherwise."

Alicia started to spread out the irregularly shaped pieces of fabric. "And I totally understand that. My older sister has a high-speed road warrior job that keeps her from even starting a regular romance, much less thoughts of children. Take a look at what I have."

Helen fleetingly remembered Max's comment about how his job kept him from entering into meaningful relationships before she focused her attention on Alicia's explanation of each of the pieces. It only took an hour for them to work out the details for the entire quilt and when she left, Helen transferred her project back to the table. Alicia said she didn't need anything to drink, but Helen felt the urge for a cup of tea and snapped her fingers to Tawny who had settled comfortably on what had become her favorite corner.

Talking with Alicia about the pattern had brought Max to mind and she opened the refrigerator while she waited for the water to boil. Chicken, of course, and a package of boneless pork chops. Hmmm, there was some thin-sliced smoked ham for sandwiches, and yes, she had Cheddar and Swiss cheese in there, too. Did she have enough potatoes to mash? If not, she had two or three rice mixes in the pantry. Veggies? There were plenty of carrots and at least one package of frozen whole green beans. Chicken or pork cordon bleu wasn't a difficult dish and it made a nice presentation. The sound of the telephone interrupted her menu planning.

"Hi, Mamma," Tricia said, sounding a little out of breath.

"Are you okay, honey?"

"What? Oh, yes, I'm fine. It just seems like carrying this load around takes more out of me every day. Would it be terrible of me to say that I'm about tired of this?"

"No, that would be what almost every woman in the world says at this stage," Helen assured her. "Do y'all want to come for dinner tonight so you don't have to think about what to make?"

"Thanks, but quite honestly, all I want to do is sit and keep my slippers on. We have some of the Brunswick stew left and it will be that, a salad, and some rolls. I wanted to call and let you know about an interesting rumor I heard today."

Helen carried the telephone to the stove where she switched the burner to low. "What's that?"

From the sound of Tricia's voice, she was grinning. "Before I get to that, I want to tell you Albert came by to see me yesterday and said to please especially thank you for your help. He said everything is fine with him and despite the fact that Jared will most probably go to jail, Boyd has apparently worked out a fairly good plea bargain for him. Johnny seems to be okay, too."

"I'm glad to hear that," Helen said, hoping Albert was correct.

"So, according to a source who shall be unnamed, but whom I trust, Steve Hillman will probably not be with us in the spring semester. It seems as if his parents have decided that perhaps a transfer to a military academy would be a better environment for him."

"Ah." Helen wasn't sure what else to say.

"I personally would prefer we catch him in something where we could take disciplinary or even legal action, but I suppose we should be grateful he'll be out of our hair."

"I don't know how much good sending him to an academy will do," Helen said, "although I imagine he won't be the only one they've ever taken in who has problems."

"Not remotely," Tricia laughed. "It would be nice to think that perhaps they can talk some sense into him if it's not too late. I suspect the nasty Hillman genes are too deeply ingrained to do much good. That's not the least bit Christian to say, is it?"

"I think you can be forgiven," Helen said. "Maybe we'll offer up a prayer for him, though, to let new wisdom guide him."

Tricia's tone was clearly doubtful. "Uh-huh. Listen, I've got to grade some papers, so we'll see you tomorrow, maybe."

They said good-bye, and with the telephone in her hand, Helen dialed Max's number before she could change her mind.

He answered on the second ring and immediately said yes to the dinner invitation.

"Are you sure you wouldn't prefer to go out?"

"No, really," Helen said, "I have everything we need here, although you could get a small dessert if you'd like."

"I insist," he said with a laugh, "and I'll bring a bottle of wine. What time is best for you?"

"Oh, let's say six thirty if that's not rushing you. Seven is okay, too."

"Six thirty it is and thank you for calling."

Helen disconnected the call with a cheery good-bye and moved to the tea box to make her selection. Dinner with Max tonight. They could finally do their reminiscing and she wondered if he would talk more about his future plans. The idea of him staying longer raised some interesting questions.

CHAPTER TWENTY-EIGHT

Helen was halfway through her first mug of coffee, and as most people do when the telephone rings at 6:22 a.m., her first thought was praying nothing was wrong.

"Mamma...," the strained voice told her almost everything she needed to know. A pause, then, "I'm okay, but we're on the way to the hospital."

Helen kept her voice calm. "Normal labor?"

"We think so," came out more as a squeak, "but maybe it's false labor."

"We'll know soon enough. Get off the phone. I'll call your grandparents and meet you there as quickly as I can."

"Love you, and Justin is nervous," Tricia said, her voice tight this time. "Bye."

Helen stood for a moment, feeling the smile on her face. The day before Thanksgiving. Of course she was delivering for real, the exact scene they hoped to avoid. Ah, well, her parents would be awake, her morning person trait having come from them. It was a quick call and they agreed it would not make sense for everyone to rush over. It was better to wait to hear from her.

Helen took an insulated travel coffee mug from the cabinet, and then took a second one down. She was willing to bet that Justin hadn't stopped to fix coffee. She rushed through a shower, not bothering to shave and didn't need to shampoo her hair. Glamor was not an issue either, a pair of pull-on brown gabardine slacks, a rust-colored rolled-neck sweater with a section of patchwork quilt on the front was fine, and her brown loafers would do. There was no need to stop and think about jewelry or makeup.

With school out for the holiday, the advantage of that hour was very little traffic and Helen was walking through the doors into labor and delivery barely forty minutes after Tricia had called. She tried not to smile when she saw him. He looked like a little boy seeing the presents under the Christmas tree. She tightened her grip on both mugs of coffee as he grabbed her in a strong hug.

"It's for real! She's five centimeters dilated." He released her and smiled as she thrust the coffee at him. "Oh, thank you so much, yes."

"She's fine though? Everything is good?"

He nodded, taking a long swallow. "Yes, well, I mean, she's in pain, but she's fine. It started around 4:00 and we weren't sure, you know, thinking it might be false labor. We were timing her and the contractions were getting close together, and I've got to tell you, she was in such pain that I couldn't stand it." He looked sheepish and ducked his head. "Oh man, that's exactly the wrong thing to say, isn't it?"

Helen held back a laugh. "You're okay as long as she doesn't hear you. Which room is she in?"

"Oh yeah, the second door. They haven't moved her into delivery yet. I told her I was coming to look for you."

Helen patted his cheek. "How about you take time to drink your coffee and I'll go in to be with her. I imagine it will be about another hour from the way it sounds."

Justin's expression was a mixture of excitement, puzzlement at this mystery of birth, and hesitation. "Aren't I supposed to be with her like every second?"

Helen laughed softly. "Trust me, a few minutes won't hurt."

"Okay," he said, walking her to the door with a grin. "I think mom and daughter time is a good idea."

When Helen entered the room and saw Tricia's damp hair plastered to her forehead, the monitors hooked to her, and the nurse taking her vitals, the memories of Ethan's and Tricia's births nearly overwhelmed her.

"Hi, Mamma," Tricia said, a grimace pulling at her mouth.

"Everything is progressing nicely," the young nurse, who must be new, said with a smile. "Dr. Fraiser is on his way. I'll leave you two together." Her name tag read Carla Lawson. Good Lord, it was Sterling's granddaughter, all grown up.

"Sorry to call so early," Tricia said, her face relaxing briefly between contractions. She reached out her left hand, and Helen moved to that side of the bed.

"Justin will be back soon, but I thought we might want a moment."

Tricia's eyes sparkled. "This natural childbirth business seemed like a better idea last week."

Helen brushed the hair from her forehead. "You're doing great and you'll be fine. You're in wonderful shape." Tricia's hand tightened to the nearly bone-crushing grip that accompanied another contraction and Helen set her mouth to keep from reacting. There, it passed.

"Guess I've messed up Thanksgiving," Tricia said with a tiny gasp, focusing on Helen's face.

"That's the last thing you should be thinking about," Helen said and they both looked over as the door opened. Dr. Fraiser entered, followed by Justin and the nurse.

"Good morning, Helen," he said cheerfully, stepping up to

Tricia. "Everything is good, but it does appear Baby Kendall has decided he or she is ready to be joining the family very soon now."

Justin stood close to Helen to be out of the way and she motioned for them to swap places, transferring Tricia's hand to his.

Dr. Fraiser patted Tricia's right hand. "I'd say another half hour or so in here, then we'll be going into delivery. Justin, you might want to change into scrubs. They're in the wardrobe, I believe. Any other questions?"

Everyone shook their heads and Dr. Fraiser and the nurse left with reassuring smiles. "I'll stay while you change," Helen said, switching places again so that Tricia's hand was grasped in constant contact.

As soon as Justin disappeared into the bathroom with the door closed, Tricia brought Helen's hand to her mouth. "Is this how you felt? This incredible sense of what's about to happen?"

"Of course," Helen said. "Although I did opt for an epidural."

"Smart woman," Tricia said, breathing hard.

Helen understood Tricia's preference for no drugs and she knew with no complications, it would all be over soon. Dr. Fraiser was experienced enough that he didn't bother to show up too long before the delivery.

Justin came out, clad in green scrubs, booties on his feet, the cap covering his hair, and seemed confused as to what to do with his clothes.

Helen let go of Tricia's hand and reached for Justin's clothes. "I'll take these and go call your grandparents with an update. You two need to be focusing on Justin doing his coaching," she said, throwing Tricia a kiss. "I'll be close by, but this is your time."

Tricia and Justin nodded, their eyes locked onto each other and Helen slipped from the room, holding the trickle of tears until she was in the hallway. She quickly swiped them away, sniffed, and neatly folded Justin's clothes to place them in the large tote she'd brought.

The small quilt she'd made as a surprise was in it, as were the pink and blue knit caps that Tricia and Ethan had worn in the hospital. They'd been knitted by Mamaw Pierce and Helen had carefully stored them for more than two decades in anticipation of this day. The little quilt that would be wrapped around their firstborn when they left the hospital was a field of pale pink, the binding blue with a large white K in the center. Blue hearts were at the top left and bottom right corners, and pink hearts were on the top right and bottom left.

Russell Mitchel Kendall emerged into the world at 8:19 a.m., seven pounds, fourteen ounces and twenty inches long, a thin covering of light brown hair, red, wrinkly, and squalling. By a little before 10:00 a.m., grandmother and great-grandparents had cradled the baby and now stood outside the nursery with Justin as Tricia drifted into exhausted sleep.

"Oh, wow," Justin said yet again, his voice incredulous, his face peering through the window.

Great-grandfather was next to him and Mamaw and GG moved several steps away so they could talk.

"A new generation," Joy said softly. "How's Tricia?"

"She's fine," Helen said. "They plan to let them come home tomorrow if there aren't any complications." She turned sideways. "What do we want to do about Thanksgiving? For real, I mean?"

Joy's eyes glinted with humor. "What's wrong with the plan that we had?"

Helen held her hands palm up. "I have no idea what time they'll actually leave the hospital and you know they'll need help getting home and settled. It could be first thing in the morning, or it could be the middle of the afternoon. I thought I'd pop over to their place this afternoon and get things cleaned up for them. I doubt Tricia has felt like scrubbing the bathrooms this week and Justin has had a lot on his mind."

"You go right ahead and don't give tomorrow a thought," her

mamma said. "Phyllis was out early this morning and saw Justin and Tricia tearing to the hospital. She called me not fifteen minutes after you did. Your daddy is going to pick the turkey up today as planned. Deirdre is getting the desserts from Lisa and will add in something small for Justin and Tricia. Phyllis will do up a turkey breast for them that she swears takes no time at all, even though I'm pretty sure the dressing will be from a box. Katie will do the sides you were going to do and will make extra servings for the new parents. The Johnsons and Raneys are bringing the drinks."

Helen was trying to absorb everything. "This sounds complicated."

Joy waved a hand. "Not really. Phyllis is in charge of pulling it together. In other words, everything for us will be brought to our place and Phyllis will drop off a complete, although small, Thanksgiving dinner in a basket at your house for you to take to the kids. You focus on them tomorrow and we'll continue with plans at our house. You know that what they're going to need most is to rest. Once you have them comfortable, you come to our place. That gives them a nice meal and a day to catch their breath and we all have a good time drinking a toast in their honor. Problem solved."

Helen pressed her hand to her mouth, trying not to laugh at the image of Phyllis in a flurry of telephone calls. "Oh my, I guess I really don't have anything to worry about, do I?"

"Not at all," her mamma said, turning back to admire Russell Mitchell. "I would say it's going to be a perfect Thanksgiving. A tad disjointed perhaps, and not all of us gathered at the same table, but perfect, nonetheless."

Helen slipped her arm around her mamma's waist and gazed at her first grandchild, the most beautiful baby in the nursery. "How right you are."

The End

More Books from AQS

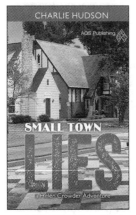

#1258 $14.95

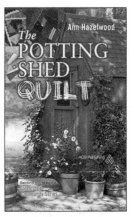

#1256 $14.95

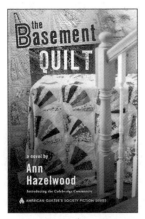

#8853 $14.00

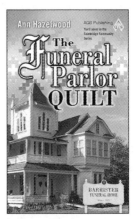

#1257 $14.95

Look for these books nationally.

1-800-626-5420

Call or Visit our website at
www.AmericanQuilter.com